CLEAN SWEEP

CLEAN SWEEP

A CRIME NOVEL
MICHAEL J. CLARK

Published by ECW Press
665 Gerrard Street East
Toronto, Ontario, Canada M4M 1Y2
416-694-3348 / info@ecwpress.com

This is a work of fiction. Names, characters, places, and incidents either are the product of the author's imagination or are used fictitiously, and any resemblance to actual persons, living or dead, business establishments, events, or locales is entirely coincidental.

LIBRARY AND ARCHIVES CANADA
CATALOGUING IN PUBLICATION

Clark, Michael J., 1969–, author
Clean sweep : a crime novel /
Michael J. Clark.

Issued in print and electronic formats.
ISBN 978-1-77041-397-9 (softcover).
ALSO ISSUED AS: 978-1-77305-171-0 (PDF),
978-1-77305-170-3 (EPUB),
I. TITLE.

PS8605.L36236C54 2018   C813'.6
C2017-906198-4   C2017-906199-2

Cover design: Michel Vrana
Author photo: Christine Bradley Portraits

The publication of *Clean Sweep* has been generously supported by the Canada Council
for the Arts which last year invested $153 million to bring the arts to Canadians
throughout the country, and by the Government of Canada through the Canada Book
Fund. *Nous remercions le Conseil des arts du Canada de son soutien. L'an dernier, le Conseil a
investi 153 millions de dollars pour mettre de l'art dans la vie des Canadiennes et des Canadiens
de tout le pays. Ce livre est financé en partie par le gouvernement du Canada.* We also acknowledge the Ontario Arts Council (OAC), an agency of the Government of Ontario, and
the contribution of the Government of Ontario through the Ontario Book Publishing
Tax Credit and the Ontario Media Development Corporation.

Ontario
Ontario Media Development
Corporation

ONTARIO ARTS COUNCIL
CONSEIL DES ARTS DE L'ONTARIO
an Ontario government agency
un organisme du gouvernement de l'Ontario

Canada Council
for the Arts

Conseil des Arts
du Canada

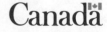

Canadä

PRINTED AND BOUND IN CANADA   PRINTING: MARQUIS   5   4   3   2   1

Happy. Paulie Noonan was wondering when he had last felt it.
Of all nights, this run-of-the-mill
Winnipeg Wednesday seemed far
from it. He was parked in front of the bus station at Pembina and Stafford, which the locals
knew better as the Salisbury House Restaurant.
He watched the goings-on within, through the
smeared windshield of his Buick Roadmaster
Estate Wagon. A group of high-school kids
were busy being high-school kids, pooling their
change for fries and gravy, maybe a few Cheese
Nips. He immediately identified the Bad Boy,
a bushy brown-haired Lothario wearing not
enough jacket for January. He was busy loos-
ening the tops on the salt and pepper shakers

for the next set of unsuspecting customers, while his friends laughed at a YouTube video on one of their phones. The blue-eyed blonde across from the bad example stared at him but saw none of it. She wanted him more than air.

Noonan looked to the left of the teens' booth. A father and daughter were winding down their evening out at a preteen concert that one of the local FM stations had been promoting all week. The girl was showing off her concert T-shirt to her dad, practically levitating off of the vinyl bench. Dad was still rubbing his left ear from one of two dins: the sound system at the MTS Centre or the screams of 10,000 prepubescent fans. The father smiled at his daughter with loving approval, the way that Noonan wished he could with his daughter. He hadn't seen her in twelve years.

The man at the table next to Dad and Daughter could have been the girl's grandfather, a bespectacled gent who had to be in his late seventies. His teeth didn't look like they fit as well as the baseball cap on his white shock of hair. Noonan had seen the hat's logo, a fist gripping what looked like lightning bolts, somewhere before, possibly the crest for the International Brotherhood of Electrical Workers. He was reading a crisp copy of the *Winnipeg Sentinel*'s Wednesday car dealer insert. Perhaps it was time for a new Buick.

Noonan's Buick was way past warranty. The woodgrain panelling concealed most of the rust. The Buick had been hiding Noonan for the last six nights, thanks to a toasty in-car warmer, a $300 sleeping bag, and plenty of empty plug-in parking spots at local retirement homes, where half the cars were Buicks. His compact frame of five feet six inches was easy to curl beneath the station wagon's retractable cargo cover. The Buick had been in storage, under a dead friend's name, for the express purpose of bugging out. He had left his ivory Escalade in front of his duplex on Rothesay Street. The house and the Cadillac had surely been searched by now by representatives of the Heaven's Rejects Motorcycle Club, a name that was usually shortened to the HRs in casual conversation, or newspaper headlines. Noonan had freelanced for most of the biker gangs in Winnipeg over the last thirty years, watching their power ebb and flow from one group to the next. Whether it was the Los Bravos, the Spartans, or the current HRs, they all had one thing in common: crossing them meant death. The HRs had a slogan in the local underworld: First, we kill you. Then we go to work on you.

The latest assignment for Noonan had gone more sideways than an Electra Glide on black ice. It had all started ten days earlier, when he took a basic gig from the HRs to guard a stash house on Mountain Avenue near the Safeway, with four kilos of cocaine, two kilos of hashish, and six Ziploc freezer bags full of ecstasy. Noonan had been dozing on and off, a rumbling space heater next to the duct-taped Barcalounger he occupied, in front of a vintage black-and-white portable TV. Either appliance could have been responsible for the fire, the one that Noonan woke up to in full force. He knew it would have been wiser to succumb to the smoke, instead of escaping with just his life. The stash went up in flames, with not even enough evidence left in the debris to present a press conference for the Winnipeg Police Service. The HRs weren't happy. Even if he had received third-degree burns all over his face, Noonan knew he would still get some breaks, as in fingers, maybe a tibia or two. Without a scratch on him, it didn't take long for the HRs to ask the question; did the stash actually burn?

Noonan's phone started vibrating in his coat pocket. He reached in to check the message, already knowing the request. "Please come home, Paulie. I miss you." It wasn't a lover, and it certainly wasn't his ex-wife. *Home* was the Heaven's Rejects clubhouse, located in a former bakery on St. John's Avenue. *I miss you* — translation: or we'll find you, and make it really, *really* painful. Not that anyone would ever find him. Winnipeg was full of missing bikers; you just had to know where to dig.

Noonan pulled down his visor for a peek at his current state. One of the vanity-mirror bulbs was burnt out, though there was just enough illumination to reveal a most frightened man of forty-seven years. His stubble was bordering on unkempt beard. His cheeks were sunken, a combination of only 145 pounds on his frame and the slim thought of eating in his current predicament. In the back seat there was a case of oversized green apple Gatorade bottles that could double as road-going urinals. The entire car stank of nervous sweat.

Noonan was waiting for the bus, a magic bus, especially if it could be the ticket out of Winnipeg, out of Manitoba, out of The Life. He continued to scan his side and rear-view mirrors for its arrival. The tap on the passenger side glass prompted him to hit the horn long enough to annoy. The teens, Daughter and Dad, and the grandfather gave the expected look at the noise: *What's HIS problem?* Noonan waited for a fat second until he turned his head to see Tommy Bosco looking through the glass. He breathed for what seemed like the first time in days as he hit the power lock.

Noonan had known Tommy Bosco for better than twenty years. The bulk of that time had involved a criss-cross of criminal activities, mostly in the field of cross-border smuggling, with Bosco at the wheel of an old half-ton pickup truck named Freddie the Ford. Noonan knew they would probably still be meeting over such matters at a neighborhood Sal's like this, if it hadn't been for January 17, 2009. That was the day Bosco was arrested at the Pembina, North Dakota, U.S. customs entry, the victim of a classic double-cross. It wasn't Tommy Bosco who was sliding into Noonan's Buick; this was Pastor Tommy Bosco. Noonan knew of many ex-cons who had made the Jesus leap while in the service of the province. Bosco's bound was the stuff of Superman.

"Did you remember everything?" said Bosco. He had assumed a position that favoured the door panel as his back-rest. Noonan nodded, pointing to a collection of personal items on the dashboard. Bosco checked the items with the help of the map light overhead. Noonan sat quietly as he watched Bosco make his mental inventory: wallet, watch, rings, receipts. Bosco was a skinny six-foot-three, with a bushy mess of salt and pepper hair under his toque that must have had a mullet extension in the late eighties. While the extension had long been removed, the same couldn't be said for the jagged scar over his left eye, a mark that Noonan had long assumed to be from a fight that Bosco had won. He wore minimal stubble, hidden partially by the pulled-up collar of his second-hand tweed overcoat. His blue-grey eyes appeared to register satisfaction as he finished flipping through the pic-tures in Noonan's wallet. He placed the wallet on the dash-board. He looked directly at Noonan without emotion. "Left or right," said Bosco.

Noonan blinked.

"Left or right?"

Noonan looked to the left, then to the right. He saw nothing. "Huh?"

"Which hand?"

"Whaddya mean, which hand?"

"Which hand do you jerk off with?"

Noonan had to think about it. He lifted both hands up by the wheel, making cupping motions with first his left hand, then his right. He was about to answer when Bosco grabbed his right wrist and sliced open his palm with a folding pocket knife. Noonan cried out. "Son of a BITCH! What the fuck was that for?"

Bosco didn't answer. He grabbed Noonan's bleeding palm and squeezed. He directed Noonan's palm over the light-grey velour upholstery. He rubbed the palm on the steering wheel, the dashboard, and the edge of the seat before releasing it. Noonan immediately applied pressure to the wound, a wound that his assailant was now trying to fix. Bosco had produced a well-worn flask from his coat. He doused the wound with a splash of pungent liquor, a mid-grade bourbon that he had acquired a taste for in the States. As Noonan winced, Bosco wrapped the hand in a hasty combo of cotton balls and adhesive gauze. "That's the first thing we do at the bus station," said Bosco. "We've got to make sure that the cops know you were at the bus station."

"Yeah, well there's only one problem."

"What's that?"

Noonan pointed at his wound. "This is the hand I jack off with!"

Bosco smirked. "Try lefty for a while. They say it feels like someone else." He gave the front seat a once-over, making sure that none of the triage items had been left behind. Satisfied, Bosco motioned for Noonan to exit the wagon. "Don't forget your shit," he said, pointing to the personal effects on the dashboard. Bosco turned off the idling Buick as Noonan left the driver's side, pocketing the keys. "Over by the Co-op," Bosco said, pointing towards what had to be the Magic Bus.

Noonan looked at the bus as he approached, a well-used white Ford Econoline fifteen-passenger model, with lettering on the side for Bosco's skid row mission. The script was anything but professionally applied. He wiped away at the dirt to read it:

THE GUIDING LIGHT MISSION
ALL DENOMINATIONS WELCOME

Noonan smirked at that. Back in the day, all denominations were certainly welcome, in the dummy fuel tank of Freddie the Ford.

The doors of the Econoline creaked in protest as the pair entered. Bosco gave the throttle six frantic pumps before attempting to crank. The van roared to life. He looked over at Noonan as he shifted gear into a hard-clunk reverse. "C'mon, Paulie. Let's get you dead."

CHAPTER
TWO

The Econoline headed south on Pembina Highway. The sound of the worn-out engine was being drowned out by whatever was stuck in the heater box. It might have been some dried leaves, the kind that fall into the cold-air duct in autumn, eventually finding their way to the blower motor. The shrieking from the fan was constant, with slight adjustments in tremolo when Bosco would bash the dashboard with his right hand, protectively wrapped in thick hide mittens, affectionately known as garbage mitts. The bashing would bring the AM radio on intermittently, with slices of a late-night conspiracy theory talk show on CJOB.

"Gimme your wallet," said Bosco, as he gave

8

the dashboard another haymaker. Noonan fished around, producing his weathered Buxton with the expected curvature of a back-pocket address. He was about to remove the wad of bills when Bosco stopped him. "Leave the money. It has to be a full wallet, otherwise it won't look like a hit."

Noonan wasn't convinced. "I gotta throw away five hundred bucks? Fuck!" He counted the bills to be sure of the truth, finding himself a twenty light. *Close enough*, he thought, as he handed the wallet over.

"Put it all in the bag and tie it up," said Bosco, pointing to a pile of empty 7-Eleven bags near the base of the engine doghouse. Noonan complied, tightly tying the bag that held his wallet, his watch, and his credit card receipts. "Bag it twice," said Bosco, pointing at the floor of the van. "Otherwise, it tears too soon." The doubled bag looked like the kind you would see in a waste bin at a public park, put there by conscientious pet owners. *Shit in a bag*, thought Noonan. That would be all that was left of him, as far as Robbery-Homicide was concerned.

Noonan found a smile then, thinking about all the wasted hours that would be spent at the Brady Road landfill in search of a finger or a leg. The new recruits from the academy, the crime scene techs with their hooded coveralls, probes, and sensors. The commercial garbage truck drivers would be complaining at the landfill supervisors, the supervisors shrugging, all for a low-level hood. *Not a bad send-off*, Noonan thought. All it needed was an open bar.

Bosco had to hold the turn signal in place for the right turn onto the Perimeter Highway. "Is there anything on this piece of shit that isn't busted?" said Tommy as he negotiated the arc. In the distance, he could see the glow from the lights at the primary city garbage dump site. He made the left onto

Brady Road, dousing the lights. "Grab that," said Bosco, as he motioned to Noonan at the long tube behind the seats.

The item looked familiar, but Noonan couldn't place its origins. Then it hit him, just like the T-shirt that had whacked him in the head and spilled his beer at the Winnipeg Goldeyes game last summer. Noonan handed the T-shirt cannon to Bosco, who had retrieved an air tank from the rear of the van. He stuffed the plastic bag into the tube, using a broken snowbrush to ensure it was at the back of the T-shirt cannon. Noonan said nothing, though every jab of the brush into the barrel felt like a steel toe to his gut. He wondered how long it would take for anyone to notice that he was gone. The first one to call would be the Manitoba Department of Corrections, wondering why he hadn't shown up for his weekly parole compliance check-in. They would start calling next of kin, finding an ex-wife full of venom, a few disconnected phone numbers, and a sixty-six-year-old mother on the crack pipe. He'd had a daughter with his high-school sweetheart, just before he got thrown into Headingley the first time, for two years less a day. He had tried to connect with her a few times over the last twenty-five years. "I have no Father!" and "You're dead to me!" were the usual responses.

Noonan could live with that. She had turned out alright, with a decent common-law husband, twin boys, and a nice trailer, in one of the nicer trailer parks. She had a job, a minivan, and no worries about knocks on the door from the local constabulary. *Not a bad life,* Noonan thought. It certainly wasn't his life.

"You wanna launch it?" said Bosco as he threw the brush into the back of the Econoline. Noonan shook his head, a shake Bosco had seen seventeen times over the past three years, from seventeen other Noonans. He whacked Noonan's head with the tube, the way you'd tap someone who was nodding off. "It might help," said Bosco, as he checked the pressure gauge on the launcher. "Out with the old, in with the new fake ID."

Noonan straightened up. "Give me a minute," he said, looking at the floorboard.

Bosco grabbed the launcher and the tank. "Don't take too fucking long. All we need is one curious cop or an RC and its done."

The RCs were the Royal Canadian Mounted Police. The Brady Road landfill site was literally on the border of the City of Winnipeg and the Rural Municipality of Macdonald. The site was still contained within city limits, though it just depended on who was more bored during their patrol. Noonan banged the busted passenger door open, slamming it hard enough to dislodge the last shard of broken mirror from the cracked side-view. He bent down to pick it up, turning it ever so slightly to catch his full mug. He hated the look of his own face. He knew what it had seen, the things it had said, and the rage it had registered against those who he professed to love. He wished he could slice it off with the shard, scab over, and start again, but there was no time. A fake ID and an electric shave would have to do.

Bosco was checking the connections of the fittings on the launcher as Noonan shuffled over. "It's ready," said Bosco, as he handed him the tube. Noonan examined the device, not quite sure of the triggering mechanism, or, for that matter, which end to aim at the landfill. "Wrong end," said Bosco, as he reversed the direction of the tube. Noonan complied, still unsure of the nuances for the angle of trajectory. Bosco motioned towards the top of the garbage hill. "Aim towards the lights."

Noonan looked up at the yellow glow from the sodium bulbs and aimed accordingly. He hit the trigger, jarred slightly by the recoil of the compressed air. They watched as the plastic bag tumbled through the night air, crossing into the canopy of light and blowing snow. They did not see it land; they didn't have to. The wheels of the landfill Caterpillars would chew open the bag in short order, as well as the curved Buxton, the knock-off Rolex, and the $480 that Noonan had called five. Something would be found, something with a name, a bar code, and a magnetic stripe that would read Paul Edward Noonan. Only then would it be done, as far as the police were concerned.

The January cold had played its usual havoc with the surface breaks on Highway 75. Paulie Noonan felt the thumps as the tired Econoline laboured to maintain the posted limit. The beat was familiar. He feigned the need to hold his fist to his chest, which would have been more than appropriate, considering his last Buick supper of beef jerky and Gatorade. He felt his heart beat through his torn woolen glove. It was keeping time with the tires below. Paulie figured it was a good sign.

The two rode in silence, watching the snow dance in serpentine fashion on the highway, bathed in the glow of the one properly aimed headlamp. They slowed as they pulled into

Morris, the weathered Stampede sign greeting them. The highway snow gates were still open, about as much of a green light as one could expect on any rural stretch of highway. Tommy Bosco spiked the brakes to comply with the town speed limit. The lone traffic light flashed in cautionary yellow. Morris slept, the way any small town sleeps: content, cozy, and forever unlocked.

"We could sure clean up here tonight," said Paulie as he eyeballed the side streets. He should have buckled up before he said it. Tommy slammed on the brakes, launching Paulie into the dash. The blood from Paulie's nose flowed quick and crimson. He looked up at Tommy, watching as he reached into the side door pocket for something. *Oh shit*, thought Paulie, *this was a double cross!* A free escape was little competition for two thousand dollars to make sure you were dead. That was the going rate in Winnipeg; they didn't call it the Wholesale Capital of Canada for nothing. Paulie closed his eyes and waited for the slug to hit.

Something hit Paulie hard, but it was definitely not a bullet. It was something a lot bigger, and a lot flatter. He opened his right eye a smidge, just in time for the second volley to land. *Did he just hit me with a book?* Paulie had been hit with a lot of things over the years — crowbars, gun butts, even an old chrome toaster by his ex-wife, but literature? This was new, and it still hurt like a motherfucker.

The swatting was interspersed with Tommy's commentary on the misguided choices that still populated Paulie's thoughts. "You-stupid-fucking-piece-of-shit-fucking-home-invasion-mother-fucker-un-grate-ful-fucking . . ." Tommy ran out of labels, finally stopping the barrage around volley twenty-two or twenty-three. Paulie had been holding up his arms in a protective defence since volley nine. Tommy threw the book onto the engine doghouse, launching a half-empty cup of Timmy's double-double onto Paulie's lap. Tommy angrily slapped the Econoline into gear, so much so that he didn't realize it was in low until he was up to fifty. The resulting correction was just as angry, finding neutral. The engine revved hard as Tommy calmed down enough to engage drive. Paulie wasn't paying much attention. He was looking at the book. It was old and black with a leather face, or at least some reasonable facsimile. Paulie remembered where he had first seen it, at The Guiding Light two days before.

Church hadn't exactly been on Paulie's to-do list in the last few years, thanks to all the whippings he had received from the nuns in Catholic school. The same could be said for higher education. Paulie had decided to fight back one day, cold-cocking the Mother Superior. It wasn't exactly the path to becoming valedictorian, or making it past grade eight.

The skid row mission block on Princess Street was something that Paulie would drive by at least once a day. He never thought that he would be opening the battered double doors to The Guiding Light at a time of personal need. Tommy had been running the place for about three years. It used to be called The Light and the Way, when it was run by a former Salvation Army Captain by the name of Bellows. The name change was somewhat required. Bellows had been running a steady string of teenage male prostitutes out the back door. Worse yet was his penchant for sampling the goods, usually after filling them up with ecstasy. He'd probably still be in business, if that one fourteen-year-old runaway hadn't run through the plate-glass window of the mission, naked, into the path of the downtown express bus. Dead kids tend to ruin everything, and right quick.

The former plate-glass window opening was mostly plywood now, with a smaller window that Tommy had received as a donation from a Mennonite community group. At least it let some light in. Too bad it couldn't let the smell out. It hit Paulie like it hits anyone who walks into a skid row mission for the first time.

Homemade benches of two-by-four construction served as seating, each one painted in whatever mis-tint paint colour Tommy could swing for free, or close to it. The food counter was doling out the gruel that they could muster for the week. The health department inspectors were hearing stories that most of the food at the Light had been 'pre-owned.' Even in the business of the skid row mission, there was a pecking order. The missions with Steering Committees, a Board of Directors, and an advertising budget would get the plum donations. These were the ones with custom-mixed paint, TV commercials, and media-savvy staff. The Guiding Light was still the home of the dead underage male prostitute, even with the name change and the new window. Most of the food inspectors turned a blind eye to the obvious infractions. The leftovers were probably getting scraped off the plates at one or more of the Chinatown restaurants, clustered closely together near Winnipeg City Hall. A couple of the cocaine dealers on Corydon had bistros as fronts, with plenty of leftover pasta at the end of the day. They were happy to do Tommy a solid, thanks to his years of faithful delivery service, and his refusal to testify against them after the double-cross. This unique fusion of Chinese and Italian resulted in a hardy stew, a touch overcooked in an effort to kill whatever bacteria might still be floating around from the previous night.

Paulie had asked one of the kitchen staff where Tommy was. "Cop or con?" said the toothless ladle handler, not even looking up from the task at hand. Paulie affirmed the latter and was pointed in the direction of the lopsided staircase.

There were only twelve beds on the second floor, with used office wall partitions on stands for some measure of privacy. The Guiding Light wasn't an official halfway house; it was more of a halfway-out-of-the-Life house. At some point, every resident had been in the system. They had gone through the rehabilitation programs, even completed stints in registered halfway houses. Most had found steady work and were in the process of rebuilding their lives when they called on Tommy. Sometimes the Light was simply a safer safe house, waiting for things to blow over, or waiting for the criminal element who had started the whole mess to get arrested.

At the back of the sleeping quarters was Tommy's space, a modified apartment of sorts, culled from three former offices. He had knocked out the walls between them and painted over the glass windows for some degree of sanctum. Two old couches looked upon a broken console television set with a cheap plasma-screen TV sitting on top. A red metal bunk bed stood at the opposite end. There was no top mattress; just a sheet of plywood in its place, stacked with office filing boxes for the Light. An oversized futon was jammed into the space of the bottom bunk. It was a far cry from Tommy's Tuxedo bungalow on Park Boulevard. He had called it the Boscalow. They still told stories about the parties.

Paulie had just lowered himself onto the couch when Tommy entered. He was wearing a thrift store–fresh houndstooth sportscoat, still in good shape, but at least twenty years south in style. The black knit turtleneck beneath it was a valiant attempt at fashion. With the jeans, and maybe a pipe,

Tommy could have passed for a university professor, if it wasn't for the scar. He was holding his vintage copy of the King James Bible, the same one that would be used to swat Paulie with later in the week. He tapped the brakes momentarily when he saw Paulie on the couch. The look on Paulie's face was clear to a reformer of convicts; I am royally screwed.

"Hey, Paulie," said Tommy, as he headed towards his makeshift filing cabinet. "And to what do I owe this pleasure?" Tommy started to rummage around in one of the filing boxes, out of Paulie's line of sight. Paulie reached inside his jacket. As he went to retrieve the item, he heard the telltale cocking of the Smith & Wesson .38. He looked at Tommy and down the barrel. "It's just my flask, man. Can't I have a drink?"

"Let's see it," said Tommy, motioning with the barrel to confirm the tale. Paulie slowly removed the flask, a cheap stainless steel job, filled with equally cheap rye. Tommy lowered the barrel. "Don't start reaching into your jacket around here," said Tommy. "You're bound to give a guy the wrong idea." Paulie took a large slug of the mix, leaning back into the couch to calm his nerves. He was about to tell Tommy the reason for the visit when there was a tap at the door.

"Tommy?" said the voice. "It's time for the eight o'clock."

Tommy returned the revolver to the box marked *Taxes*. The gun had been empty for as long as it had been in his possession, though there was no need to let Paulie know that. "I'll be right down, Cindy." He reached up on the post of the bunk bed to retrieve a homemade wooden cross with a leather-laced necklace. It looked like the type of item that might have been sanded and lacquered in the grade-nine wood-shop class that Paulie had missed out on. He grabbed the King James, almost seeming as though he would leave Paulie in peace.

"C'mon, you evil fuck," said Tommy. "Let's go save your sorry ass."

Paulie reluctantly followed as Tommy descended the stairs. On the wall, he noticed a poster of what he thought was Jesus Christ. It was a full-sized blow-up of the Buddy Christ, from the movie *Dogma*. Paulie didn't know the movie, but the irreverent thumbs-up pose of the teacher was enough to make any former Catholic boy smile.

Tommy rounded the corner at the bottom of the stairs, where the hungry homeless began to clap in pitiful unison. He headed to the opposite end of the hall as the ovation continued. Paulie watched as Tommy climbed up on a makeshift stage. Behind them hung a hand-knitted cobalt blue quilt with the words "God Don't Make No Trash" spelled out in shimmering gold fabric.

Tommy motioned for the crowd to calm themselves as he switched on the microphone. "Alright, simmer down now so we can save you fuckers." The shock value commentary drew the expected laugh of a comedy club audience, not a God-fearing congregation. Tommy began his makeshift homily, with little use of the King James.

"For those of you visiting us for the first time, welcome to The Guiding Light. We're not your regular Charlie Church deal, and we're not trying to be. We're not going to give you some bullshit answers about why God has fucked you in the ass. You fucked yourself in the ass, and that's why you're here." Paulie expected a gasp from the audience. Instead, Tommy's sermon was met by applause and cheers. "God loves you," said Tommy. "Jesus loves you. The apostles, saints, and all those angels upstairs love you. But they can't fix your shit. That's your job."

The applause continued as Tommy held up his Bible. "There's a lot of good shit in this book. Shit that can help you figure shit out. This book will give you the answers." Then Tommy slammed the King onto the podium. "But YOU'VE got to do the fucking work!" The enthusiasm continued unabated as Paulie found himself compelled to join in the applause. "You wanna know what Jesus would do? Jesus would tell you to go out and DO something!" Tommy scanned the crowd. "Who worked today? Show me some hands!" About a third of the room raised their arms to confirm. Tommy held up an old Heinz Ketchup can, the style used in the food service trade. "Then fill 'er up, you fuckers!"

There was no hymn for this community offering. Instead, the buzzy speakers of the PA system started up with a Doobie Brothers standard, "Jesus Is Just Alright." Paulie smiled as the parishioners hoisted the can through the room, throwing in whatever spare change they could, or whatever could be spared from their budget allotment for malt liquor or the tried-and-true paint thinner that the shadier area merchants would sell out the back door. It cost the same as a two-six of rye, though many of the attendees would argue that the thinner was the better high.

Paulie was starting to feel a little high himself that night, a feeling that even his life was still valuable enough to save. Tommy kept up the blue sermon for another hour. When it was done, he spent another hour-and-a-half in fellowship with his guests. Chewing on a day-old donut, Paulie watched Tommy from across the room. As Tommy spoke to his parishioners, Paulie noticed how he would connect glances with him. They seemed to assure him that everything would be alright. Just like Jesus.

As the semi-permanent residents headed up to bed, Tommy motioned to Paulie and said, "Help me with the bleachers. We've got to set up the folding tables for breakfast." The tables were old church cast-offs, each one feeling as heavy as a pair of stone tablets. Paulie thought that exhaustion might overtake him before he had a chance to explain his visit. On the eighth table, he dropped his end to get Tommy's attention. "Tommy, gimme a minute here. I, I gotta ask you something."

"Yes."

"Yes what?"

"Yes, I'll get you out. How bad is the heat?"

Paulie gave his best regional answer. "August long at Grand Beach."

Tommy put his end of the table down. "That's pretty fucking hot. When can you jet?"

"Whenever you say. I can lay low. Got the Roadmaster."

Tommy smiled. "The Royal Buick Hotel. Beats a Super 8 for sure." He reached into his coat pocket and threw an item about the size of a half-deck of cigarettes. Paulie caught it and looked at the little black box with a knowing grin. "You gotta be kidding me. It actually works?"

"Of course it works," said Tommy as he walked over to Paulie, flicking the side-mounted power switch of the numeric pager to prove it. "It's a Motorola."

CHAPTER FOUR

After Tommy got nabbed at the border, the consensus amongst the local criminal community was that he would turn. It was nothing personal, just the obvious next step for anyone arrested on drug-trafficking charges. Having it all go down at an international boundary made it a sure thing. Tommy would turn, go into the U.S. federal system, spill the beans on the Minneapolis connection, and then get extradited back home for the Canadian mess. It would probably take a good eighteen months, depending on the backlog. They knew he'd be in protective custody on either side, making a jailhouse assassination difficult. There were other ways. There was Park Boulevard.

While Tommy sat in a Federal office in Fargo, his seventeen-year-old son Jeremy thumbed his way through Grand Theft Auto on his PlayStation. The HRs were the first to fire, with three automatic assault rifles, through the picture window at the big screen's glow. The sunken living room was like lying in a bathtub for protection, which was exactly how Jeremy had been coached. Jeremy had accepted the life as normal — a lot more normal than the wife swapping and swinger parties that his classmates' parents indulged in. He waited for the fog of upholstery dust to settle before he poked his head up. He figured it was over. He didn't know that the Minneapolis contingent was coming down the boulevard from the opposite direction. Their spray of bullets took out the rest of the picture window, the table lamps, and Jeremy's skull. Tommy didn't cry when they told him. He knew that he was the one who had pulled the trigger. He didn't think of revenge or packaging them all up for the respective Feds. He thought of Jeremy's skull blown wide open, the spray of his brain matter against the big screen as the *Game Over* script cycled over and over.

The hidden cameras were a lot smaller than Tommy remembered, which is why he didn't succeed with his shoe-lace hanging attempt while in holding. It was while he was restrained and doped up on better drugs than he could get on his own that he met the Padre. He couldn't remember his name, or the scripture, or even the names of three of the apostles. What he did remember was how this Padre spoke. It wasn't the typical God-has-a-plan stylings.

He confirmed that it was as Tommy suspected; it was his fault entirely. "What are you going to do about it?" asked the Padre. Tommy offered the usual answers of retribution. The Padre responded with the King James, square across Tommy's face.

"What are you going to do about it?" shouted the Padre, continuing his attack as Tommy flexed the restraints.

"I'M GOING TO KILL THEM ALL!"

"Wrong answer," screamed the Padre, as he hit Tommy again with the thick hide. "What are you going to do about it?" Tommy tasted the blood from his nose. He felt his eyes beginning to swell. He didn't want to kill anyone. He just wanted it all to stop. What Tommy wanted came out as an unintelligible whisper.

"What did you say?" said the Padre, showing no sign of slowing. "I didn't quite get that."

"I want it to stop."

"Stop what exactly?"

"All of it."

"All of what?"

Tommy mustered up what was left of his strength, and his dignity. "The fucking life!" he shouted. The Padre stopped mid-swing as Tommy began to sob and repeat his desire. "I want it to stop," said Tommy. "I want it to stop for everybody. I don't want anyone to feel this. Nobody should ever feel what this feels like. Nobody."

"Good," said the Padre. He pulled out the homemade wooden cross, the same one that Tommy wore during his services. "My son made this for me, just before they got to him and his mother and his sister and the pizza guy who stumbled into the whole thing." Tommy held the cross to his chest. This was no ordinary Padre. This was the man he would try to become.

Getting there took about eighteen months, a few finger-points at low-level/no-retaliation drug dealers, and all his assets as proceeds of crime. He worked at a damaged goods warehouse on Logan Avenue after his release. He made fast friends with the owner, Sidney Guberman. When he told him about his idea for a mission, Sidney called in a favour to the owner of the Light and the Way property, which had been vacant since the front-page incident. If Tommy agreed to look the other way on the building code violations, spruce it up, and keep the prostitution trade reputation in the past tense, the space was his for $500 a month. That included the living quarters in the back for him. You could hardly rent a flea-infested studio apartment for that number. And with that, The Guiding Light was born.

CHAPTER
FIVE

Noonan figured they had to be about ten minutes from the Emerson border crossing when Tommy made a left onto a gravel side road. They passed a sign that read "Pembina Crossing First Nation," slightly obscured by blowing snow pack. "Yeah, it's a crossing alright," said Tommy, as he corrected a slight skid from a patch of glare ice. "The whole rez butts up right against the border." The new chief, David Clear-Sky, had done a good job of cleaning up the reserve's reputation with snowmobile patrols that discouraged crime. There was still smuggling going on, though it wasn't drugs or guns; it was people. Clear-Sky had had his run-ins with the law, having done some time in Headingley Correctional for receiving stolen property. "I met him in Headingley when I was nineteen," said Tommy. "I had six months on a break-and-enter. When I saw his name on a list of cons, I thought he was Ukrainian: *Clearsky*." Like Tommy, Clear-Sky knew how hard it was to start over, and he knew that some of those people couldn't stick around in their old postal code to do it.

The Econoline crested the next hill, greeted by three Ski-Doos with flashing blue LED lights. Chief Clear-Sky rode the centre unit, flanked by one of his constables on each side. He smiled as Tommy emerged from the van, topped with a hand-knitted toque to guard against the wind.

"How's that toque my grandmother made for you, White Bitch?" said Clear-Sky. White Bitch was the standard name lobbed by Aboriginal prisoners at Caucasians who were spending time in the Canadian prison system.

"Itchy as fuck," said Tommy, as he removed the garbage mitt to shake Clear-Sky's hand. The Chief was a beefy presence, about six-foot-two and 350 well-fed pounds, with jet black hair and a moustache that bordered on Tom Selleck. Tommy always took a dig at the obvious. "How's that low-carb diet working out? Too many perogies?"

"Fuck you, White Bitch," said Clear-Sky, smiling wider. "The store needs to start bringing in those low-fat chips. Besides, chiefing is hard work!"

"Stressful, too," said Tommy, as he handed him a bottle of Alberta Premium rye. Clear-Sky pulled the bottle out of the paper bag to confirm. "My favourite firewater," he said, stroking the label like the wool of a newborn lamb. "It's the only way I can get through the band council meetings." He stowed the two-six inside his parka. "So who's on tonight's departure list?"

"Just Mister X here," said Tommy, pointing to Paulie, who nodded at Clear-Sky while keeping his hands firmly in his pockets.

"That ain't no proper kind of Ski-Doo suit," said Clear-Sky. He retrieved the plastic garbage bag that had been attached with bungee cords to the rear of his Ski-Doo. Paulie removed the black suit, noticing that the reflective arm and leg stripes had been removed. "Suit up," said Clear-Sky. "Just don't wave your little white dick at us while you're doing it." The constables laughed at the jab as Paulie stripped off his coat for the suit. There was the sound of another snowmobile approaching, though the surrounding blackness offered no visual evidence until the blacked-out vintage Polaris sprang onto the roadbed. There were no lights on the Polaris, just a rider, clad in black, with a matching helmet that had been modified to hold some form of oversized night-vision goggles. He motioned at the constables. "Turn off your fucking lights!" said the rider. "It burns my fucking eyes!"

The constables complied as the rider removed his helmet. A scraggly blond mullet emerged. Paulie figured that the rider had to be of Norwegian or Swedish descent, as many North Dakotans were. He rubbed his eyes incessantly. "How fucking hard would it be for you guys to turn off your fucking lights when you hear me fucking coming?"

"Cause it's fun blinding you, White Bitch," said Clear-Sky. The nickname wasn't just for Tommy, Paulie realized; Clear-Sky called every Caucasian White Bitch.

"Hey Svenn," said Tommy. "How you been keeping? Are those the Russian surplus goggles?"

"Yeah," said Svenn Tergesen, as he fiddled with the make-shift battery pack fastened to the side of his helmet. "The battery life sucks, so I RadioShacked this one on." Svenn was about forty, lanky, with a family farm about ten miles from the border. He pointed to the gas cap. "Who's got the gas?" One of the constables produced a five-gallon jerrycan from his Ski-Doo. Svenn began topping off his tank, ignoring the safety issues of a running engine. "Cargo, please," said Svenn, motioning to Paulie. With that, the cargo eased himself onto the back of the Polaris, careful not to rip the Ski-Doo suit, an easy two sizes off. There were no grab handles and no strap to steady him.

"Hang on to me," said Svenn, shouting over the din of the engine. "It doesn't make you gay." Paulie took one last look at Tommy as he complied with the request. Tommy nodded the type of nod that says, "Hey, man. It's cool. You're welcome. Get the fuck out of here. Have a nice life." Then Svenn gunned the throttle, launching the Polaris off the roadbed and almost losing Paulie in the process. The tune of the engine continued to fade as the blackness swallowed them whole.

CHAPTER SIX

While Tommy Bosco drank in the band office, a rusty brown Chevy Caprice idled across from the Driftwood Apartments on Osborne Street South. Ernie Friday waited patiently in the driver's seat, scanning through radio stations in a futile attempt to find something he hadn't heard a million times before. He settled on a college station. He didn't know the band. He didn't really like the progression of the beat. The singer sounded like a boy and a girl all at the same time. At least it was something new.

Ernie was about sixty, and everything about him said so, except for one thing: his hair. While his face had sunk, his belly had expanded, and his eyes were assisted by bargain bifocals, his hair had remained black, lush, and full. The running theory amongst those who knew him was that it had to be a rug. A couple of years ago, a drunken bouncer at the Stock Exchange Hotel decided it would be fun to find out. Ernie gave him the Vise Grip, as his neck clutch had become known. In his younger days, Friday would have lifted the offender off the ground, squeezed till he was unconscious, and then thrown him through the nearest plate-glass window. After three heart attacks, Ernie simply squeezed the would-be rug snatcher to sleep and returned to his rye and 7 as he hit the floor. Ernie had mellowed. The offending bouncer learned to behave, after a month in a neck brace.

The front passenger door handle started to jiggle. Ernie hit the power lock, allowing entry for Teddy Simms. Teddy had been known for his solid B&E work when he was sober, which was about ten years ago. He wasn't good for much these days, especially after getting a tire-iron beating by a couple of fifteen-year-olds behind the neighbourhood Safeway. He managed to get by on the stupidity of others, the kind that still populated the suburbs. Simms was amazed at how many people forgot to close their garage doors for the night. With the disability check, plus whatever he could steal and pawn, Teddy could easily handle the rent, plus the one-gallon jugs of swish whiskey he would buy from a barrel connection at the Seagram's Distillery in Gimli. The old Crown Royal barrels could still produce a palatable rye, without the colour or texture of the store-bought mix. Two twenties bought eight litres, delivered in the plastic water jugs that were emptied into the barrels to leach out the whiskey. Teddy reeked of the mix.

"You better not be completely fucked up," said Ernie as he handed Teddy a double-double. "I can't move this fucker all by myself." Teddy looked towards the direction of the unseen corpse in the trunk of the Caprice. "Anybody I'd know?" said Teddy as Ernie pulled into traffic.

"You've been out of the loop for a while, don't yah think?" said Ernie, as he headed south on Dunkirk. "You probably think the Wilsons are still cooking up the primo meth."

"Hey, I may be a drunk, but I'm not completely stupid," said Teddy, as he opened the coffee lid. "I saw the news."

Ernie didn't answer as he signalled for the right onto St. Mary's Road. Teddy kept looking at the trunk. "So, who is it?" said Teddy.

"Nobody important," said Ernie.

"He had to be important enough."

"Important enough to what?"

"Important enough to end up in the trunk."

Ernie slowly exhaled in frustration. Teddy scanned the streets as the Caprice rumbled down St. Mary's. He seemed to get excited as they approached River Park South, knowing that even in January there would be at least one garage with $200 worth of snatch-and-grab tools, open for business. Probably not a good idea to ask for a side trip, Teddy thought, especially with a fresh body in the trunk.

Ernie tapped the brakes for the slow-down to the Perimeter Highway. As he pulled up, he noticed a marked RCMP Crown Vic approaching from the opposite side. They waited in their positions at the red light. Even after more than forty years of successful criminal activity, Ernie's stomach always tensed up when he saw a marked car. It was not the first time he had disposed of a body or had been involved in some form of illicit cargo transfer. For whatever reason, there had always been a cop at the threshold. Not to catch him, simply to remind him of where he could be going if he made a mistake. He still remembered the first one he'd faced down; a mid-seventies Plymouth Fury, black and white, from the old West St. Paul police force. The light went green. The Crown Vic turned right. Ernie breathed.

The greenhouses of St. Mary's Road were in various stages of closed for the season. A sanding truck and a group of kids going too fast in a minivan were all that presented themselves. Ernie flicked on the right turn signal, heading over the Red River Floodway gate. As they approached Red River Road, they saw a brown community-based organization sign bent at a forty-five-degree angle that read Howden Community Centre. The Caprice turned right towards it.

"Is there a hole?" said Teddy as the Caprice drove past the oversized homes, a popular place to build thanks to the rural tax breaks.

"Not unless there's a jackhammer in that trunk with him," said Ernie as he slowed to a stop just outside the parking lot of the community centre. He flipped open a battered brief-case that occupied the centre of the bench seat. Inside was an aftermarket backup camera system, a cheap Canadian Tire model that Ernie had bought on clearance. He plugged in a power lead to the cigarette lighter socket. The small screen flickered to life with an image that wasn't of the road behind the Caprice. Like most businesses on a budget, the centre was using a wireless security camera system, a popular alternative to the expense associated with a closed-circuit set-up. Ernie could see inside the centre, a grainy black-and-white image that confirmed that nobody was home. He couldn't see the locations of any outdoor cameras, though Ernie knew that most kits came with four, if Amazon Canada could be believed. Teddy watched as Ernie produced a black box. It was connected to a series of small antenna mounts that were wired together with a homemade harness, with some form of external battery pack. "What the fuck is that?"

"It's a Freedom Box," said Ernie.

"What the fuck is a Freedom Box?"

"It keeps me free, and out of the box." Ernie placed the antenna array across the flat top of the Caprice dashboard. He switched the power switch on the box to the on position. Ernie watched as the screen showing the interior of the Howden Community Centre started to flicker, then fuzz like the screen of an old television. Then he saw the image he was waiting for from the Howden wireless security system: *SIGNAL LOST.* He put the Caprice into drive.

The lot needed plowing, though it was not impassable. He drove the Caprice towards the back of the centre, dousing the lights and hitting a darkened toggle switch on the dashboard. The switch glowed red, an indicator to those within that the brake lights were now as dark as the rest of the Caprice. An old three-ton box from a U-Haul rental truck stood on a platform of wooden pallets. *It was obviously a storage locker of sorts*, thought Teddy, *maybe for extra tables or folding chairs*. It would also make for a good body dump. This would be a public dump, meant to send a message to others. It would probably take a few days for one of the retired volunteers at the community centre to head to the box. It wasn't that he wished for it to happen, but Ernie had often thought that it would be quite amusing for someone like that to find the body and drop dead at the same time. Talk about confusion; the place would be littered with police vehicles, news vans, and a big white tent to cover it all — very public indeed. Sometimes, the message was obvious to the police, the media, and the public at large. Bad guy, with bad-guy buddies, gets whacked by other bad-guy buddies, because he wasn't a buddy to the bad guys no more. The case would usually go cold before the large overhead crime-scene lights had gone out. Still, it made for great TV.

Ernie killed the motor, handing Teddy a pair of rubber work gloves with winter lining. He reached into the glovebox, hitting the power release for the trunk. The two exited the Caprice, Teddy moving the half-pace slower of a man not ready to see what was in the trunk. The trunk light was either loose or verging on replacement. The lamp flickered over the contents, a large blue hockey bag presented itself, with the Toronto Maple Leafs logo centered, in white silkscreen.

"Oh, great. A Leafs fan," Teddy said, with a hint of snicker. "Wouldn't that make this a mercy killing?"

Ernie wasn't in the mood. "Just grab that end," he said, motioning to the right. Teddy gave the bag a tug. It was heavy, at least 200 pounds. The duffle was large, though anything but a natural fit. Whoever was inside was broken up good. "Get the door," Ernie motioned as they rolled the bag out of the trunk. It hit the snow-packed ground with a sickening thud. Teddy kicked the latch open, finding that the cold had done little to jam the door rollers. They dragged the bag into the centre of the box, dropping it with little thought to its cargo.

"Hey, Teddy, you wanna take a peek?" Ernie asked, panting. Teddy was confused. Usually, a simple dump would be a couple hundred bucks and maybe a double-double, depending on who called you. The rest was usually kept anonymous. Who needed the nightmare? As dead as whoever the stiff was, it didn't make sense to tempt fate. Plus, Teddy had done four other dumps with Ernie over the years. He had never asked if he wanted a peek before. Maybe it was someone important. Maybe it was worth a look.

Teddy bent down, slowly unzipping the duffle. The top was layered with black plastic garbage bags. Teddy pulled back the bags, already squinting in anticipation of the damage or decomposition that would be present. What he saw was yellow, a lot of it. The duffle bag was full of paper. No body, just a stack of expired phone books. Teddy looked up just in time to see the first muzzle flash from the silencer on Ernie's Beretta. A slight fluff of down insulation leapt forth from his jacket as the first slug entered his chest. He fell back against the wall of the box. Bullets two and three were clustered close to the first, to ensure maximum internal bleeding. Teddy looked up at Ernie, hopeful for some form of explanation in his final moments.

Ernie wasn't forthcoming. He didn't have to be. Teddy had been doing low-level snitch work for the Vice division for the past few months. He had tried to be careful, fingering the soldiers of the various criminal organizations around town. He figured he had played it smart, since most of them were too junior to turn. They needed a bit of prison time under their belts to establish credibility. He hadn't bet on one of them being chatty enough to bring down a sergeant-at-arms with the Heaven's Rejects. The soldier "committed suicide" at the space-age Remand Centre, where even multiple cameras and bed checks were no match for dirty guards ready to look the other way. Teddy, like everyone with a contract on their life, was the last to know.

"That's the great thing about Winnipeg," said Ernie as he raised the Beretta to line up with Teddy's forehead. "You can get anywhere in fifteen minutes." Ernie was right. One more shot shipped Teddy straight off to eternity. Ernie stacked the old phone books in the corner, a little hard to carry without a helper. He decided not to double back on his initial route to

Howden. No sense in tempting fate with the RCs, he thought. He put the empty duffle bag back in the trunk, removing a folding sweeper as wide as the Caprice, with bristles cut from old semi-trailer mud flaps. The metal framework that held it together was welded to a trailer ball mount. He plugged the mount into the receiver on the Caprice with the usual cursing and fighting that occurs with old, cold metal. He drove around the parking lot three times, making sure to stagger his tracks to erase any forensic evidence. He knew it was overkill. Overkill was what separated him from freedom and wearing a number at the Stony Mountain institution. The Caprice would go to the scrap yard in the morning, to be shredded.

About a half mile south of Howden, heading towards 75, Ernie stowed the sweeper in the trunk. When he reached the intersection to the highway, he sat idling for a moment at the stop sign. He could have gone — the approaching headlights were at least a minute away — but this was typical Ernie: take a moment to process. Was it a clean dump? Did anyone notice his detailing of the snow? Were the tail lights working on the rusty Caprice? Ernie checked the cut-off switch to make sure, checking the glow in the rear-view mirror. A deep exhale followed. Ernie fumbled in his coat for his pack of Peter Jacksons, a harsh finish for a harsh deed.

The nicotine pause was long enough to bring the oncoming headlights close enough for Ernie to yield as Tommy Bosco's beaten Econoline rumbled past. Ernie knew it was Tommy, with the cockeyed headlight and the Guiding Light lettering on the side. He floored the throttle of the Caprice to find traction for the icy takeoff. He managed to catch up to Tommy as the two slowed for the traffic light for the entry into St. Norbert. He stayed back half a car length. This wouldn't be a "Hey, son, how you doing? Let's get a coffee at Timmy's" kind of deal. This wouldn't be anything at all, just like their relationship had been for years.

Unlike most of Ernie's contemporaries, Tommy was encouraged to enter The Life instead of legitimate pursuits. Tommy's mother had died in a drunk driving accident when Tommy was two. Discipline occurred, though only for getting caught. The last belt-lashing happened at age twelve. Ernie bought Tommy a car for his sixteenth birthday after he successfully stole his twentieth car. It was far from *Father Knows Best*, but it seemed to work until Tommy fell in with the hard-drugs trade. Like an old Mafioso in an old Mafioso movie, Ernie believed there were just some things you didn't do. Killing was okay, if there was a valid reason. Pimping was allowed — it *was* the world's oldest profession. Soft drugs weren't as big of a deal, but cocaine, heroin, and the new synthetics, like fentanyl, would bring in overdoses and unwanted attention. Ernie used to say that it upset the natural balance of honest crime. That's what he believed in then. He still believed it now.

Tommy going straight had caused the rift between them. He couldn't turn a blind eye, nor could Ernie expect him to. They tried the Tim Hortons coffee chats for a while, but there just didn't seem to be anything to talk about anymore. Ernie wasn't exactly politically correct when it came to the redemption of failed criminals. He saw them as dumb cons without discipline. "Nobody ever has to get caught," he would say to Tommy during a game of catch with stolen gloves from a truck heist. "You always choose. And it's usually some stupid bitch who gives you away." Shortly after their last Timmy's meeting in 2012, Tommy officially changed his last name to his mother's maiden name. He had been using it as an alias for much longer.

In the north end of the city, a veteran of the red-light district was using an old screwdriver to pry open the catch of a Pritchard Avenue basement window. Claire Hebert was pushing thirty-five, an age when most hookers would be considering a much-needed retirement. In the sex trade since fourteen, Hebert, or "Claire-Bear" as the johns knew her, had risen through the ranks of local prostitution, from the Higgins Avenue low track to the fur coats and hush-hush escort services of Albert Street. In a town known for wholesale, Claire Hebert didn't come cheap. $1,000 got you three hours, anal, if that was your thing, and a squirt show that could rival whatever you could download off the internet. Add another thousand, and she'd bring an equally adept friend.

Claire wasn't sure about her background. Her Ukrainian-Scottish mother referred to her absentee father in terms reserved more for his character, though it was obvious to any mirror that she had aboriginal blood in her veins, the kind of Métis mix that a white-run advertising agency would use for a marketing campaign. She pushed back and forth on the old basement window, using it like a snow shovel to clear away the crisp white powder, just like the high-grade cocaine on the mirror upstairs, with the rolled-up Borden, next to the body of the freshly late Jimmy Stephanos.

Claire wasn't a fan of the underworld john. The pluses of ready cash, quality drugs, and a relatively safe working environment could just as quickly erupt into violence. Most of them could hold their liquor and coke and wouldn't cross the line with a fist or a gun. Every five years or so, a Claire-Bear wannabe would turn up, usually face down on Pipeline Road or the outer reaches of Community Row. Dentals and prints were the identifiers, as the faces were usually beaten to a bloody mash. The last one was a girl that Claire had stood alongside on Albert Street, near the Duke of Kent Legion. An HR recruit took her ecstasy-laced comments about his manhood too personally. After strangling her, he took her to a wood shop and introduced her to an industrial planer. Claire couldn't remember if her name was Sarah or Sandy.

Stephanos's blood flow had slowed from his neck, the razor still embedded just past the left carotid slice. In his final moments, he had tried to dial his new bodyguard, who was idling unaware in front of the well-kept bungalow. Stephanos was known to complain about his cell phone at executive meetings of the Heaven's Rejects. "I gotta figure out how to use this speed-dial bullshit," he would mutter as he tried to remember the phone numbers of key associates. Most of them wouldn't keep numbers like that stored for fear that a lost or confiscated phone would give Vice or Robbery-Homicide key information on open cases. Stephanos figured he didn't have to worry. Misguided or not, he was the president of the local chapter.

With only four numbers keyed, Stephanos's final spasm hit Send. The "call cannot go through" chatter had ended, along with the fast busy. There was nothing but dead air. Dead Claire-Bear would be next. It was only a matter of time till the bodyguard checked in; he would find the body, the hooker missing, and Stephanos's briefcase gone. That would happen in about two hours, twenty minutes past the three-hour maximum.

The Pritchard house was known as the HRs' Fuck Palace amongst Winnipeg Vice, and the rear door had been barricaded to combat possible raids, making the basement window Claire's only exit. As tiny as she was in frame, the pratfalls of breast augmentation made the exit difficult.

"Stupid fucking tits," she said as she finally shimmied out of the opening. Her coat was busy, soaking up blood on the living room floor, along with her burner phone, which had fallen during the melee. The thin cashmere sweater she was wearing wouldn't provide comfort for long. The briefcase was another issue. It was one thing for a Native-looking girl with a fresh shiner and no jacket to be walking down a North End street. The $400 Jack Georges leather briefcase would look out of place to a patrol car or a neighbourhood low-life looking for an easy mark. She pulled a half-full green garbage bag out of the AutoBin in the back lane. The inside of the bag was fresh with the funk of spoiled foodstuffs. After emptying the bag's contents, she stuffed the briefcase inside the North End suitcase, tying a double knot to secure it. She hoped that it held enough drugs and cash to get out of town.

The back lane was tricky for three-inch-heel boots. The house was mid-block, with McGregor Avenue the best bet for a bus or cab. The cold helped to numb the pain of the shiner. A cap had become dislodged from an incisor. Claire couldn't remember if it had been spat or swallowed. She didn't remember much of the rage that had occurred, only that it seemed out of place for Stephanos. When she arrived, he was a different kind of edgy; not the expected emotion from the cocaine, but the "something's up" kind. Still, there were no crimson red flags. Claire had taken a hit offered by Stephanos. Feeling the buzz, she kicked out her legs in appreciation, knocking the coffee table hard. The jostle sent the briefcase over the other side. That's when Stephanos snapped. The sucker punch found her right eye, then a left-bound haymaker to the jaw. *Community Row*, she thought as Stephanos put his hands around her neck. She reached into her boot for the razor. It was a reflex. She had heard cops talk about how they had never pulled a gun in twenty years on the force, but they knew that they could if called upon.

A veteran working girl from Albert Street had given her the razor and had taught her how to use it. "You want to be able to retire one day," said Jasmine Starr as she explained the need for protection in the Blue Note Café. "Not as a picture in the missing persons section of the *Sentinel*." Jasmine had successfully retired about seven years earlier. She had put her previous work experience to good use, opening a sex shop on Main Street called The Other Woman. She had never pulled the razor, as far as Claire knew.

Claire had pulled the razor and had swung it hard into

Stephanos's neck. She didn't know what she had hit, other than the obvious main line to his brain, as the telltale sign of the blood spatter on the wall would illustrate to any crime scene investigator. The speed of the upwards slice caused the razor to lodge in the jawbone. Claire watched for a moment as Stephanos bled out. He tried to reach for her, but there was no blood available to move the extremities. The gasps were almost amusing. With each one, the razor handle would quiver as it followed the movements of his jaw. He tried to speak.

"Y-y-you f-f-fu-fu-fu-cking c-c-cunt," he said as he felt his tank reaching empty. Then he was quiet. Even though Stephanos's driver hadn't seen the skirmish through the blackout curtains, Claire knew that time wasn't on her side. Just enough time to grab the bag, lose her jacket, jam her clutch in the front of her jeans, and bolt towards the basement.

She was on McGregor now, trying to keep from breaking an ankle on the poorly plowed sidewalk. There were no convenience stores with a phone nearby. About the only friendly public spot would be the fire hall at McGregor and Redwood, though she would probably be kept on the other side of the door, thanks to a couple of firefighters from the Maple Street Engine Company who in the past had been caught with Higgins Avenue working girls in the storage shed behind the station. The best bet was a cab, if it was the right company. Jimmy's Taxi was the largest fleet, which meant it carried most of the hooker trade, placing it in deep with the criminal element. Buddy's Cab wasn't much better. What she needed was an indie, and there were only four left in the city. She scanned the traffic for a roof-mount lamp. Traffic was brisk, with plenty of the cabs she didn't need. Then she saw the white Dodge Diplomat. White Taxi, the oldest independent in town, with the oldest cabs. There were only six cabs in the

White fleet, with the average driver age in the low seventies. Their only innovation was their no-cash policy, which kept knives out of backsides. The drivers would call in the credit card number before the cab rolled. Claire pulled out her clutch to flag him down. The cabbie pulled up at the cut-out to the back lane and rolled down the passenger window.

"Evening miss," said the darkened gravelly voice. "Little cold for sweater weather, isn't it?"

Claire nodded. "I need a lift."

"Sure thing," said the cabbie. "Remember, we don't take cash, just plastic."

Claire didn't have a credit card, or a debit card, or even a bank account, one of the drawbacks to living life off the grid. She did a quick scan of the cabbie. Not too big, no Virgin Mary figurine on the dashboard, and a well-worn wedding ring on his left hand. Perfect. She pushed back her hair, hoping that her impromptu snow wash and the old man's eyesight would miss any sign of her recent facial carnage. She mustered up the bravado.

"How about a hummer?"

The cabbie grabbed an old paint stirring stick, with a u-shaped indent on the end. He flipped up the passenger door lock. Claire entered as he picked up his two-way.

"Cab twenty-four to Dispatch."

"Go ahead, twenty-four."

"Going to stop for coffee at Robin's on Redwood."

"Gotcha twenty-four. Out."

The Diplomat pulled away from the curb. Claire breathed.

Through all of this, Freddie the
Ford slept.

Freddie was cold steel, just like the
lathes and drill presses that took up the adjacent
space in the century-old machine shop on Jarvis,
near the north ramp of the Arlington Bridge. If
Freddie could hear, it would be the cacophony
of the Canadian Pacific rail yards, the squeal of
massive brakes, the low register of diesel loco-
motives, and the soul-jarring impact of train cars
being coupled. Freddie heard none of it. Freddie
slept.

It had been at least a year since Freddie drew
breath. Tommy would visit on occasion, with
the keys and a freshly charged battery. Keeping

the truck was becoming more of an involved process. Freddie was stored in Jaime Bachynski's machine shop, and space was becoming a bit of a premium. Jaime had just purchased an industrial drill press, a relic of the over-built 1950s American military complex. It had served at a Midwestern university, constructing all manner of world-ending components. Jaime wasn't one for computer-controlled systems; he was an old-school machinist. He had the touch needed to operate the oversized beast, mostly for specialty pieces for Manitoba Hydro projects. The new-old press meant a short trip for Freddie, to the east wall of the shop. The 1989 Ford F-150 XLT Lariat was covered with miscellaneous debris; a few tow straps, some scraps of angle iron, and an old set of booster cables rested on the hood. The old Ford was too ugly to catch anyone's eye; it looked like the definition of an old piece of wheeled junk.

Freddie wasn't junk; Freddie had history. Most observers would see a weathered light-blue pickup truck, equipped with top-down paint peel, rusting panels, and a cracked wind-shield. Three patches of lubricants were evident at floor level; engine oil, transmission fluid, and differential sweats. The signal switch was broken for left-hand turns. Tommy would have to hold it in place to make the blinkers fire. Freddie cer-tainly didn't look special. No one would have ever thought that this old Ford was a millionaire ten times over.

In his prime, Freddie the Ford had been an important link in the chain that was cross-border smuggling. Freddie and Tommy had made bi-weekly runs to Minneapolis, having to stop much more regularly for fuel than a proper dual tank half-ton Ford should. Tommy was running a semi-legitimate business on the St. Paul side of the Twin Cities, selling air bag suspensions and custom wheels. Most of the customers were in the drug trade, and the nicer the ride, the better the drugs, as well as the size of the territory that they maintained in the metro area. Tommy had never been a full-patch member of any gang, though he was a level-one friendly of the Heaven's Rejects. One errand grew to two, then three, then bankrolls for fronts. Tommy's Winnipeg operation did custom bike work — performance modifications and elaborate paint jobs on Harley-Davidsons — plus automotive wheel repairs. The money from the local criminal operations would flow into the Winnipeg shop, where it would be stashed in the dummy fuel tank and head south. On the return trip, Freddie's dummy tank would carry new cargo — cocaine, heroin, and the occasional supply of gun parts, such as conversion kits for full automatic firing.

The side streets in the Twin Cities would do quick and consistent damage to oversized custom wheels. The trade required specialized equipment, much of which hadn't been built for decades. Custom paint colours and air brushed accents ensured repeat business with the Twin Cities customers, along with a well-timed act of arson against the only wheel-repair shop in St. Paul. The tale was plausible for the go-ahead nod from Customs agents at the border crossing — a truckload of repaired wheels heading south, an equal load of broken ones heading north. Tommy would sometimes have to purposely damage new wheels on the U.S. side to top off Freddie's load.

The dummy tank still held gas, though the quantity was considerably less than the owner's manual specifications. The filler neck flared out as it entered the tank, much like the profile of a chemist's beaker. A casual sniff at Customs wouldn't tip the hand; even a swipe of a wooden test stick would draw out enough fuel to send Freddie the Ford out of the inspection bay. Getting the money together involved numerous Heaven's

Rejects soldiers, shady currency houses, even a few legitimate banks asleep at the switch. Cash loads averaged between one hundred and two hundred thousand dollars, depending on what was getting bought for the return trip.

Underneath, Freddie's underbelly still looked factory. The fuel lines, supply hoses, even the corrosion on the lines looked correct for the vintage, thanks to one of the airbrush artists who worked on the Harleys at the Winnipeg shop. The release mechanism for the contraband cargo hold was incorporated into the straps that held the tank to the under-carriage. When the straps were unbolted from their factory holes, hidden hinges concealed inside the tank allowed it to swing down for access. The trick was making sure that the bolts keeping the tank closed were properly tightened. On one of the initial runs, the vibrations of Highway 75 loosened the bolts free. The dummy tank flopped wide open at about 109 kilometres per hour. Two thirty-nine-cent lock washers made sure that Tommy wouldn't have to fish bags of contra-band or cash out of the ditch.

And so it went. Five years, three months, and sixteen days' worth of successful cartage, as Tommy pulled into the Emerson–Pembina border crossing on January 17, 2009. There was no tipoff, just a non-threatening request from the officer on duty to proceed to door two of the U.S. customs inspection garage. Tommy had just finished placing Freddie into park, when he felt the Glock pistol muzzle, its handler pushing the imprint hard into his left temple. A lot of yelling and screaming accompanied the proceedings. Every face was hoping that Tommy would do just one thing; flinch. That was the problem with many U.S. customs officers. Only one in five ever saw service in the military, and that was usually on the home front in the highly classified areas of the motor pool and the mess hall. *Please,* they all seemed to mouth. *Please give me a reason to blow out the side of your skull. Please.*

Then, the leader of the U.S. customs posse reached in behind the bench seat, removing a brick of hashish duct-taped to the vinyl. He threw it at Tommy's head.

"What the fuck is this?" asked Officer Posse.

Tommy sniffed at the package. "Some guys save up balls of string. That's a brick of your Mom's pubes."

Tommy would have thrown in Merry Ukrainian Christmas for good measure, if not for the Winchester butt that slammed into his face. Even before the gun butt sent him for a nap, he had already figured out the chain of events; it was the woman scorned. This was why most of Tommy's circle settled on the young and the dumb, the girls with fake breasts, painted-on rubber dresses, and an appetite for partying. Tommy started a relationship with the one woman you never should: a hooker. Claire Hebert liked it rough, and often, as did Tommy. She also liked the free cocaine that circulated amongst the HRs' inner circle a little too much for Tommy's liking. It was fun at first, though after a baker's dozen rescues from the penthouse balconies of various apartments, Tommy had had enough. Unfortunately, Claire hadn't, and a combination of unwanted detoxification, a bag of hydroponic weed, and a week of steady hits of vodka led to a revenge brick of hashish taped to the backside of Freddie's bench seat. Tommy bet it had been stashed in her apartment so long that it was starting to resemble an unwanted fruitcake. There was no sense in screwing someone over with anything good; it just had to be illegal.

Freddie the Ford avoided the usual vehicular strip search, thanks to the easy bust. As Tommy languished, so did Freddie, in a compound just outside Pembina. It spoke of camera surveillance and guard dogs, though the cameras had yet to be hooked into an endless loop recorder and the resident German Shepherd was at the vet, thanks to Paulie Noonan and some ex-lax–laden peanut butter. Paulie knew the procedure well enough for Freddie's underbelly, even had the right-sized socket wrench for the dummy tank bolts. The HRs would have assumed that the cash had been found in the bust; it was forgotten money. When the dust had settled, it would help with the upstart fees on The Guiding Light. First, it would pay for Jeremy Bosco's funeral.

Through a glitch with the Manitoba Public Insurance title department, Freddie the Ford was listed as having two owners: Tommy Friday, aka Tommy Bosco, and his father, Ernie Friday. Freddie had originally belonged to Ernie, an insurance write-off that was fixed on the cheap. The family relation meant that Tommy didn't have to get the old Ford safety inspected. When Tommy got arrested, it was a safe bet that Freddie would wheel his way to a U.S. Drug Enforcement Agency–seized property auction in Bismarck, North Dakota. The ownership issue gave Freddie a reprieve. Ernie had a cartage company tow the truck to the Emerson side of the border. When Tommy got back to Winnipeg, his old Ford was waiting for him. Tommy wasn't ready to part with his rusty steed, though he wasn't ready to make him a daily driver, either. The next twelve hours would change that.

The cabbie took forever to finish, and Claire didn't exactly have much time. She told the cabbie to drop her at the Anderson Apartments, which was about three blocks south of The Other Woman. The door on the Anderson was seldom locked, even less so during the winter months when the ice jams of slush and grit kept it from being secure till late March. Claire exited the cab, heading up the walk with purpose, fumbling with a key that she wouldn't need. The cab didn't pull away, as if the driver was watching her enter, assuring some modicum of safety for her illicit services. She headed up the stairs to the second floor, using her peripheral vision to eye the Diplomat through the stairway glass as it pulled away. She ran the entire length of the hallway, descending the staircase in a flurry that seemed more like a choreographed fall than concentrated steps. The rear door closure had been disconnected for an earlier move-in. Claire hit the door hard and swung into the fender of a soiled Pontiac. The Pontiac started to screech and wail, as most inexpensive car alarms do. Panic, snow, and high heels are never a good mix. Claire made a slippery beeline for the back door of The Other Woman as all the lights came on at the Anderson.

Jasmine Starr was busy putting bogus Canadian compliance stickers on a shipment of Chinese dildos when the buzzer rang. She took a drag on her Peter Jackson as she looked up at the grainy video image. Starr was younger than forty but looked way over fifty. The adult store had allowed her to relax in the ways of health and implants. She was now around a size fourteen, which put her in the minority at the plus-sized boutiques, or the "Large Marge" as she would call them. Her website took care of most of the trade, since suburbanites were still too scared to admit that anything but the missionary position was occurring in their cab-over splits. Her makeup was thin; her hair pulled tight and convenient in a French braid. It took her another ten seconds to check the other cameras before she buzzed Claire in. The thermal shock was a welcome sensation. Claire ran straight past Jasmine, dropped the bagged briefcase, and collapsed on a pull-out sofa that looked anything but comfortable.

"Tough day at the office, dear?" said Jasmine as she surveyed the all-too-common fetal position of a distressed Claire Hebert.

"I'm dead," said Claire, as she tried to pull some magical warmth from the decorative afghan that covered the sofa upholstery. "I'm very, very dead."

"You look very much alive to me." Jasmine had already gone back to the label task, assuming this was nothing more than a bad trip or possibly a bad john freak-out episode. Jasmine had the Claire-Bear box set. What could possibly be new here?

"I killed a guy."

Jasmine looked up, still affixing the label as she aligned her deadpan gaze. "He probably had it coming. Was it anybody important?"

Claire continued her search for warmth. "Jimmy. Jimmy Stephanos."

Only those who knew Jasmine Starr could have seen the momentary pause. While she was a sort-of friend, Jasmine knew Claire was as good as dead. If it had been a simple case of an adventurous suburban john who pushed his luck, she would have offered the expected support, or at least a proper blanket. There had to be a reason, a really good reason, to invite the full fury of the Heaven's Rejects. Jasmine noted the roughed-up face. Claire shook with a tremor beyond that of narcotic withdrawal. Jasmine knew it would be at least a Community Row type of ending, if they found her. The question at this point was how much time Claire had to run like hell.

"What cab did you take?"

Claire was starting to calm down. "Indie, White."

"How?" said Jasmine. "You don't have plastic."

"I blew him." Claire was muffled now, having turned in to the back of the cushions.

"At least you didn't take the main lines," said Jasmine. She tossed a wrapped mint at Claire's head, which bounced off her cheek with no reaction or protest. "Where'd he drop you?"

Claire motioned. "Anderson Apartments, went out the back."

Simple double-back stuff, thought Jasmine. A grade-school kid could do it, which also meant a grade-school kid, or a Heaven's Reject, could figure it out. Claire had to disappear, maybe not tonight, but soon. The longer she stayed with Jasmine, the better the chance that someone would come looking. Jasmine finally noticed the bag.

"What's that?"

"What's what?" The muffling of the couch was taking on the nuances of a new language for Claire-Bear.

"The fancy bag you rolled in with."

Claire rolled towards the voice. "It's Stephanos's. Girl's gotta get paid, right?"

Jasmine managed a smirk. She wondered how long she would be amused with her couch surfer.

Detective Sergeant Miles Sawatski wouldn't be sleeping tonight, or tomorrow.

His Robbery-Homicide cell phone had started vibrating on the nightstand around three thirty a.m. Thursday morning, about a half hour after the first marked car in District Three had responded to the 911 call. The detective sergeant was now seated in the leather chair adjacent to the couch that displayed the Stephanos corpse. He had the expected look of cop curiosity as he studied the razor's final resting place. Every so often, his eyes would cast upwards, following the blood spray on the wall, then back to the razor. *Not too many working girls use razors anymore*, Sawatski thought. He did remember one from the early two-thousands on Albert Street, when he was working Vice, a Jasmine something-or-other.

Sawatski rubbed his eyes without removing his glasses. He had put on about forty pounds since his divorce last year. The breakup had accelerated the thinning of his hair and the veneer of his good nature. There were two complaints outstanding on him: one from a welfare mother whom he had pushed while looking for her son during a gas station hold-up investigation and one from a desk sergeant at the District Three station. A mix-up had led to the release of a person of interest in a home invasion-turned-bludgeoning of an eighty-eight-year-old Holocaust survivor. Sawatski had thrown the book at him — literally. The Yellow Pages had only glanced off the shoulder of the sergeant, landing on a full cup of coffee. Maybe that's why the spatter looked so familiar. He had two years left until his twenty-five. Sawatski wished it was two seconds.

A voice bellowed at the open front door. "Make sure you tape off the back yard," said Constable Gayle Spence, the newest member of Robbery-Homicide and Sawatski's new partner. She was a ten-year veteran, thick but muscular, with a short bob of jet black hair. Spence had grown up poor and Cree in the Manitoba Housing projects on Dufferin. She had seen her fair share of police tape. She also knew which side of it she would be on if she stuck around. Gayle kept as low a profile as possible until she could enlist in the Canadian Forces. She escaped serious injury when the Gelandewagen she was driving triggered a roadside bomb outside Kandahar. Stitches and light bandages seemed horribly insignificant as she watched the caskets of her two passengers being loaded onto the military transport. It was the one time that she was on record for having wept.

Sawatski continued his gaze unabated as Spence broke the silence. "I wonder how much pressure it actually is," she said.

Sawatski jumped off his thought train. "How much what is?"

"The pressure," said Spence, "you know, of blood in the human body." Spence approached the spatter, being sure to avoid contaminating the blood-soaked items of interest at floor level. "Whaddya think? Five, ten pounds per square inch?"

"I don't think we have placards on our asses like a car does for tires," said Sawatski. "Besides, it's a big artery. Probably runs higher pressure to the brain, especially for all the she-nanigans this shit was up to."

Spence turned in mock disgust. "Hey, Sarge, a little respect for the dead shit please."

"A thousand pardons, milady." Sawatski enjoyed having a female partner, his first since his rookie days in Traffic. He was starting to mellow, maybe even starting to enjoy her company. He still hadn't decided if a friendly drunken sex romp was out of the question. That would take time and an eventual near-breakdown by either party, resulting in a late-night phone call, a short drive, a sympathetic ear, and half a box of condoms. There was plenty of precedent for it, even if most of that precedent came from a Hollywood scriptwriter.

"Steph's bodyguard was pretty helpful. Hooker's name is Claire Hebert." Gayle said, then looked at Sawatski. "Is that *the* Claire Hebert?"

"AKA Claire-Bear," said Sawatski. He put on gloves to examine the coat left behind by the alleged murderess. Fur hadn't exactly been in vogue for a decade or more, and yet, this particular mink had held up exceptionally well. It was ruined now, soaked with Stephanos's blood. Sawatski checked the inner pockets. No bills, parking stubs, or receipts. Clean, just the way a pro lived. The Reiss Furs tag showed its wear, continually being scrubbed by hair or clothes during the winter months. He tried to casually sniff for a scent of perfume. Spence caught him.

"Miles's got a girlfriend, Miles's got a girlfriend."

"Fuck you, partner."

"Not without dinner and a show." Spence turned back to her task of feeling around in the cracks of the sofa cushions, looking for anything that might have fallen in during the melee. Stephanos's corpse occupied the centre cushion while she worked. She provided Sawatski with the play-by-play.

"Hmmm . . . popcorn, pen, smokes, a lot of soiled rubbers." There weren't any rubbers, Spence was just looking to get a reaction out of Sawatski, who had started jotting down items of interest: the obvious struggle, the severity of the wound, the bloody footprints leading to the basement door, and an equally bloody handprint on the door casement. There was Stephanos's cell phone, still cycling through its screen saver of green code from *The Matrix*. Beneath the scribbles, Sawatski wrote one word in block letters: WHY.

"Where the fuck are those techs?" Spence had started to grow restless. There was still a raft of photos to take, measurements to measure, swabs to be soiled. "We'll be lucky if we get out of here by seven."

"More like eight." Sawatski had risen, stretching out his back muscles with a dramatic groan. "They have to do the basement, plus the backyard, and the lane. Maybe more like nine."

"Well, that's just fucktacular," said Spence, as she mimicked the Sawatski Stretch.

Everyone in Robbery-Homicide knew the Stretch. It had started when Sawatski had requisitioned a new desk chair for his back trouble. The more red tape he had to cut through, the more dramatic his groans would be in the squad room. It used to piss him off something fierce when fellow members would do their impressions of the Stretch. These days, Sawatski would judge the impromptu competitions with genuine delight. It felt good to have colleagues who considered his presence important enough to rib.

The silence was broken by the vibration of Sawatski's phone against his car keys. He reached into his pocket and checked the caller ID. "Shit."

"What is it?" said Spence.

"Tyrannosaurus Ex."

"Oh."

"Give me a minute."

Spence smiled. "For you Sawatski, I'll give you five."

Sawatski turned towards the door, answering the phone as he hit the stairs. There was enough activity around that no one would be listening in too intently. "Sawatski."

A male voice responded. "Are you there now?"

"Yeah, some hooker named Claire-Bear, old pro. Stephanos is as dead as disco."

"He isn't my concern," said The Voice. "Was his briefcase with him?"

Sawatski did a quick mental picture. No case, no gun, no ID. "There was nothing in the house. I'll check with the bodyguard."

"Good. I'll call you in two hours."

"Lucky me."

Sawatski turned in the direction of the bodyguard who smoked nervously next to the driver's door of his ivory Denali. A fresh-faced rookie was running his driver's license for wants. Sawatski made a beeline for him, his jacket open, right hand on the butt of his Glock.

"Step away from the car!"

The bodyguard bristled. "What the fuck for?"

Sawatski repeated, with gusto. "Step away from the fucking car now, asshole." He remembered his recent transgressions. "Please and fuck you."

The staged drama caught the attention of the rookie constable, who quickly exited the Crown Victoria. He moved up to Sawatski quickly, mimicking his gun butt stance. Sawatski gave him a quick nod. "What's your name kid?"

"It's Steiner, sir." *Christ*, thought Sawatski. *The kid's voice sounds like a fucking squeak toy. That should come in handy for domestic disputes.*

"Steiner, did you search this shit sandwich?"

Steiner adjusted his stance, in search of cop bravado. "Yes sir, nothing on him."

"Did you search the vehicle?" Sawatski looked at Steiner. He knew he hadn't. What threat could the bodyguard have posed? He was the one who'd made the 911 call, an expected occurrence when a high-profile member of the gang had been murdered. Why would he suddenly reach in, grab a gun, and start laying waste until he was taken out?

Sawatski looked at the bodyguard with conviction as he barked at the rookie. "Steiner, I want you to take this witness into protective custody. Cuff him and put him in your car while I search this vehicle."

"Fuck you," said the bodyguard. "You got no reason to search shit."

Sawatski tilted his head like an inquisitive dog. "No reason? You're telling me I've got no reason? There's about a gallon of your boss's blood soaking through the floorboards in there. Maybe you set this whole fucking thing up. Maybe you killed him and made the call and put this bullshit story together about

some ninety-eight-pound-soaking-wet skank taking him out."
Sawatski pulled the Glock halfway out of his holster, keeping
it visible only to the bodyguard and the wide-eyed rookie. "If I
was you, I wouldn't give me any more reasons."

The bodyguard relented. The rookie led him away as
Sawatski opened the driver's door. An overflowing ashtray
was starting to spill out onto the carpet, already marked
from previous burns. Sawatski popped open the console: a
few party packs of weed, the remnants of an eight ball in full
view. He closed the console and reached under the driver's
seat. He felt the barrel of a 9 mm automatic, not enough to
brand it. The back seat was empty, save for the fast food bags
of a week's lunches. There was a sawed-off in a compartment
under the cargo floor. No briefcase. Sawatski closed up the
Denali and instructed the rookie to turn the bodyguard loose.
Sawatski glared at him as he passed. The bodyguard grinned.

"Don't you fucking smile at me," Sawatski growled.

"Sure you didn't find anything, Sipowitz?"

Sawatski moved in closer to emphasize his opinion of the
bodyguard. "Nothing important, nothing I can't find again."
He felt the need for composure swell, even if it was as fake as
a twenty-dollar Fabergé egg. "Thanks for your, uh, coopera-
tion. Have a nice day." The bodyguard watched him with a
quizzical look as Sawatski walked back to the house. He was
almost at the steps when he heard the double-honk. He turned
in time to see the driver's door open on the *Winnipeg Sentinel*
Cavalier and the suspension rise two inches as its occupant
exited. *Here comes the fucking circus*, thought Sawatski.

The circus had a name: David "Downtown" Worschuk, the
Sentinel's crime reporter. He had been covering the crime beat
for about seven years, an appointment courtesy of an awful
lot of drinking with the newspaper's publisher. Worschuk

had first appeared on the pages of the *Sentinel* with a freelance series dubbed Barbed Wires. He had been working for almost a decade with a large fencing firm, which had been tasked with maintenance on fences at correctional institutions throughout Manitoba. Prisoners with sunny dispositions were chosen to assist with the work. Casual conversations turned into posts on Worschuk's Facebook page, then a blog, then the column. After a think piece aired on CBC Radio One about the column, the *Sentinel*'s publisher, Kyle Morgan, decided to cozy up to the ingenue, inviting him to the drinking parties with the press operators during the nightly run. He took an even bigger shine to Worschuk after sampling his uncle's moonshine, a mix that still bubbled on the family farm near Komarno. Morgan reciprocated with his drug of choice: cocaine. On one such bender, Morgan told Worschuk to show up at the City Desk on Monday. He had to yell the directive at Worschuk three times, thanks to the mandatory ear protection that they were wearing. After Worschuk had switched careers, word had filtered down through Manitoba Corrections that he had been under investigation for smuggling drugs into Milner Ridge. Remnants of empty drug chargers had been found near various fence locations at the facility on dates that corresponded with his visits. No one was sure how many chargers Worschuk could carry at one time. At six feet and a scale tip of at least 375 pounds, he certainly had plenty of cargo space. It also meant that he went commando, or had the loosest boxer shorts imaginable to direct the chargers out the bottom of his pant legs. The complaint had come from a serial fraudster incarcerated at Milner Ridge. It died quickly, after Kyle Morgan threatened the corrections department with a series on inmate suicides. It had been rumoured that some of the "suicides" were actually the result of illegal choke holds by overly aggressive guards.

Sawatski had long made a point of practising the punctuation of his "No comment" statement, just in case Worschuk showed up. Nothing pissed him off more than a crime reporter who thought he had a place amongst cops, especially one who saw no problem with freelance drug-mule work. Sawatski pondered his current dilemma. Wasn't he just like Worschuk? *No, it's not the same thing*, he thought. Whatever mess he had fallen into was simply the transparency of the thin blue line.

Until now, the calls from The Voice were for minor requests. Many of them lacked any obvious criminal element or intent, though it was still information from crime scenes or arrests that wouldn't be made public. The calls always came through his department cellular line, always Unknown Caller on a WPS phone that had been programmed to list even unlisted numbers and payphones. Sawatski knew that getting caught would still mean immediate suspension, or worse. Still, an extra $500 per request, in cash, made the support cheques to his ex-wife easier to scrawl. There wasn't a cop on the force who could say that they had never seen some benefit from the badge. This wasn't corruption; this was a typical shift. The only thing that bothered him was the briefcase. It was the first time The Voice had made a request for a physical piece of evidence.

"Hey, Miles," said Worschuk, as he adjusted his ample belted overhang. "Where's the fire?"

Sawatski feigned interest in a blank notebook page. "You're a little confused, Dave. That would be the guys with the shiny red trucks."

"Would it kill you to call me Downtown?" Worschuk was always trying to get cops to call him by his nickname, a throw to his Downtown 24/7 crime beat column. It seemed more important than the volleys at his intellect.

Sawatski wasn't in the mood. "I'm busy, David. And there's no news to tell."

"That's not what I hear." Worschuk fumbled in his outer pocket for his digital recorder. Sawatski grabbed the pocket, pulling Worschuk up close and personal. The grab was hard enough to dislodge Worschuk's Domo Gas toque, revealing a messy shock of curly red hair, courtesy of his Irish mother. The clownish topping was how he had received the nickname that Sawatski preferred.

"Listen carefully, Clowntown, you don't hear shit, you don't see shit, and you don't know shit." Sawatski snapped his notebook closed for effect. "And you won't get shit from me. And yes, you can quote me on that." He started back up the walk to the stairs.

Worschuk managed to put two and two together, more or less. "Are you still mad at me? And it's Downtown, not Clowntown."

Sawatski stopped but didn't turn. He thought about Worschuk's story, the one he'd written about Sawatski's old partner. A career-ender with enough damage for a dismissal before his twenty-five: a low-track hooker crying cop rape. The star witness recanted about two weeks after the story ran and a week after Sawatski's partner ate his gun. His name was Jerry Klein. He left a wife, three kids, and a houseboat in Kenora. Sawatski turned with his right hand firmly gripping the butt of his Glock, his jacket open to make sure Worschuk saw it, and looked at the reporter. "No comment."

Tommy eased the Econoline into its space behind The Guiding Light, using the wall as the parking stop. He had to, unless he wanted to come out in the morning to a missing battery. He gathered up the bulk of the important gear for Paulie's "disappearance." The Light had a rear entrance that led to a staircase that wouldn't wake the guests. There were no exterior windows, assuring the casual observer that this staircase had been added years after the initial construction. The only light in the stairwell came from the windows on the original building, which after lights out was the glow from the vintage fire exit light bulb covers. The windows used chicken wire mesh sandwiched in the panes. If the bulbs could flicker, it would give the illusion that the Light was on fire. Tommy had often thought about dropping that match.

The door at the top opened into a storage area jammed with blankets, toilet paper, and outdated magazines with the covers torn off to discourage resale. He deposited his gear in the corner; it was just loud enough to let someone on the other side of the makeshift curtains in his room know that he was home. He found a meagre smile as he heard her stir. Tommy peeked through the curtains at Cindy Smyth. At least, he thought it was Cindy; with three comforters piled high atop her, it was hard to tell.

Cindy and Tommy went way back, almost too far. Calling it a relationship seemed weak. Calling it a union of soulmates seemed way over the top. They had come up with a name for it once: kindred observers. It seemed that when anything really bad happened, Tommy and Cindy would find each other. Tommy had put the pieces back together and delivered a beating on each of those involved after Cindy was gang-raped at a party. Cindy had pulled the Smith & Wesson out of Tommy's mouth when he first returned to Winnipeg and had thoughts of joining Jeremy. They had never considered themselves to have dated. That would have involved such suburban niceties as dinners, movies, and sorting socks. They marvelled at how amazing the sex was without all of that annoying mental foreplay. They dated other people, lay down with their share of strangers. They watched as their faces sunk, their parts sagged, and their hair greyed. It was a marriage; Smyth and Bosco–style.

Tommy went for the customary peek to confirm the clothing situation. Cindy pulled the covers back in protest. "I'm fucking freezing in here!" Cindy whispered as loud as she could without waking up the neighbours. "Did you pay the hydro?"

"Two days ago," said Tommy. He noticed her flannel pyjamas on a nearby chair and grinned as he dropped his pants to the floor. "Maybe you're just a frigid bitch."

"Maybe you prefer the little boys, like the last guy here."

"Supercunt."

"Felchfairy."

Their lips met hard. Tommy reached underneath the covers, grabbing her left breast and twisting her amethyst nipple ring. Cindy pushed the covers back, rolling over on her side just enough to present the tattooed image of Icarus, drawn with a face that mimicked Tommy's, in the not-so-obvious sense. Tommy bit into her nape, hard enough to leave a mark and an approving coo. She loved his hand work, and he obliged, ensuring that she arrived strong. He found his way inside then, cupping both breasts as he contemplated the quality of the Icarus artwork with his thrusting. Loose file folders slid out of an overturned box above them, falling one by one to the floor. A few of the Guiding Light guests on the other side of the glass joined in with muted solo performances. Tommy was still feeling his spasms when Cindy spoke.

"Did it go off okay?"

"What? You didn't feel that?"

"No, dipshit. Paulie!"

"Oh, yeah. He's gone." Tommy started to get up to grab Cindy's pyjamas and an extra blanket. She always felt colder after, at least since turning forty-two — the joys of pre-meno-pause. Cindy pulled him back.

"It's okay," she said. "Just stay close. I'll be warm enough."

"Are you sure?"

"Yes, I'm sure."

"Goodnight, Supercunt."

"Goodnight, Felchfairy."

It was about five a.m. when it happened. Experience had taught Tommy to simply hang on to Cindy as tight as he could, stay quiet, and ride it out. Cindy was experiencing what they called sleep-raging. Waking her was dangerous; that's how he got the scar over his left eye. Simple utterances of comfort would unleash her fury. It felt like Cindy was having some form of convulsion, though this was anything but textbook. It was as though she was reliving every horrible occurrence in her life, word for word, page for page. The rapes, the molestations from foster family and caregivers, the demeaning acts in search of acceptance, the blood on her hands.

Cindy was a killer. It was all over the papers; even hit the national TV newscasts when it all went down. Some had called her a hero, though she knew better. A domestic argument had spilled into the streets of the West Kildonan neighbourhood, near Kildonan Park. Petrified onlookers watched in horror as the knife-wielding man, a Heaven's Reject soldier, chased his estranged wife along the grassy centre median. He was on top of her, on stab number six, when Cindy knocked him loose with her Triumph Bonneville. Even with a compound fracture on her left leg, Cindy still managed to lift a loose hunk of curbstone, most likely dislodged by a snow-clearing crew. She landed the stone three times before a park police officer wrestled her down. The case and the Heaven's Reject's casket were closed tight. Coming to the aid of the woman, who later died in hospital, seemed textbook heroic. Cindy had wanted to kill for a very long time; she just wasn't sure if it would be herself or someone else. The circumstances surrounding her actions, and their acceptance by the media and the public at large, made it far worse. Tommy couldn't comfort her as she recovered from her suicide attempt at the Selkirk Mental Hospital. He was in Federal U.S. custody at the time. Tommy had discovered that rubbing the scars on her wrists during the convulsions seemed to help. He would bury his head in her brown and grey tresses, keeping his lips pressed against her neck. The silence. That was always the weird part. During every convulsion, Cindy never made a sound.

Cindy had helped Tommy to paint The Light before it opened in early 2011. She had been there ever since. She took novice care of the books, kept an eye open for the inspectors, and prayed. She would always recite her prayers after the sleep-raging. Tommy never knew for sure if she was awake.

"Hi God, it's Cindy. Thanks for today. It was a good day. Thanks for timing the food delivery after that prick, I mean, gentleman from Food Protection had left. Thanks for no fights today with the guests. Thanks for keeping the low-lifes and the cops out. Thanks for helping Tommy get Paulie out. Thanks for Tommy. Thanks for Tommy." Cindy paused. "And thanks for a sober day. Amen."

Tommy pulled her close. He smiled at the thought that the day was only an hour and a half away from starting.

CHAPTER
TWELVE

Sawatski sat idling in a light-green Crown Victoria outside Spence's well-kept bungalow on Atlantic Avenue. She had taken her personal car to the scene and wanted to keep it from getting damaged in the Public Safety Building garage. The parkade had been crumbling for years, dropping tiny chunks of salt-eaten concrete from the seams as cars passed overhead. Sawatski was past the point of caring about his car, or much else. He watched her through the kitchen window, quickly preparing a healthy lunch that he should have been having himself. He would probably end up at The Line Up on Albert Street, in the Exchange District. They had the best fish and chips under ten bucks in town.

He wondered why Spence didn't just park in the Vice Division parking lot. The Vice building was a converted hydro power station, about three blocks south of the PSB, the Public Safety Building. This was the temporary home for Robbery-Homicide, thanks to the discovery of asbestos at the PSB. The administration had decided to move the police service into the main post office building on Graham Avenue, which was being vacated for a new post office distribution centre at the airport. The problem was that both buildings were of equal vintage, which had put the entire transformation a year behind schedule and millions over budget. Sawatski thought it would be easier to work from The Line Up, and probably healthier, at least for his respiratory system.

The first floor of the temporary Vice address had been converted into service garages for police vehicles, with a separate investigation area for fatal accidents and vehicles that needed additional investigation by forensics. Even in the early morning hours, the second floor was always crowded. Sawatski smiled as a mixture of Vice and Robbery-Homicide members did their best Sawatski Stretch as he entered. He turned his head to Spence as he walked. "Your turn to pick."

"Aww, c'mon. I always pick the lamest one."

"I'm feeling like a John Lithgow over-the-top this morning."

"Then that'll be Bangster for sure."

They rounded a corner of filing cabinets and came upon Constable Billy "Bangster" Sangster, in full Sawatski Stretch. One of Billy's girlfriends had turned him on to yoga, and his newfound flexibility had made for some comical smart-phone screen savers. He was sitting on the corner of his desk, with his right leg pointing at the ceiling, almost touching his ear-lobe.

"Al-most there," said Sangster, doing his best to smile while keenly aware that he was dangerously close to pulling something important.

Sawatski started to clap. Spence flipped a toonie at Sangster, who grabbed it with his left hand, almost losing his balance. "Enjoy your double-double, Bangster." Sangster had earned the nickname from his known prowess with the emergency room nurses at the Health Sciences Centre during his rookie days. He stood just over six feet, thin but sculpted, with a tight salt-and-pepper buzz cut. "Tim Fucking Hortons medium doo-blay-doo-blay! Sweet nectar of life!" said Sangster as he lowered his leg, with just a touch of painful grimace for the approving crowd. He handed a healthy file to Spence. "Here it is: The Fast Times and Most-Likely Short Life of Claire-Bear Hebert."

"You've probably got that right." Spence flipped open the file, noticing the tally of arrests, old mugshots, and hand-drawn statements. Much of this would be in the WPS database, though history had taught that a cryptic scrawl or notation could mean the difference between an arrest and a skip.

"Gotta love a gimme," said Sangster as he balanced the toonie on his nose, like a third-rate street performer. "It sure helps with the clearance stats." Sangster checked on the status of his current double-double. He frowned at the weight and the ambient temperature. Everyone on the second floor knew that Sangster would squeeze a drop of Timmy's out of a salt-stained floormat before another brand of coffee touched his lips. His cubicle was littered with past and present shards of Roll Up the Rim prize attempts.

Sawatski looked up from his comfy chair, slightly annoyed. "It ain't a gimme unless they walk into the PSB. And something tells me this one will hit the basement of the HSC first."

"True that," said Sangster. "Got an address?"

"Doubtful," said Spence. "Looks like off-the-grid shit. She's probably sharing a place with another working girl, maybe an alias on the lease." Spence flipped through the file. "Last known was a general delivery in Fisher Branch. I'll check the latest to be sure, but I'm not hopeful."

"When was the last arrest?"

Spence was already at her computer, checking the stats. "Not since '99. She's a smart skank, I'll give her that." She checked a little further into known associates. "All of her friends are dead, in jail, or missing."

"If only I were so lucky," said Sawatski, massaging his neck. It was coming up on eight a.m., still two hours away from The Line Up's lunch start. The techs were still processing the scene, so it would be at least an hour until someone sent him the pictures. He flipped open his cell, a Blackberry Pearl with plenty of nicks and scrapes, consulting the pictures he had snapped before the techs arrived — at least there was one advantage of the digital age. The Robbery-Homicide inspector wouldn't be thrilled to know Sawatski had taken them. The WPS was still exercising damage control from a crime-scene snapshot that had made its way onto a Facebook page. It was a double slaying at a known crystal-meth lab. The issue had more to do with identifying key members of the task force, who were now riding desks. Sawatski looked at the close-up of the razor in Stephanos's neck. It seemed downright vintage, the type favoured by the boutique barber shops that had popped up over the past two years. Most of the high-class prostitutes were carrying small calibre automatics at this point. Sangster relayed a story about a disgruntled john, dead of a heart attack, with a Taser prong stuck in each testicle. Sawatski wondered if the john had paid extra.

The banter was broken by the buzz of Sawatski's cell phone. He flipped it open, expecting a tech from the scene. "You got my pictures yet?"

"I'm more concerned with fine luggage," said The Voice. Sawatski had learned not to react when he received these calls. He also knew how to get those around him to provide a buffer of personal space.

"Sheila, for Christ's sake, I mailed the cheque on Tuesday. How the fuck should I know where it is?" Sangster and Spence heard the exchange, turning to see Sawatski shaking his head. They nodded in unison, taking the file and laptop into the conference room. Miles did his best to portray the role of beleaguered ex-husband while having a very different conversation. "I told you that I would call when I had something."

"It's been almost three hours since you arrived on scene," said The Voice. "Let's just say that our expectations were much higher."

"What you're paying me should be a lot higher!" whispered Sawatski as harshly as possible.

The Voice was calm. "Miles, everyone in this fair town knows that a dollar under the table is practically three on the books. We'll look at your compensation upon the conclusion of this adventure. Have you located Miss Hebert? There is much concern for her whereabouts at this time."

"I'm working a theory."

"Work it well, Miles. Your stipend will be at the usual location." The line went dead. Sawatski closed his phone, hammering the table with his fist loud enough to signal the end of the call to the squad. "Fucking bitch!"

Ernie Friday was kicking the snow off his boots at the back door of his Bowman Avenue shanty when his pager went off. He had resisted the move to a cell phone, convinced that it would somehow be his undoing. Though anything but advertised, the paging network was still alive and well through Manitoba Telecom Services. He dropped the license plates from the Caprice, which had just been picked up by an outfit called Dawn to Dusk Towing. The company was adept at one thing: getting your dirty car to the front of the line at the Selkirk scrap-metal shredder. Any physical evidence of Teddy Simms and his brief appearance in the rusty Caprice would soon be in the foundry smelter. The plates would be fastened to an '86 Pontiac Parisienne, about as rusty as the Chevy that had just left. It was a tight fit in the old garage. Ernie had already wired the brake and running lights with kill switches and had replaced all the headlights and marker lamp bulbs with fresh glow. The Pontiac was a bargain: $200 cash on Kijiji, with a bad water pump that Ernie had fixed himself with plenty of cursing. There was plenty of room on the bench seat for his jammer briefcase.

The house was dark except for the fluorescent glow from the stove console. Ernie grabbed a tea towel to wipe the winter fog from his glasses. He brought the pager up to a distance of legibility. 586-1042. It was a phone number to most, especially a nosy cop. The number was also legitimate; it belonged to a drugstore on McGregor Avenue. The code system had been in place for years and was one of the carefully guarded secrets amongst the local criminal element. "86" was to eighty-six, a hit. "10" was the target category, in this case a prostitute. A drug dealer was an eighty, as in eight-ball. A snitch was a seventy, only because the number and the category started with the same letter. There were some categories that the hired hands would avoid, out of principle or preference. A witness was a twenty, for the two eyes they should have kept shut. The worst of the category codes was forty. The letter shared was F. Family.

The "5" and the "42" made up the bank branch number. Those who were regular contractors maintained safety deposit boxes at various city banks. When a hit was sanctioned, a package would be deposited in the safety deposit box of the key contractor, part of which would contain the information on the subject, plus any outstanding payments for services rendered, such as the $2,000 now owed for the late Teddy Simms. Murder was the least-used code. Most numbers had to do with drug shipments, cartage thefts, and disciplinary action against those who needed it. The HRs had resurrected the old pager system after too many career-ending taps on both landline and wireless phones.

Ernie filled the kettle and placed it on the one free burner, surrounded by pots with recent, but congealed, cooking. A grey long-haired cat made his presence known, pushing up against Ernie's legs. "Yes, Chico, time for breakfast." The meowing reached a fever pitch as Ernie engaged the electric can opener. As Chico ate, Ernie poured the kettle's bounty into a cup of instant coffee grounds. He pulled down the metal tackle box from atop the fridge and removed his Beretta from his coat. The tackle box held his cleaning tools and gun oil, and in between sips of black instant, the Beretta was treated to its usual high-class service.

The sunshine portion of Ernie's Thursday morning had started at nine sharp, with a quick stop to the insurance agent on Watt Street, updating the Caprice tags for the Pontiac. Next stop was the Winnipeg Credit Union at Notre Dame Avenue and Arlington, home of the nearest safety deposit box, which would have the directions to his next two grand. The Pontiac had a handicapped placard in the glove box — out of date but good enough to hoodwink the parking authority. Ernie threw in a bit of a limp as he walked towards the door. There was no teller at the wicket for the safety deposit boxes as Ernie tapped his fingers on the desk. A woman close to Ernie's age appeared, thin, well dressed, and with almost enough black hair dye to qualify as a close Friday relative. She smiled, the kind of smile reserved for regulars.

"Good morning, Ernie. How's my favourite cat?"

Ernie grinned. "Chico says hi, Merle." Merle wore a nametag with the credit union logo and a stick-on nodule that spoke of thirty-five years of service. "Need to get into my safety deposit box."

"Four-thirty-four," said Merle from memory. "Right this way."

She led Ernie down a narrow corridor to the rear stairs, taking the steps slowly, thanks to shoes reserved more for a night on the town than eight hours standing on a marble floor.

"These bloody hips," said Merle, as she gripped the well-worn rail. "I think I need a new pair."

"Must be all those dance partners at the Legion," said Ernie. He never was much of a dancer, though he would often run into Merle and her friends at the Army Navy Air Force hall. There was always a good meat draw, and the video lottery terminals must have been wired for payout. "What's your favourite dance, Merle? The Horizontal Mambo?"

Merle stopped and swatted him in his well-fed belly. "Ernie Bloody Friday!" she scolded, as she continued down the stairs to the safety deposit box cage. Ernie found the light switch for the customer room. A moment later, Merle appeared with box 434. It was the longer-sized box, though it didn't seem to be full enough to involve a struggle of effort.

"Four thirty-four," said Merle as she laid the box in front of him. "Full of pearls and gold bars, and rubies the size of your nose."

Ernie grinned. "That would be one ugly-looking ruby."

Merle turned to head up the stairs. "Call me when you're done massaging your platinum tie bars." Ernie listened as she ascended the stairs, each step punctuated by her heels. He waited until she was at the top, or what he thought was the top, about thirty steps. He opened the long top cover of the box, half-wondering if Merle knew how the information was deposited. The manager was an underworld friendly, carrying out the duties of criminal postmaster. The packet would arrive via local courier, attention to the manager. Within the thick manila envelope was a second envelope of the bubble-wrap variety. Within this were two standard letter envelopes; one blank, with five hundred-dollar bills for the manager, the second marked with a computer-generated label with the box number. Ernie removed the envelope and easily opened its fresh adhesive strip.

The picture was folded in half, with the particulars handwritten on the backside of the photo paper. He recognized the name without a sign of emotion. Ernie had never been a fan of Claire Hebert, especially after what she had done to Tommy and how it had put Jeremy in the crosshairs. Just like a movie rating, the name was accompanied by five badly drawn red stars. Ernie had heard about the Stephanos murder the previous night on the CJOB morning drive, concerned at first that they were talking about Teddy Simms. The North End location calmed his nerves. They hadn't released the name, though Ernie knew of the Heaven's Rejects clubhouse on Pritchard. Five stars: the most any future corpse could get. Teddy Simms had only three. Five stars meant the job was open, with a one hundred percent premium. Four grand was enough for a proper vacation down to the Shooting Star Casino on the Minnesota side, maybe even that Dominican all-inclusive that Merle raved about every winter.

There was another picture inside the packet, though it wasn't a second someone in need of a few Beretta slugs. The picture was of a book, some type of cheap store-brand ledger that Stephanos must have used to record the HRs' business transactions of the day. If it fell into the wrong hands, and could be deciphered, there could be dire consequences for the future of the HRs in Winnipeg. A simple notation had been written on the photograph in black Magic Marker — *To be discussed*.

It was anyone's guess as to what the ledger retrieval notation meant for payment; maybe a lot, maybe a little. For now, it was a four-grand hit, which meant that every amateur shooter in town was going to be gunning for Claire Hebert. Most were of little consequence; they didn't have enough contacts or smarts to unload a clip at a gun-club target, let alone Hebert. It wasn't them who Ernie was worried about, it was the Two Pauls — Paul Bouchard and Paul Lemay.

Every city has its complete psychopaths, even a place like Winnipeg. While without official affiliation, Ernie knew that the Two Pauls could be counted on for one thing: making a deadly mess of the person on the contract. Ernie always tried to keep things clean. The smaller calibre of the Beretta meant that even a head shot would be relatively easy for a funeral director to patch — not an easy task when large-calibre weaponry is used. The Two Pauls weren't concerned with calibre, clip size, or pearl-handled grips; they prided themselves on one key element, and it was about as Winnipeg as you could get: the cheapest kill possible.

Ernie had read about the latest budget body in the *Sentinel*. It was a true puzzler, found frozen solid on the top of the Smith Street parkade. Stranger still was the autopsy upon thaw. The victim had drowned, though there was extensive dental damage and inner throat lacerations. The lungs had traces of an industrial grade tire cleaner, car wax, and liquid soap. The break for Robbery-Homicide was the discovery of a dental partial at a coin-operated car wash in the West End. They even found teeth marks on the wash wand. There were no usable prints or fibres, not even off the change in the coin box. The medical examiner figured that the water volume that killed the victim was less than one full cycle. It was less than one loonie. That was still cheaper than five rounds from Ernie's Beretta.

The Two Pauls were veterans of the auto-dismantling trade, with two decades of criminal freelance between them. Paul Bouchard had the look of blue-collar respectability, a clothes horse in an industry that soiled your attempts on an hourly basis. He had five Carhartt yard jackets and went through a washing machine a year diluting the grease stain patchwork. His steel-toed boots were a combination of scuff and multiple coats of Arctic Dubbin. He favoured black knit skullcaps, a necessity in the chill of the outdoor wrecking yards. Beneath was a thin pattern of blond stubble and a tightly trimmed matching goatee. A shop mishap some ten years before had cut the vision in his left eye to borderline blindness, making it a milkier blue than the movie-star tint of the right. Fix the eye and remove the acne scars, and his muscular six-foot-two frame could have easily graced the pages of a work-apparel catalogue. Ernie had first met him at the counter of an auto-parts recycler. He remembered how he had told Bouchard to go fuck himself after he quoted a ridiculous price for a radiator support for a 1989 Ford F-150 that Ernie was fixing on the cheap. He had recently been laid off, which freed up time for his cocaine deliveries. He had the perfect cover: delivering food hampers on welfare cheque day to the so-called needy throughout the North End.

Ernie had put eyes on Paul Lemay about a year ago at a towing compound auction. He kept his distance after he passed him getting a hot dog from the compound canteen, and for good reason. Lemay carried the stench of three days of sweat at all times, with a fifty-pound overhang, bad teeth, and greasy salt-and-pepper locks that had never known a comb. Ernie had heard that Lemay was an artist with a cutting torch, so much so that the wreckers he worked for never dared to complain about the hours he chose to keep, or if he showed up at all. His car dismantles were clean and precise, in stark contrast to his manner of dispatch for the unfortunate. While Bouchard favoured Ernie's belief that less mess is more, Lemay was simply unhinged, with a creative lilt. He had suggested the inland drowning technique. Bouchard would hold the victim in a full nelson, looking the other way, as Lemay performed his life-ending work. Rumour had it that it was his victims' eyes that fascinated Lemay. It never ceased to amaze him how something so full of movement and emotion in their final throes could become so equally still and empty in mere seconds. He never looked away.

The Two Pauls were KTP, known to police, but not for these reasons. The current local drinking establishment ban tally for the Pauls was eight. They would drink themselves into oblivion, and then break into boisterous song, with or without a karaoke system on the premises. It would start off as amusing but would eventually require a call to the police service for public intoxication as the Pauls ended with their off-key rendition of "The Wreck of the Edmund Fitzgerald," while being loaded into the paddy wagon. Ernie had heard that there was only one assault charge on the books for Lemay, and it depended on your definition of assault: a Main Street Project care worker lodged the complaint, after a shower of Lemay's projectile vomit. It ended as a public mischief charge plus a dry-cleaning bill.

Ernie had reason to be concerned about the Pauls. It had been less than two years since a freelance contractor was found next to a contract corpse in a similar state. The contractor had been suffocated, courtesy of an entire roll of duct tape concealing his head. It was later determined that the contractor had completed the deed and was checking for vitals on the victim when a cinder block knocked him out cold. Dead men can't spend, and the first to make the contract claim gets the cash, regardless of how many bonus bodies are present. That event had resulted in more specific contract management amongst the various criminal groups. The Claire Hebert job was the first open contract since the bonus-body incident.

Ernie stowed the items in the safety deposit box. They would be destroyed by the bank manager within the hour. The last known addresses were committed to memory, though Ernie knew those would be of little use. Claire Hebert was surely underground by now, protected by the friendlies in the sex trade. The goal would be to get her out of town as quickly as possible, which would be anything but easy with the Robbery-Homicide unit bearing down. Five stars. *That's the concern,* Ernie thought as he held the guardrail for his ascent. *The punishment doesn't exactly fit the crime.*

CHAPTER
FOURTEEN

Claire Hebert hadn't moved a muscle on the musty fold-out as Jasmine Starr searched for her instant coffee grounds. Her plug-in kettle lacked a whistle, though the boiling gurgle and switch shut-off were easily heard in the rear of the shop. She still took care to keep the spoon from making too much clank, with a dash of sweetener to take the edge off. The briefcase was now on the floor, un-bagged, with Claire still hanging on to the shoulder strap.

Once the instant started to charge her, Jasmine noticed that the strap was removable. *Fair game, and a fair price to pay*, thought Jasmine, *for keeping Claire safe*. Keeping up with the offshore online sex-toy suppliers had been whittling away at The Other Woman's profit margins for the last two years. Jasmine had sold her cabin at West Hawk Lake, even shaved staff hours to the bone. She was also sick and tired of black instant.

The clasps on the bag were spring-loaded, which kept the rustling to a minimum. The contents were relatively minor: a few pens, a cheap RadioShack calculator, a few receipts for gas, some lottery tickets with the Please Try Again paper slice. No sign of drugs or cash; not even a laptop in the laptop compartment. A stiff wind could have knocked over this bag, Jasmine thought. She gingerly pulled open the Velcro strap where the laptop would have resided. A thin journal presented itself. There was no writing on the exterior. Jasmine figured it was the usual goings-on of any criminal enterprise: drugs, payments for drugs, and who was behind on their payments for drugs. There could also be prostitution, cartage theft, possibly some high-end cars jacked for HR friendlies in Montreal. A River Heights BMW could end up on a pier in Nigeria for a fifth of retail. Jasmine hesitated slightly, wondering if it was worth opening, wondering if it was worth knowing. She wondered if it was truly worth her life.

The entries, as legible and neat as they were, offered no obvious clues. Each entry had a date, then a long string of digits, with a separate amount that may have been some form of total. Jasmine had seen such ledgers like this before, and they didn't tend to be too hard to crack. She remembered one such book, where the "code" for the cartage thefts was the license plate of the trailer that had been fleeced. The dates went back about eighteen months, right up to the previous day. Each date had twenty entries. The first string of digits remained the same for all individual entries, which probably pointed to a location of some sort. The rest seemed jumbled, with different sequences, even the odd letter or symbol. Jasmine figured it had to be some way of recording cash transactions without being too obvious.

Jasmine would have read further, were it not for a new piece of reading material that had just slammed into the side of her head. She fell to the floor, dazed, her left cheek stinging. Claire was very much awake. She tossed the White Pages aside, pulling the bag away from Jasmine's reach. Claire did her best to keep one eye on Jasmine as she groaned, using the other to scan the contents of the bag. She was not pleased. Jasmine's left ear was now bleeding, wounded from the contact of the phone book with her array of earrings. Claire reached down, pulling on the damaged ear.

"Where's the fucking coke, you thieving cunt?" Claire pulled the ear open, to make sure Jasmine heard. She did, and responded with an old steering wheel club that had been left under her desk. The club hit Claire square in the jaw with the business end of the lock assembly. The key was long lost, and the arc of the motion sent the top portion of the Club flying, destroying a glass display shelf next to the couch. A few of the newly freed dildos switched on as they hit the floor, vibrating on the broken glass. The women panted as they made the necessary physical and mental checks that occur with recent injury. Jasmine assessed her ear, looking at the amount of blood on her hand. Claire rubbed her jaw, concerned with the possibility of a fracture. It didn't hurt too much to open. She flicked her tongue around her mouth, checking for loose teeth. She found two, spitting them to the floor in unison. This was not the first time the two had fought; it was simply the first time that they had fought each other. Jasmine stared up at the flickering fluorescent fixture.

"Stupid lights," she said, as she brought herself up to

sitting level, still with laboured breath. "Hydro wants me to change them."

Claire brought herself up slowly, still checking for errant teeth. "Is that the Power Smart shit? Like on the billboards?"

"Something like that. Save the planet or something."

"That flickering is annoying."

"You're annoying."

Jasmine's dig caught Claire off guard, enough that a laugh seemed appropriate. In a life coloured by far worse, the melee had all of the lasting damage of a suburban pillow fight. Jasmine picked up the briefcase and slammed it into Claire's chest, just hard enough to get her attention and knock out a puff of air. "There's no coke, and I didn't take anything out, except for that." She pointed to the ledger, still resting on the floor, still open to the page Jasmine had been reading. Claire rubbed her jaw and groaned. She looked at the ledger. She knew it was the wrong thing to have.

"Oh, shit!"

"You're damn right, oh shit."

"I was just looking for coke and cash!"

Jasmine picked up the ledger, flipping nonchalantly through the pages. "These are the worst things to get your hands on. Some coded bullshit that any eleven-year-old could crack." Jasmine kept flipping, not seeming to be looking for anything important. "The HRs must know you've got it by now, and they've probably put an all-points bulletin out on your ass. You should go to the cops."

Claire's bravado was returning. "Oh sure, go to the cops. Gee, I wonder how that chat will go. Oh, hi Mr. Policeman, I found this book written by a borderline retard badass." She grabbed the ledger from Jasmine, performing an amateur ballet dance of sorts, finally turning to face her for the grand finale. "Oh, and about the retard — I stuck a razor in his neck, just like Jasmine Starr taught me."

Jasmine stood in front of her, arms now crossed, like a disapproving mother. "Well, you can't stay here — you or your stuff. Somebody wants that back, and I want nothing to do with it." Jasmine rubbed her temples, unable to maintain her composure anymore. "Fuck! Why didn't you just root through the bag while he was draining out?"

Claire was back on the fold-out now, her head in her hands. "I don't fucking know!"

Jasmine kept up her volleys. "I know. I know exactly why you didn't. Because you're a fucking cokehead, and you don't fucking think!"

"Fuck you!"

"Fuck me? Fuck you!"

"Cunt!"

"Hosebag!"

The pair erupted into laughter that lasted a good minute. The laughter ended when Claire opted for tears. Jasmine wasn't sure whether it was an emotional release or the withdrawal symptoms from Claire's unofficial fifth food group. She walked up to her slowly, Claire rocking back and forth on the corner of the fold-out, a low moan sustained throughout her motions. *Nobody ever cried sexy*, Jasmine thought as she held Claire's head to her side, stroking her hair as maternally as she could. She restated the facts as softly as she could. "You can't stay here, Bear. They'll find you and they'll kill you."

Claire wiped her eyes and nose with her cashmere sweater, showing little concern for the garment. "Can you help me get outta here?"

"No," Jasmine whispered as she stroked her hair. "But I know who can."

Sawatski kept his right hand over his collar as he walked briskly east on McDermot Avenue. He would usually walk down King to Bannatyne, if it wasn't for the north wind that greeted him as he exited Vice. He was early, about fifteen minutes before The Line Up opened for the lunch crowd. Spence had offered up a generous portion of her homemade Greek salad, which Sawatski had refused with a bogus claim about his constitution and feta cheese. He hoped that the slight curvature of the buildings on Albert Street would offer a windbreak as he turned north, only to be greeted by an equally insulting blast of winter chill. The door at The Line Up was locked, as it should have been. Sawatski saw one of the kitchen staff cleaning the grill. He pulled out his badge, tapping on the glass with the city crest. The worker seemed to be engrossed in his task, even as Sawatski punctuated the beats. He turned momentarily to see Sawatski and called to someone in the back.

A heavy-set woman appeared, fumbling with her hairnet as she approached the door. She was in her mid-fifties and had a sunken face from a habit of two packs a day minimum for forty years. She raised her head, recognized Sawatski, then turned on her heel as quickly as she could, with a hint of humour in her gait. She was on her third step of retreat when she turned back and headed to the door, a sly grin firmly affixed to her standard looks.

"We're closed," she said, pointing to an invisible watch on her left arm.

Sawatski pleaded. "C'mon Deidre, it's only seven minutes. And it's a police emergency."

"Is that so," said Deidre. She folded her arms in front of her, revealing poorly done tattoo sleeves. "What kind of police emergency?"

Sawatski exhaled the chilled vapor from his lungs, resting his nose against the glass. "I'm the police, and I'm freezing my fucking ass off, so it's an emergency."

"No, I think it's an ass-clown with a badge who doesn't know how to tell time." Deidre unlocked the door as Sawatski leaned against it, almost dumping him onto the floor. He cursed expectedly. "Fuck!"

"Kiss your mother with that mouth?" Deidre had moved behind the counter, checking the fryers. Sawatski was too busy to comment, shaking his glasses in a vain attempt to remove the foggy film. Deidre dumped the haddock into the fryer. "Breakfast of champions, I presume?"

"You presume right," said Sawatski, leaning against the guardrail that directed customers around the counter. "I gotta hit the head."

"I'll bring it out to you," said Deidre as she adjusted her hair net and threw in the fries, violating at least a paragraph in the health code. "And turn on the fan this time!"

Like most buildings in Winnipeg's Exchange District, The Line Up was a mix of two buildings, assembled long before a building code existed, or at least before it was being enforced. A steep stairway with an overhead metal sign announcing its descent opened up into the larger eating area, about four feet below street level. The windows were oversized, making it a great spot to people watch. There wouldn't be anyone there until the lunch crowd started trickling in around 11:30. Sawatski enjoyed the quiet time, for solitude and other things.

The single-stall men's room was roomy enough. It was never clean when the door first opened for the day. Sawatski figured that it was the job of Deidre's indifferent co-worker, so it probably wouldn't get re-spooled with the cheapest of toilet paper until eleven. From the toilet tank, he lifted out the Ziploc bag, shaking off the excess water before removing the white envelope within. It was folded in a way that spoke of the size of currency. As with the times before, five crisp hundreds presented themselves. Sawatski pulled out a few paper towels to dry the bag that he would take with him; no sense giving an indifferent bathroom attendant something to wonder about.

His fish and chips were waiting, with extra tartar sauce and a large coffee in a takeout cup. He took a swig, watching the windows, wondering when the show would start.

CHAPTER
SIXTEEN

Tommy awoke to the sound of the morning rush. Cindy had already joined the ladle scuffle. He could hear her shouting orders at both kitchen staff and patrons. *That can't be right,* he thought as he looked up at the time on the sunburst clock on the cracking plaster. Tommy had managed three hours of sleep, more than expected. It was almost like a lazy Sunday sleep, the kind he had once enjoyed at the Boscalow. He rubbed his eyes as he swung himself off the bed, grabbing the nearest clothes. He would help with the breakfast and see if anyone needed his counselling. There would be the usual calls to the suppliers of freebies, be they clothes or food, and the look-the-other-way friendlies in the various branches of city and provincial health inspection. What could be pushed off, what needed to be hidden, and how much it would cost to make it go away for another sixty days. There was also The Mail.

The Mail had been devised to help those in need of transition from being identified, by police or the criminal element. While the Winnipeg Police Service had legitimate means of acquiring both cellular and landline phone taps, the Heaven's Rejects had their connections, usually on the cellular side. Few known-to-police types had cell phone contracts, unless they were tied to semi-legitimate businesses, which were usually monitored by the law and the unlawful. The practice was highly illegal in the eyes of the Canadian Radio and Telecommunications Commission, though almost impossible to enforce, especially with an equal amount of legitimate enquiries by police agencies. Even payphones were not immune. In fact, they were easier to monitor with the onslaught of the modern wireless phone. The police service had a special name for the tactics: an anonymous tip.

Tommy hit the power switch on the computer tower, which still carried the sticker that identified it as government surplus. The rounded CRT screen flickered to life, along with a start-up screen for a bootleg version of Windows XP. He struggled with the old mouse, finally opening the browser. The home screen for Kijiji appeared, with Saskatoon as the location. He clicked on the Personals link, changing the search parameters to the newest ads. What came next was the usual collection of bored husbands and housewives, looking for a fling, a three-way, or a might-be-gay. It was too hard to use a regular tag line, such as Bored and Hot in Suburbia or Adventurous Couple Seeks. There was a pattern that Tommy was looking for. It was the third ad from the bottom.

"Exotic, discreet, and I NEED it bad! Married 23-year-old female wants too talk dirty first, Get Me off and maybe more! 36/24/36, blonde, no tats, laying my cards Out on the table. Married OK. Email for pix."

For those looking for that sort of thing, the ad seemed normal enough. For Tommy, it was the string of words and their placement within the message that spoke to him. The NEED was the first clue, capitalized for emphasis. The spelling error: too talk dirty. The dirty talk had no bearing on the message; it was the incorrect *to* that was the tip. All that was left was the Get Me and the Out. The Mail had been delivered.

The use of the email method was concerning. Most of Tommy's passengers to the after-the-life weren't being pursued with such fervour. Paulie Noonan simply strolled in. He could have probably avoided detection for a month or two, until he got lazy, assuming that the HRs hadn't somehow forgot about him. He would have made his way back to a regular haunt, where a well-placed Borden with an underworld informant who knew how to dial would be all that was required for an Ernie Friday, or one of the Pauls, to collect an easy two grand.

Tommy's concentration was broken by the *Winnipeg Sentinel* dropping onto his desk. "Looks like your ex had a busy night," said Cindy as she pointed at the front page.

Tommy looked at the headline. "Blood Pool on Pritchard, Heaven's Reject Prez Slain." The headline was laid atop a picture of the body pick-up team from the medical examiner's office as they rolled the gurney down the sidewalk. In the picture, a crime technician, in full protective gear, was exiting the front door, carrying what appeared to be a blood-stained fur coat. Tommy knew the coat. So did Cindy. Cindy also saw the open Kijiji page.

"Did the stupid bitch already put up an ad?"

Tommy highlighted the ad. "Yep. Came in around seven this morning."

"Shit!" Cindy took the front section from the rest of the paper, flipping inward for the rest of the story. She found it on the third page, next to the headshot of David Worschuk and his Downtown 24/7 column. Tommy knew that Worschuk had something resembling an entourage, a group of Remand Centre guards, beat cops, and provincial sheriffs who would meet up at the Black Stallion on Kennedy Street, near the Law Courts Building.

They would drink themselves into oblivion, telling exciting lies about their work day, then drive home, success-fully evading their badged brethren. About once every three months, Worschuk would do a lifestyle write-up on one of his cronies. It was the kind of thing that was treated to a fine custom frame by the subject in question, and the entourage patiently waited for their respective turns at the spotlight — so patient that they would often leak information to Worschuk on ongoing investigations. Cindy read the key words aloud to Tommy.

"While the Public Information Officer for the Winnipeg Police Service did not offer any information on the identity of the assailant, sources close to Downtown 24/7 have revealed that the killer was most likely a prostitute, due to the use of a straight razor in the killing." The ink on the page seemed to transfer easily onto Cindy's fingers. Worschuk was known for his last-minute press stops at the *Sentinel*.

Tommy had already started responding to the ad. To acknowledge the receipt of the message, all Tommy had to do was reference light, be it lunch, a bulb, anything at all. That was the cue for the subject to deliver themselves to The

Guiding Light as discreetly as possible. Cindy put her hand on his right shoulder as she watched him type. "This one's going to be tough."

"I know."

She leaned in closer. "Then why do it?"

Tommy glanced to the left of the computer screen, where a simple frame held a picture of him and Jeremy at Rae and Jerry's Steak House, on Jeremy's fourteenth birthday. "Because she asked me to."

"Even after she fucked you over? Even after she —"

"She didn't do that, Cindy. I did."

"But if she hadn't . . ."

"It still would have happened."

"You don't know that."

Tommy exhaled. "Neither do you, Cindy." He hit the enter key. Cindy looked away to hide her quiet weeping. Tommy heard it just the same. He rose to embrace her, but Cindy would have none of it. She headed for the door, fighting the tears. "I've got to get lunch started," she said. "And you've got a delivery coming."

Claire Hebert sat in front of Jasmine Starr's laptop screen. Jasmine had told her to refresh the page every fifteen minutes or so, checking for an email response to her Kijiji ad. Fifteen had become ten, ten had become five. Now it was down to every sixty seconds.

"Didn't your mother ever tell you about a watched pot?" Jasmine was standing over the sink, dabbing her wounds with moistened paper towel. She had removed her earrings, which had not fared well in the attack. She could see Claire in the reflection of the mirror. "And you owe me some earrings, bitch."

Claire didn't answer. She was more interested

in the message that had just popped up. "I got something!" she blurted.

"Don't respond!" Jasmine shouted as she approached, still dabbing the torn ear. "We've got to make sure it's him. What's it say?"

Claire squinted at the screen. "It says, 'Hey baby, how you doing, blah-blah-blah —'"

"The blah-blah is important," said Jasmine. "Read the whole thing, word-for-word."

Claire looked annoyed, but complied, slow and heavy on the punctuation of the text. "'Hey baby, liked your ad. I'm six-foot-two, twenty-four, work out, tongue stud . . .'" Claire stopped. "This is just some horny fuck!"

"'That's how it's supposed to look," said Jasmine. "Read it. Don't leave anything out."

Claire continued. "'I like to give/receive oral. Can go all NIGHT till the morning LIGHT. I like to —'"

"Right there!"

"Right where?"

"The light. It's him."

"Why? Just because it's in caps?"

Jasmine squinted at the screen. "EXACTLY because it's in caps."

"Bullshit!"

Jasmine looked at Claire with harsh eyes. "It's not bull-shit, Bear, it's a system. A system that works. It's a system that those fuckers at the cell phone companies can't mon-itor, and it's a system that's going to save your stupid ass." Jasmine pushed Claire aside and started to type the response. She motioned to the closet. "Pull out a couple of old sleeping bags from there."

Claire winced. "Sleeping bags? Where's the hideout, a campground?"

Jasmine kept typing. "They're not for camping; they're for comfort." She hit enter and closed the laptop. "How are you with tight spaces?"

Claire smirked. "I fucked a guy in a Smart car once."

Jasmine returned the smirk, chuckling slightly. "Then you're gonna love this." Jasmine walked over to the closet where Claire had just removed the sleeping bags. She pulled out a few more garment bags, revealing a plywood panel. The panel was held in place by four storm-window latches. Jasmine opened the latches, dislodging the panel. She passed it to Claire, who immediately noticed the rough hole cut through the cinder block wall. Jasmine huffed as she backed herself out of the passage. "Grab your shit," she panted. "And don't forget that fucking bag and book. I don't want that coming back on me."

Claire grabbed her meagre belongings, plus the two sleeping bags. Jasmine crawled through first. Claire hesitated at first, wondering if it was a hands-and-knees entrance to eternity, with a hot slug to the back of the head as she emerged to a perceived safe haven. The next building had been converted into storage, even though a retail canopy for a defunct drugstore remained out front. The space was owned by the laundromat next door, jammed to the rafters with washing machines, dryers, and related parts. Jasmine had something of a thing going on with the married owner. She would service him bi-monthly, usually in the storage area. It kept the rent down. She had requested the passage a year ago, for Underworld Railroad purposes, as well as discretion for liaisons. The laundromat owner lived on the second level of the building with an increasingly nosy wife on the prowl.

A roll-top door had been installed at the rear of the space. Near this was a large commercial washing machine on a pallet. Jasmine picked up an electric screwdriver on the workbench. "I suppose we should put the setting on delicate," she said, as she removed the rear panel.

Claire wasn't amused. "How the fuck am I supposed to fit in there? It's all full of wires and motors and —" Claire quickly re-thought her concerns as Jasmine moved the panel aside. It was empty except for pieces of heavy metal plate bolted to the floor. The added weight would give anyone moving it the impression that it was a real washing machine. Claire looked at the front of the machine. It looked like the typical load door, though when she tried the handle, it wouldn't open. In the window appeared to be the drum interior. She was still trying to figure out how when Jasmine broke her concentration.

"It's just a picture," said Jasmine as she threw the sleeping bags inside. "It's something to do with the glass and the lens or something." She checked the clock on the wall near the workbench. "Shit, they're going to be here in like five minutes."

"Who's going to be here?"

"Cartage company. It has to look legit. You better get in."

Claire started to, but hesitated. "You're sure I'm not headed for the car crusher, like in some old movie?" Jasmine smiled, and threw the bag of the late Jimmy Stephanos in, almost hitting Claire in the head.

"You're going to Tommy's," said Jasmine as she grabbed the panel and her screwdriver. "He'll get you out. He gets everybody out.

CHAPTER
EIGHTEEN

The Exchange District was relatively quiet that morning, with the only disturbance of note being the hammering on the glass of The Line Up by Miles Sawatski. The Voice had followed his journey from his perch on the third floor of the Albert Street Cocktail Company. He knew that Sawatski would be back at the Vice division by now, leaving the pie slice of Albert and Arthur Streets to the locals. The Voice knew how the rest of the morning would play out. There would be a steady growth to the lunch crowd, emerging from the upper levels of the Artspace Building, the warehouse lofts, and the commodities brokers on the other side of Main Street. The panhandlers would be ignored, with cell phone conversations and Canada Goose parka hoods used to shield the nine-to-five workers from the eventual insults of "white bitch," or worse. Eventually, the sirens would approach: first responders from the Winnipeg Number One fire hall. The siren's wail and bleating of the horns would ricochet off the stately granite and rounded cobble. It was seldom that the paramedics wouldn't end up at or near the Woodbine Hotel to attend to the losing side of an altercation or a collapsed drunk on the sidewalk.

The third-floor room was sparsely decorated, with a vintage metal desk and a single chair of well-worn ash. The Voice toggled through his Blackberry as he leaned against the window frame. No new messages. He was about six-foot-two, a well-kept fifty-something, with salt-and-pepper hair in a ponytail. With his grey horn-rimmed glasses and his dark-blue pinstripe suit with a crisp linen shirt, he could have passed for one of the area commodities brokers, an inspired cover. Even with the long-sleeved attire, aged ink from prison tattoos would peek out momentarily as the Blackberry was pressed for news. When none came, the ringer did. The Voice answered quick and cool.

"Talk to me."

"I'm at her apartment," said the accomplice. "Had to kill the roommate."

"Does she use?"

"More tracks than Symington Yard. It will look like a classic OD."

"Good. Associates?"

"Nothing on that. Looks like Hebert got her fun-time toys from that old broad at The Other Woman, about half a dozen receipts in her drawer."

"Run it down."

"For dildos? Really?"

"Run it down. Six receipts are a friend, not a storekeeper."
The man pressed End, stowing the phone in his breast pocket
as he headed for the door. He was almost ready to turn
the handle when he stopped, turned back to the desk, and
retrieved a ledger from the top desk drawer, a cheap store
brand.

David Worschuk was trying to remember if it was ten feet
or metres, the distance he had to be away from the *Sentinel*
for a cigarette. He didn't spend too much time there, thanks
to what staffers referred to as Publisher Teflon. The *Sentinel*
had moved into a former garment factory on Fife Street in
'89, the Eastern border of the Inkster Industrial Park, near
the homes of the rival *Winnipeg Sun* and the *Winnipeg Free
Press*. The move had been necessary after an embarrassing
level of asbestos had been found in the ductwork of the original building. Worschuk had only known the new building.
His spotty attendance wasn't an issue. As long as his column
found its way into the City Desk email inbox before deadline, he was considered to be on the job. He had squeaked
the Jimmy Stephanos murder piece in with twelve minutes
to spare. He had stopped in to catch up on his snail mail
when the publisher had requested a chat. This always worried Worschuk. He had thrown his weight around for so long
now that even he could see that his days were numbered. Few
had challenged him when he first arrived, as they knew that
Worschuk would simply text the publisher about any fric-
tion, making the complainant's life an eight on the Richter
scale. The problem was recent managerial changes and pressure from the newspaper's owners over slipping revenues.

He even had to come in twice a week to do page layout. For Worschuk, this was starting to feel too much like a job.

The front doors to the *Sentinel* slid open as three employees emerged, most likely on their way to lunch. The doors had started to close when they stopped and retreated, as Kyle Morgan stepped into the cold. The publisher of the *Winnipeg Sentinel* wore a heavy black cashmere coat and a red silk scarf. He was in his early fifties and stood a tired and worn five-foot-eight, with a two-hundred-dollar haircut on his dirty-blond locks, which helped to offset the appearance of his pockmarked face. The sun struck him, sending his designer glass frames into auto-tint. The coat was open and the scarf hung around his neck with little thought to appearances. He eyed Worschuk. He looked annoyed.

"That doesn't look like ten metres, Downtown," said Morgan. Worschuk hesitated mid-drag, analyzing Morgan's face for the tell. Morgan smirked. "Or maybe its ten feet, I can't remember." Morgan patted his pockets, in search of his brand. Worschuk hastily offered up his DuMaurier pack, so quickly that it could have been mistaken for the offers of smoke made by old-time suitors in black-and-white films. He offered up his Zippo just as fast.

"Thanks," said Morgan, inhaling deeply. "I'd rather talk out here. Too many shit-disturbing ears in this fucking place." Worschuk felt his heartbeat drop ten beats as Morgan let out a well-earned exhale. "Good piece this morning. It's like they always say . . ."

Worschuk finished Morgan's sentence before it had any steam. "If it bleeds, it leads."

Morgan chuckled. "Ain't that the truth?" He took a thick drag as he formulated his next thought. "If I could get away with it, I'd send a meth-head with an Uzi into a day care every day, just to keep the fucking owners from carving a new chunk out of my ass."

Worschuk nodded, opting for a drag instead of a comment. So maybe this was the preview of what was coming. He appreciated the intel, though Worschuk was more concerned as to how he was going to keep up the payments on his Escalade, his Ski-Doo, and the new Can-Am Spyder if the paper closed its doors. Winnipeg was a one-newspaper town at best. It was anyone's guess who would shut down their presses first.

Morgan took one last long drag, flicking the thrice-smoked cigarette to the ground with a slight hint of disgust. "This HR murder is a good opportunity. Need to show the blog babies out there that news and paper go together like peanut butter and chocolate, and stick it to the *Sun* and the *Freep* at the same time. How much dirt can we dig up on that hooker?"

Work — maybe it isn't all that bad, Worschuk thought. He could dig deeper into the sex trade, call girls, and drugs. It was pure entertainment value. "I've got some leads," said Worschuk, knowing full well that he didn't. "I can hit up the cops, ask some of the guards at Portage Correctional. They've got the hookers. Someone's got to be able to get me close."

Morgan slapped Worschuk's back as he headed back in. "Just make sure you wear three rubbers in Portage," said Morgan, as the door slid open. "Better make it four, if the girls are local." Worschuk watched him disappear into the catacombs of half cubicle walls, chuckling as he went, enjoying the dig at the neighbouring Manitoba hamlet. Worschuk lit another cigarette to calm his nerves.

CHAPTER
NINETEEN

Claire Hebert did her best not to breathe, keeping her frame in a tight fetal position as the delivery van carrying the mock washing machine rumbled down Main Street. Or maybe it was Arlington. She couldn't say for sure, though she had tried to monitor the roll and pitch of the van, assuming that she could somehow internalize some type of positioning for her general location. *Not that it will do me any good*, she thought as she felt the van stop, then power through what must have been a four-way stop. She still couldn't say with certainty that Jasmine hadn't sold her out; the price must have been enough to mobilize most of the Winnipeg low-lifes out of their holes. Would she be safe, or slain? She would know soon enough.

The van was crawling now, the speed of which was feeling back lane to Claire. It was definitely an area of town that was in need of serious infrastructure work, with even the snow and ice doing little to fill the potholes. The van stopped suddenly. The warble of the reverse warning speaker began to echo in the cargo chamber. The two cab doors opened and shut as the delivery men trudged in stereo to the rear. The hydraulic lift descended, picked up the pair, and ascended to the roll-top door. Their conversation seemed benign enough: talk of the hockey game, beer after work, which strip club to visit. There was no talk of how to kill and dispose of the girl in the oversized washing machine.

She heard another roll-top door, though this one seemed to be more light-duty, the kind on storage lockers or delivery entrance points on buildings. She heard a familiar voice.

"I hope this one doesn't fuck up like the last one," said Tommy as the two delivery men grunted with the load. "It pissed all over the floor."

"Yeah, but you should be used to guys pissing all over the floor," said one of the delivery men. He was young, Claire thought, and very unaware of whom he was talking to. She played the image out in her mind: the dig at the patrons of The Guiding Light, the steely cold glare of Tommy Bosco, a defence of his tenants that was beyond any words; the kid, realizing he had gone too far, trying to recover. The silence lasted an eternity. "Give me that fucking clipboard," said Tommy, slapping it against the top of the machine. It was so loud, Claire almost cried out. She knew she didn't need to. She was safe, for the moment.

Tommy removed the last screw with the cordless drill, shifting the panel to the side. He looked in at Claire Hebert, still huddled in a protective pose. She looked smaller, certainly far less threatening than the woman he had once known. He remembered those times, when he had looked upon her in similar moments. There was a peace within her now. *Everyone has one*, thought Tommy, *even the ones who couldn't live a day without some form of self-lit explosion.*

"Is she awake?" Cindy broke the silence, startling Tommy. "I don't know how you could sleep in that thing."

Tommy bent down and saw the briefcase as he looked further inward. "C'mon, Bear. You can't forward your mail to this box."

Claire turned to look at Tommy. He looked older than she had remembered. A lot more tired, but he still had a glimmer in his eyes. She noticed Cindy observing the interplay. *So, this is the new one*, she thought, as she started to shuffle out of the metal box. Claire was still trying to decide whether she cared one way or the other. She honestly couldn't remember. Those days were anything but sober. She was still feeling the effects of the current withdrawal as Tommy helped her to her feet. "Welcome to The Guiding Light," he said. "And may God protect your dumb, murdering ass."

Claire assessed the surroundings. She was in a loading area of some type, at the rear of the Light. Food service boxes, plastic dairy cases, and empty white buckets were piled ceiling high. She could hear the bustle of the lunch rush. It reminded her that she would eat from time to time, usually when she ran out of coke. Her request was as meek as a first-time john. "Do you, uhm, think I could get, uh . . ."

"We'll bring you some food in a few," said Cindy. "First we've got to get you safe."

CHAPTER
TWENTY

Ernie Friday idled in front of a dental-supply office on Cumberland. He adjusted his rear-view mirror for a better look at the action at 411 On the Park, the latest catchy name for a most notorious high-rise. In the right city, 411 Cumberland Avenue would have easily commanded half a million for a park-like-view studio condo. It may have been called Central Park below, but it was nothing more than a wading pool of syringes, used condoms, and blood trails from recreational stabbings. A studio condo could be had for about ninety thousand at 411, not a bad deal if you never intended on leaving the house again.

The crime scene technicians should have

had their own parking spaces up front at 411, as visits were frequent. The identification van was flanked by unmarked detective cars, all with lights flashing from their visors. Ernie had planned on making a visit to unit 723. Claire Hebert was living off the grid, but she wasn't off the security cameras. Almost a third of the prostitution trade lived, worked, or crashed at 411 Cumberland Avenue. Ernie figured it was as safe a bet as any for finding an off-grid girl, so he called up a friend at the security company that managed the building. The friend was an ex-con, with no interest in getting found out and booted from his minimum wages. Ernie described Claire and asked him to check the four-to-five-a.m. time block. That was the hour when most premium girls were done for the night. It was the "big stupid tits" comment of Ernie's that found her dropping her keys. She was too drunk or too stoned to operate them. She did remember her apartment code number though. To make sure, she recited it aloud for the security camera microphone to pick up.

Ernie figured that he was too late for four grand, though he couldn't be a hundred percent sure. He killed the engine and walked across the street to the payphones. One of the five was operational, good odds for Central Park. He flipped open his little black book, cradling the phone on his shoulder as he punched in the digits. As he hung up, he kept an eye on the medical examiner's van. The black van had been parked in the opposite direction of the one-way Cumberland, next to an unmarked detective car near the lobby. A pair of heavy-set men in their late twenties emerged. They called themselves the Ferrymen, tasked with a job that few would ever apply for: the retrieval of Winnipeg's dead. Ernie didn't know their names, and he didn't want to. He needed them for confirmations, to avoid chasing ghosts.

Ernie had met the Ferrymen about six months ago on a side street near Waterfront Drive. The divers had just pulled out a floater near the Provencher Bridge, and the Ferrymen were heading back to the morgue, when a flat tire on the meat wagon had prompted a changeover. Ernie had pulled up behind the van, its rear doors open to access the spare. The Ferrymen tried to shield the bodies within as they lowered the spare tire. Friday had been following the van for most of the morning, trying to come up with a way to get a peek at the first body pick-up. It was an apparent suicide — one that had been probably brought about by the victim's gambling debts to the Heaven's Rejects. It was a rough-up job that Ernie wouldn't be collecting on.

Ernie exited his car of the month, a rusty Delta 88, holding a tire iron in his right hand. The Ferryman keeping the door from swinging open had red hair — that was all the name he needed.

"Hey, Red," said Ernie, as he approached the van. "Need a hand with that?"

Red looked up from watching his partner wind down the spare, somewhat annoyed. "No thanks, old man," said Red. "I think we got it under control."

"That's alright," said Ernie, as he gently rocked the tire iron in his hand. "I'm not here to change your fucking tire." The comment got the attention of both Ferrymen, with the Tire Winder stopping in mid-crank to see what the interruption was about. Ernie smiled. "Now that I have your full attention, I need to see inside bag number one."

Tire Winder jumped in. "Uh, we don't like, uh, have a number one."

Red interjected. "Well, we kinda do. The top left."

"That's not number one; that's number three."

"Not the way I count 'em"

"That's not proper."

"To who?" Red pointed at the bags within. "Do you think they give a shit?"

The Tire Winder got up to explain. "It's like the floors in a building. First floor, first body. Second floor, second body, third —"

"What about the other side?" said Red. He was smiling at his newfound ability to outsmart Tire Winder. "So, you're saying we got two first bodies, two second bodies —"

"That side is four-five-six."

"What building starts on the fourth floor?

"One with a parkade of course." Tire Winder gestured to Ernie, expecting at least a shrug of agreement. Ernie wasn't interested.

"I'll let you ladies figure this out on your own time," said Ernie. "Right now, I need to see the suicide." He opened the top corner of his jacket, revealing two fifties poking out of his shirt pocket.

"I don't know about that. It was made to look like, but definitely was not, a suicide."

"Like you know," said Red. He looked at Ernie as he thumbed at Tire Winder. "He watches that fuckin' *CSI* shit like its porn — thinks he's the M-E."

Ernie whacked the fender of the Oldsmobile with the tire iron, hard, making sure not to break the turn signal lens while still achieving immediate attention. "The suicide. Which one is it?" The Ferrymen pointed at the bag of interest.

"Bag one," said Red, pointing to the top left.

"Bag three," said Tire Winder, pointing to the same location. Ernie rolled his eyes, motioning to the bag with the tire iron. He handed Red the fifties while Tire Winder pulled open the bag, wincing slightly at the summertime stench of decomposition. Ernie didn't look at the face; he lifted up the head by the dead man's hair. He smiled, setting the head down with an action resembling respect. He reached into his other shirt pocket, producing a pager. "Takes double As," said Friday. "Cheapest at Costco." He walked back to the Oldsmobile. As he opened the door, he stopped and looked at the Ferrymen. "Make sure you keep it on."

As Ernie pulled away, the Ferrymen decided they needed to know. Red lifted the head and smiled.

"What's it say?" asked Tire Winder. Red lifted the head a little higher to show him the tattoo.

Tire Winder smirked. "Born to Lose," he said. "No shit."

The Ferrymen's pager had been used about eight times since the tire change. Red fumbled in his pocket with the new vibration as Tire Winder readied the gurney. They knew the drill. Once the body was loaded, the Ferrymen would take the long way back to the city morgue in the basement of the Health Sciences Centre. Higgins Avenue was close enough to the crime scene to keep the time impact to a minimum, in case anyone was keeping track. Next to the CPR yards, the street surface changed from bumpy to potholed, which kept traffic flow to the bare minimum. It was about as discreet a spot as one could hope for in broad daylight.

It took about fifteen minutes until the Ferrymen emerged with the body. Ernie watched the load-up in his rear-view. For some reason, he hoped it was Claire Hebert. The money was good, a lot better than he had seen for some time, but the years were getting harder. The last check-up hadn't gone well, with Ernie off the charts for bad cholesterol, plus the hips, and his heart. There was even a slight shadow on his right lung, found during a chest X-ray. It was time. He hoped that some new young buck had done the deed, which would start to diminish the invitations. He had enough saved up to join the snowbird set, maybe a nice mobile home in Mesa, Arizona, with a carport. It might only be for a couple of years. *At least they would be peaceful*, he thought, as he pulled away from the curb.

The Ferrymen got to Higgins Avenue first, with Ernie tardy by about ninety seconds. Red stayed in the van while Tire Winder took care of the fifties and the reveal. Ernie studied the naked corpse from suite 723. It wasn't Claire Hebert, at least that much was certain. Even with the onset of rigor, it was easy to see that the girl was of Asian descent, with dyed blonde hair and a teardrop tattoo below her left eye, the kind applied with whatever is handy in juvenile corrections. Ernie checked for working-girl cues. Her arms were pockmarked with needle tracks, both recent and vintage. It looked like the classic overdose, almost too classic at a time like this. *This was some serious punishment for simply sharing a sock drawer with somebody on a hit list,* Ernie thought.

He returned the blanket to the corpse. He had seen a tattoo above her left breast: Cherie. He bade her safe travels. He knew no one else would.

Ernie was about to give Tire Winder a goodbye nod when he heard approaching wheels spin on ice. He turned around in time to see the Two Pauls slide to a stop. Bouchard drove an old Ford Ranger parts-delivery truck, still sporting the aftermarket parts cage instead of a pickup box. The Ranger cab was a tight fit for Lemay, though he still managed to exit the truck with the speed of a man half his size. He smiled at Ernie. "Hey, old man. I figured you were in to Cold Ethels."

Ernie glared at Lemay while Bouchard stayed by the driver's side fender. Ernie could tell by the bulge in Bouchard's yard jacket that he had at least a 9mm automatic in his right pocket. "What's this?" said Ernie, pointing at the gun bulge in Bouchard's pocket. "I thought you guys were the Wholesale Hitters."

Bouchard looked at his pocket, feigning surprise. "Oh, that? I'm just happy to see you, Friday. Thank God it's Friday." Bouchard moved up to the passenger fender. "If you're looking for fresh meat, you should try Cantor's on Wednesdays."

"Fucking heebs," said Lemay. "Miller's on St. Mary's kicks ass."

"Tastes like ass," said Bouchard.

"Tastes like your Mom."

"Watch it, shitbag."

"Hey, watch this," said Lemay, flipping Bouchard the finger.

Ernie was starting to wonder if they had remembered what they had come for. "It's not her," he said.

"Not who?" said Lemay. "Whoever could you mean?"

"Whomever," said Tire Winder. "I'm pretty sure it's whomever."

Lemay shot Tire Winder a look that read *you're not supposed to talk, ever.*

"Or whoever," Tire Winder said. "Whatever works."

Lemay opened his coat, revealing a snub-nosed .357 stuffed in his ample waistband. He looked at his gun, then at Tire Winder, then gave an obvious nod to the van door. Tire Winder complied. Lemay threw back the blanket, revealing Cherie's breasts. He grabbed one for a cursory check. "Fake, just as I suspected," said Lemay. He rocked her head to the side, not really knowing what he was looking for.

"What are you doing?" said Bouchard, his impatience growing. "I can tell from here it's not her."

Lemay ignored him. "Could be a clever disguise, you know, maybe even one of those movie masks that peel off." Lemay looked for some sort of break in the skin to confirm his theory. He pulled at some of the neck skin. Nothing budged. "Looks like original, numbers matching, except for the tits."

Bouchard rolled his eyes. "It's not a '67 Camaro, dipshit. It's a dead hooker, and it ain't the right one, so let's get the fuck outta here." He looked over at Ernie, flashing a fake smile. "If you need some help on this, old man, just let us know. I'll cut you in for twenty percent if the lead works out."

Ernie kept his cool, as much as he would have preferred not to. He wanted to unload a Deluxe Vise Grip on Bouchard's neck for his insolence, though now that they were packing, it simply wasn't worth the extra hole that Lemay would undoubtedly provide, even if it took three shots to get there.

"I'll keep it in mind," said Ernie as he fumbled for his lighter. "Happy hunting."

Lemay smirked as he turned to enter the truck. The stereo was loud enough to hear outside the cab. The song was "Sister Christian" by Night Ranger. Their heads bobbed calmly as the lyrics approached.

"Motoring!" sang the Pauls. "What's your price for flight?" Bouchard revved the tired engine and popped the clutch, spitting up snow and sand as the pair spun away in song. Ernie and Tire Winder watched in silence.

"Who are those guys?" Tire Winder asked when they were out of sight.

"Ass-clowns," said Ernie. "Ass-clowns with guns."

CHAPTER
TWENTY-ONE

Claire Hebert wasn't doing so well. The initial sweats of withdrawal in the back room of The Other Woman had reached a fever pitch as she rocked in the fetal position on the fold-out couch in Tommy's office. Cindy had been keeping an eye on her while Tommy attended to a surprise visit by the food inspection branch. Claire wasn't swearing as much anymore, preferring the sound of her sustained moans as she shivered beneath the blankets. The briefcase and the ledger were open on the computer desk in front of Cindy. She chewed on an apple as she tried to make sense of the encoding, punching random sequences of the information into Google. Nothing lined up. Some portions came back as parts numbers, for everything from replacement fenders to washing machine motors. Others identified telephone numbers in non-volatile places, like Des Moines, Iowa. The glare from the monitor was starting to take its toll when Tommy walked in with a warning letter from the food inspector. Cindy looked perplexed. "I thought you paid him off," she said.

"I did," said Tommy. "This is a lightweight, so it looks like he's doing his job and not getting greased." He handed her the notice, with checkmarks on a leaking fridge seal, a soiled ceiling tile, and an out-of-date fire extinguisher. Cindy opened the drawer with the blank fire extinguisher inspection tags and adjusted the date to her liking on the adjacent rubber stamp. "Sorry Bosco," said Cindy. "I thought I had done this one."

Tommy looked over at the tossing and turning of his former lover. "Is she doing any better? We should get rolling no later than eight tonight."

Cindy glanced over at her for a moment. "Well, she's down to calling me a cunt only three times per hour. Two hours ago it was around thirteen."

"Now, that's what I call a Supercunt," said Tommy as he headed for the relative comfort of the bottom bunk. He rubbed his eyes as Cindy typed. "Any headway on the code system?"

"Nothing yet," said Cindy as she maintained eye contact with the flickering screen. "Someone actually put some effort into this one. The sequences are the same, but it doesn't bring anything up. I've reversed the digits, dropped things that looked like a shield against identifying what it is. No one is supposed to figure this one out."

Claire bolted upright, as much as anyone bolts upright

during the various stages of detoxification. Her makeup had run, and was approaching that of a Stephen King clown. Her hair was a matted mess. She looked nothing like her price. "I feel like the floor of the men's room at the bus station."

Cindy turned to assess the remark. "Looks like it was a long, lost decade of weekends," said Cindy. Claire turned to her, her left eye half open. It was feeble, but she was still able to flip Cindy an obvious finger.

Tommy grabbed a bottle of water from the half-used twenty-four pack under the bed. "Drink up, buttercup," said Tommy, holding the bottle out to Claire. She winced at the thought of liquid. Tommy insisted. "You're still detoxing, and you've got to flush that shit out before we travel." Claire relented, fumbling with the cap like an octogenarian. She took small sips, concerned that too much swig would bring yet another thunderous vomit. She was only batting about .250 for hitting the wastebasket placed by her head. She held the bottle to her forehead. Even the coolness of the room-temperature bottle was enough to release a soothing sigh. The sigh was interrupted by Claire's own spotty memory. She looked at Tommy with eyes glazed, but wide. "Has anyone come looking for me?"

Tommy smiled and grabbed a nearby chair to sit closer, though not close enough for projectile vomit to reach him. "You're safe, Bear. Nobody knows you're here except for Jasmine and us." Cindy worked the computer, though her glances towards Tommy and Claire were increasing. Perhaps she was simply guarding her territory, even though the territory had never been truly defined.

Tommy started to rummage through what little contents remained in the briefcase. Cindy knew Claire's off-grid situation was going to be a problem for getting her out of town with relative ease. The Brady Road Package that Tommy assembled would usually contain some remnants of identification to help with the presumed confirmation of death from the police service. The computer and printing equipment at the Light was as ancient as the floorboards. Fakes were getting harder to duplicate, especially with holograms and security elements. Cindy had tried to make a few, using the free computers at the Millennium Library to do her research, keeping the Guiding Light computer clean from criminal activity searches. She quickly realized she was out of her league, with most of her attempts bordering on scrapbooking. While adept at their work, the local forgers were a little too chatty with other criminals. The right slip to the wrong person could bring everything to the doorstep of The Light by dusk, or sooner. Cindy knew that it was a safe bet that the top three had already been given an underworld all-points bulletin.

Tommy suddenly stopped the search, looked at Claire, and smiled. "You still got a thing for monograms?"

Claire smirked and proceeded to remove her bra from within her sweater. She tossed the custom-made unit at him. Tommy looked at the straps. The Claire-Bear handle had been embroidered in gold, with Claire on the left strap and Bear on the right. "It's on my panties, too," said Claire-Bear. She looked over at Cindy. "I guess I can swap them out for some of your granny gitch."

Cindy didn't look over at Claire, nor did her gaze waver from her computer monitor. She was still able to flash a proper middle finger at Claire's good eye.

David Worschuk rolled up in front of the Black Stallion on Corydon Avenue in his equally black Escalade. The Little Italy location had been open for about six months, though weak reviews had kept it from being a force amongst the Italian eateries. The restaurant may have been quiet, but the lounge was well attended, already half full twenty minutes after opening. The bartender gave Worschuk the classic I-Know-You nod. Worschuk returned it in kind.

"Just coffee, Phil," said Worschuk as he scanned the room for his party. Phil grabbed the carafe and poured, offering no eyebrows as to why the order was just coffee without the usual shot of Jack Daniel's. Worschuk tossed a toonie into the tip mug as he headed towards the back of the L-shaped space.

There were six booths at the rear of the lounge, insulated to a slight degree from the bank of video lottery terminals. Pub-style partitions kept the conversations cozy. The first booth was occupied, with three area residents speaking in boisterous Italian about the global story spread in the morning *Sentinel*. The next four were empty, with menus strategically placed in the hopes that customers might be filling them. The last booth had company: a heavy-set man in his late fifties, still sporting a full head of brown hair. He had the look of an ex-cop with few visits to the police association gym that was free for retirees. He was more intent on adding pepper to his pea soup than acknowledging Worschuk's bumpy slide into the booth. He stirred the bowl with one of the hard bread-sticks provided.

"You might want to get a bowl from the top of the pot," said the man. "You're bound to get some of the burnt bits from the bottom by the end of the lunch hour."

Worschuk took a swig of his coffee and removed a cellophane-wrapped breadstick from the community bowl. "Maybe I'll just dip into yours," said Worschuk, as he made a play for the green goodness.

The man looked at him hard, with a glare that was three degrees right of Don't Even Think About It. It stopped Worschuk cold. The man took a few initial slurps of soup before speaking again. "So, it's a hooker you're looking for, is it?"

"You know it is, Wilson." Wilson looked at Worschuk with even more disgust. He had hung on to a tidy collection of photocopied files from his days in Vice. Worschuk would tap Wilson for information when the need arose.

He was meticulous in his recall of events, especially details from crime scenes. He had never learned to turn it off, even after seven years of pension. He would usually grab a couple of Bordens for the requests. Using his name would usually require a third as a penalty.

"I'm sorry Wilson, I just —" Worschuk realized he had just broken the Wilson Law twice. "Can I get your lunch?" As if on cue, the waitress approached the table. Wilson smiled at her.

"What's the best thing you have today that isn't on special?"

The waitress seemed puzzled at first, until she saw Worschuk. Figuring it was his treat, she suggested the rib-eye. "Medium-rare," said Wilson. "And two fingers of Johnny Walker Blue, neat." The waitress finished her shorthand and gave Wilson a regular customer smile on her way to the kitchen. Wilson looked at Worschuk with a superior grin. "You want to throw a dessert in there too while you're at it, Downtown?"

Worschuk took a few seconds to compose himself, reminding his mouth of the non-name policy. "Do you have anything on her?" He slid the two hundred-dollar bills to Wilson. Worschuk was more than hopeful for a return on his investment. His enquiry to Portage Correctional had been met by deaf ears and a quick hang-up. He was still trying to recall what he had written about them for the quick disconnect.

Wilson smiled, stowing the bills in his shirt pocket. He reached into his jacket pocket and produced a small coiled notebook with a dog-eared finish. It had been in use for some time, as his notations for Claire Hebert were at the end of his page run. "Miss Claire Marie Hebert, aka Claire-Bear. In the system for prostitution, bawdy house, career hooker. Last known on her was 411 Cumberland, apartment 723, off-grid. I heard they pulled a body out of there this morning."

Worschuk looked surprised. "This morning? When the fuck did that —" Worschuk was more upset that he hadn't received a tip from one of his fluff-piece confederates. It didn't play well for Worschuk to be the last to know of a fresh homicide.

Wilson glared at Worschuk. "Keep your voice down!"

"Was it Claire —"

"No, and keep your fucking voice down!"

Worschuk composed himself as Wilson explained. "I've still got some teeth in my head, and people still like to tell me what's going on." Wilson took another slurp of his soup, now cold enough to produce a reaction of disgust. He put the spoon to the side. "An emergency scanner does wonders, too." Wilson looked hopefully towards the front of the restaurant, knowing it was far too soon for a steak to appear. "Looks like the roommate was in the wrong place at the wrong time, or an OD, whichever you prefer to believe."

Worschuk leaned back as far as he could in the tight booth. Even he knew it was far too much effort occurring in far too little time for the crime. "She must have something pretty big on somebody to get this kind of attention. This isn't just the Stephanos whack." Worschuk considered another breadstick, withdrawing his fingers from the bowl at the last second. "Did she have pictures on somebody? Video? A list of johns?"

"Maybe," said Wilson as he swirled his cold soup in search of pockets of steam. "She wouldn't be the first hooker with an insurance policy. The problem is that very few of them ever cash in. Most of them have a habit the size of Transcona. That makes it a hard juggle to hide, run, and score, plus stay alive. Most end up in Brady Road, a ditch on Pipeline, or face down on Community Row."

"You mean face off," said Worschuk, in search of cop-worthy darkness. Wilson maintained his deadpan, enjoying the Worschuk squirm. Wilson turned to his notebook, flipping through the pages in a form of file search that only he could understand. "Brady Road," he muttered. "You know, funny thing about Brady Road."

Worschuk leaned in. "What's that?"

Wilson flipped a little more to confirm his suspicions. "We never had a body put in a dump before Brady, and when you think about it, not the smartest place to dump anything. They're always pushing, dragging, scooping up garbage. You'd think they'd find a piece of somebody — a foot, a leg, anything. Then, about three-and-a-half years ago, they start finding shit — wallets, IDs, a few dental partials, but no meat, not even enough to make a cheeseburger. And get this — every one of them was on the active Missing Persons list." Wilson flipped some more. "Plus, every one of them was known to police."

Worschuk rubbed his morning whiskers for inspiration. "Did they declare them?"

"Every last one of them." said Wilson. He flipped a little more. "That's seventeen bodies we never found, and those are just the ones who were reported missing. They've found other IDs in there, but if they weren't missing or wanted, they probably chalked it up to folks who haven't read the news on why you should chop up your old credit cards. Or, what they did was so dumb that they weren't going to stick around to see how it played out. If nobody misses you, we're not going to start looking for you."

The tale was starting to move into Worschuk's element. He understood convicts better than most cops with badges, even ex-cops like Wilson. Someone was helping these cons get out of the Life and out of town. The question was who would be crazy and/or dumb enough to invite such notoriety. "Any particular trade?" said Worschuk.

"Naw, it's all over the map," said Wilson. "Hooking, B and E, a few HR wannabes." He leaned out of the booth, hopeful that the zephyrs of charred meat were heading his way. "It doesn't look like they knew the same people or hung out in the same places. They were just . . ."

Worschuk couldn't wait for Wilson to complete his thought. "They were just what?"

"Garbage," said Wilson. "Grade A, prime cut, economy-sized packs of human garbage. Somebody was gunning for every single last one of these fuckers. When that happens, your choices are somewhat limited for your survival. You can pull a suicide or face the music, which is usually just another form of suicide. Or, you can disappear." Wilson dabbed a freshly opened breadstick in the soup. "There's a magician in town," said Wilson. "And he's really, really good. Dean Gunnarson–good."

A magician. Worschuk let the idea roll around in his head for a moment as Wilson gave an annoyed lean-and-glance towards the kitchen. *This is one hell of a smoke-and-mirrors operator*, thought Worschuk. It almost smelled of cop involvement, especially with the quick-pronounced missing persons. Worschuk tried to think of anyone who could be an obvious candidate. Nothing clicked. He knew it was someone sympathetic to the cause, perhaps a social worker or a parole officer with a heart of gold. They may have wanted to help, though getting found out would surely mean the end of a career, or worse. This was charity that seemed more like a winning lottery ticket in its level of generosity. He rubbed the bridge of his nose as the waitress arrived with Wilson's over-marbled rib-eye. Wilson had no gristle fears as he devoured the first cut. Worschuk started to deduce out loud. "It has to be someone who's con-savvy, someone who gets them. Maybe even one of them."

Wilson nodded. "That would play, but whoever it is, they better hope that no one finds out how much of a stand-up guy they are." He took another bite of the mediocre steak as he formed his next thought. "It's a dead man's hand, no matter how you play it."

Worschuk contemplated why this person would incur such risk. How had they avoided detection by criminals? He was still staring off into space when Wilson snapped his sausage-like fingers at him. "411 Cumberland," said Wilson as he finished the chew. "They'll be on scene for at least another hour."

Traffic on Osborne Street South was relatively light, though that didn't keep The Voice and his silver Chrysler 300-C from maintaining a twenty-kilometre-per-hour premium on the speed limit. He slowed at the obvious photo-radar intersections and spiked the brake whenever he saw a late-model Dodge Caravan idling in a no-parking zone. These were the mobile photo-radar units, which were technically marked units with parking enforcement labels adhered to the rear curbside windows. The only ones who ever saw those markings were pedestrians.

He tapped the signal for a left on Morley Avenue, coasting through the remaining stop signs towards the Riverview Health Centre. The centre was born from the remnants of two vintage brick structures, the former King George and King Edward Hospitals. The old buildings had long since been demolished, with a new care facility and a mandate aimed at the booming growth in the elderly populace. It had become a respected palliative care centre and an Alzheimer's research facility, plus something of a clearing house for the longest of long-term patients with debilitating ailments of a bygone era. Little remained to tell visitors about the polio epidemic that swept through the city in 1953, though there were still a few iron lungs in operation in less-travelled wards.

The Voice, clutching a zippered leather folio, melded easily into the corridors. He kept a brisk pace, the kind usually reserved for those with military or law enforcement backgrounds. The staff and security officers made the obvious assumptions: drug rep, medical supply salesman, syringe-pump pusher. He was acutely aware of the security camera locations, dodging them with precision without seeming evasive. Eventually, he found a slight inner hallway with a stairway that should have been marked for authorized personnel. It was steeper than standard inclines, descending to the expected labyrinth of hospital piping and conduit. It was still the lunch hour, which The Voice had planned for, to avoid detection.

It took fifty-three steps to reach the door, emblazoned with a biohazard warning sticker. The Voice produced a key and entered into the room quickly. The aroma was part medication, part saline, part dead tissue. It had little effect on his olfactory system. He produced a key card and approached the rear of the room, placing him at the northern most tip of the new facility. There was no card reader; at least, not one that could be seen or swiped. He held the card at a height of approximately seven feet, and waited.

The wall started to slide open, without the grinding effects associated with grave robber movies. It was a polite, almost silent movement. The opening was approximately four feet wide and could easily accommodate a hospital gurney. He stepped into a hallway of standard width, lit with the brightness normally associated with a budget apartment block. The floor had been expertly polished, the walls painted with generous coats of putty grey. There was no whiff of mold, no scampering rodents to contend with, just the polite hum of the overhead air-exchange system.

The tunnel was constructed of many angles, easily confusing the actual earthbound direction after the fifth turn. It took about four minutes to navigate to a blind corner, made safer by the addition of an overhead convex mirror. Once rounded, the walls connected to the remnants of an old foundation of massive limestone blocks. In the centre of this transition was a smudge-free door of machine-turned stainless steel. He held the security card to the blue glow of an LED at the right-hand side of the door frame. The steel panel whispered open, leading to another secure inlet. Once the panel had slid shut, The Voice closed his eyes for the security scan, which bathed him from head to toe in a matrix of blue LED light. A small panel opened in the ceiling, lowering a dual retinal scanner to eye level. The Voice removed his grey horn-rimmed glasses and positioned his eyes in the hovering goggles. A mechanical whirring sound signalled the opening of the next door, easily a foot thick, with a locking system that spoke more of a bank vault than insulated steel.

The scent of fresh-cut flowers beckoned from within, mingling with the initial notes of the "So What" cut from the Miles Davis masterpiece *Kind of Blue*. The interior walls were finished in cherry oak panelling from floor to ceiling. The floor was an artisan work of complementary terrazzo tiles. Crystal sconces cast subdued lighting, though it didn't take long to notice that the entire ceiling was a fully-lighted panel, most likely required for the needs of emergency resuscitation. It stood dark for the time being. There were minimal furnishings, which were easily eclipsed by the highly polished Emerson respirator in the centre of the room. The iron lung had been treated to the utmost care for its patient, a patient who was being spoon-fed by a nurse when Mr. Ponytail arrived. She was dressed like a nurse would have dressed in the 1950s, replete with a navy cape, temporarily draped on a nearby settee. The makeup and hair were also period correct, though she surely hadn't been alive during the ravages of the polio epidemic. She looked up at The Voice with a thirty-something face, giving a cordial nod before storing the feeding items in an insulated lunch bag. She donned her cape and headed briskly for the exterior passage. He took her chair, still engulfed with her warmth.

He looked at the exposed head of the man in the respirator — pale and well populated with wrinkles and age spots. His eyes were closed, though not in slumber. The remnants of his hair were cut short, almost, but not quite, stubble. The steady exhale of the respirator and the Miles Davis sextet were the only sounds for the next minute, until the man spoke. "Volume, twenty percent," said the man, with an authoritative tone. Miles and his masters complied. He opened his eyes, revealing sharp, piercing greens. "Good afternoon, Nathaniel," said the broken man. "I trust that this current matter is now behind us."

It wasn't, though Nathaniel still hoped that the explanation he was formulating would at least suffice for the moment. "We have confirmed the identity of the sex trade worker who was responsible for the Stephanos murder, as well as the theft of the briefcase with the ledger. A search of her place of residence yielded strong clues as to the identity of a key member of her inner circle. I have an operative en route to confirm as we speak. As a precaution, the roommate of the subject was terminated, after it was determined by the operative that she possessed no information as to the subject's whereabouts. All key points of exit from the city are under twenty-four-hour surveillance. Intersection and downtown camera feeds are being monitored. We anticipate a capture, termination, and recovery of the ledger within the next twenty-four hours."

The broken man sighed as hard as he could in an iron lung. "That was some very impressive bullshit Nate — some of your best work. In other times of crisis, it would have sufficed. But today, of all days, that simply won't do. The current matter is not behind us, Nathaniel. It is still very much alive. And it threatens to destroy more than you can possibly know." He closed his eyes again. "It threatens to destroy our legacy in its entirety."

"I understand," said Nathaniel, also nodding at the closed eyes of the broken man. "There shall be no such outcome."

The broken man gave the slightest smile. "That is all, Nathaniel," he said. He opened his eyes to coincide with his forming lips. "Dave Brubeck Quartet, 'Take Five,' volume fifty percent." Wherever the system that heard him was, it understood.

CHAPTER
TWENTY-
FOUR

Miles Sawatski idled in front of 411 Cumberland, consulting his notebook more to pass the time than to solve a murder. Gayle Spence was standing near the front door, speaking with the lead on the homicide of Claire Hebert's roommate. Sawatski rubbed his eyes to focus on his notes. The cameras were on the fritz, of course, with no footage recorded from six p.m. on for the previous evening. The techs weren't sure on the intercourse prelim, as it would take a while to determine how many clients had gained entry. Semen was noted, both vaginal and anal, a growing trend amongst adventurous johns, who would pay premiums for bareback service. Sawatski thought momentarily about some faceless housewife in Linden Woods, unaware of the potential threats of disease that her well-heeled husband was bringing into their marriage bed. He wondered if that's where the next homicide call-out would be from, the snow-blown driveways and Christmas lights of suburbia. He was still smiling to himself when Spence entered the Crown Vic. She immediately caught the happy tell.

"You shouldn't be smiling that big at a crime scene," said Spence, adding a comical yet dour tone to a deadpan look. "One of those freelance long-lens hacks for the *Sentinel* might put you on the front page for shits and giggles." Recent pictures and television coverage had shown members of the traffic division's fatality squad smiling at a three-death pile-up near the University of Manitoba. Whatever the joke, the grins weren't welcomed by the grieving parents, which resulted in paid suspensions plus a strongly worded communiqué to the rank and file: dead meant deadpan.

They both looked towards the playground structure of Central Park, a handy perch for a media shooter. It was empty, as were the sidewalks, except for neighbourhood onlookers with nothing better to do. The meat wagon was gone. The shots that mattered to deadline and six p.m. newscasts were already in the can. Sawatski decided to heed the warning and drove a half block down Carlton Street for some idling chat in front of a fire hydrant.

Sawatski was getting concerned, which luckily had not shown up as a tell. He had received the fresh meat text from Spence as he walked back from The Line Up to Robbery-Homicide and hopped into the Crown Vic as she pulled into the exit driveway of the former hydro station. While they weren't the primary, there was enough evidence pointing to this apartment as Hebert's key residence. Her roommate's bedroom was an obvious home office, in both paraphernalia and decor. Hebert's bedroom was a sanctuary, with a simple elegance to it. The room could have been easily deposited into many a suburban home; it was almost open-house clean. Pictures of family from happier times and a teddy bear collection on the bed allowed a smile to shine through the darkness of her chosen trade.

The money from the Line Up toilet was still in Sawatski's pocket. He thought it would jump out at any moment and start talking about his clandestine activities to his partner. Spence flipped through her notes, hoping for something that could determine the next stop on the search for Claire Hebert. "Gotta hand it to her," said Spence as she flipped slowly through the key pages. "The girl doesn't leave much of a trail. Whatever she's got for a john list must be with her." She flipped a little more while Sawatski rubbed his eyes. "Even I have more sex toys than what she has in her drawers!"

Sawatski would have said something amusing to cap off Spence's statement, but his mind was elsewhere. Spence noticed. "What's up, Mileage?"

Sawatski yawned as part of the buildup for his fabrication. "Sorry partner, I'm just running on fumes. Besides, this whole thing is bullshit anyway. Claire-Bear is either underground or under the ground by now."

Spence flipped forward. "Was Claire-Bear a user? I didn't see a kit in her room."

"Probably," said Sawatski. "It may not have been regular hardcore, but you can pretty much include the recreational stuff. I don't see how you do this gig without it, plus the pharmaceuticals, and the vodka."

"Well, the roomie OD'd on some quality shit," said Spence. "The techs are just going off field tests for the residue, but they're guessing ninety percent pure, just off the colour." Like with most street-level heroin, Winnipeg's addicts were lucky to get twenty percent purity after the mix had been cut down and cut down again at some point, usually during the transfers from Montreal.

Sawatski was skeptical. "If that smack is ninety percent, I doubt it's even local — sounds like it came out of a Hollywood movie."

Spence rubbed her eyes, a mannerism Sawatski realized she'd picked up from him. "Are they filming any movies right now in the Exchange?" The Exchange District had been used extensively over the last twenty years as a period backdrop. "What was that one that Brad Pitt did here?"

"Wasn't it that Jesse James thing?"

"Yeah! I saw him one day on Bannatyne!" Spence smiled as she remembered her brush with fame.

Sawatski snapped her out of it. "Need a moment?"

"No, I'm good. I haven't seen all those white movie trucks around on a shoot lately. No radio chatter for street shut-downs either." She thought the angle would end there. Then it hit her, and Sawatski felt a smack in his chest from her notebook. "Music! What about a band at the MTS Centre?"

The city had seen a growing number of big-name concerts at the MTS Centre. Perhaps a member of an entourage had employed the roommate, shooting her up with purity beyond her normal limits. When the overdose was in full swing, he ran. The Centre was close, only three blocks from Cumberland. "Who's playing right now?"

Spence did a quick check on her phone. "This week it's Willie Nelson."

Sawatski gave a low, quick snicker. "They won't be on anything stronger than weed."

The tap on the passenger side window was enough to jar Sawatski and Spence into the initial stages of a Glock reach, until they noticed it was David Worschuk. "Hey, guys," he said, muffled by the closed glass. "Got anything new on Claire-Bear? I hear her roommate OD'd last night."

Spence took the initiative and hit the power window control. "Why don't you talk to the PIO like everybody else? You know we can't comment on an open." The usual protocol for any press interactions with the police service was to first enquire with the Public Information Officer by phone, and then follow up with an email. Most of the PIOs wouldn't offer information until the official release, keeping the story uniform throughout the local media. Worschuk had done a River Kwai to that bridge, though he did have a knack for taking the slightest offhand comment at a crime scene and inflating it with just enough eyebrow-raise to prompt a slew of unique visitors to the *Sentinel*'s website. The new reality of newspaper had even prompted the creation of a smartphone app for the Downtown 24/7 column plus regular tweets. The rest of the story would be peppered with comments by onlookers, neighbours, anyone who could make the tale taller than it really was.

Worschuk pounced on the one word that mattered. "Open, you say?" he said as he quickly scribbled in his notebook. "Sounds like it may not be another tragic tale of a sex trade overdose. How —"

"Who told you it was a fucking overdose?" Spence had already lost this battle and simply didn't know how to get out of it. Every word and every gesture just fanned the flames of Worschuk's story.

Worschuk scribbled with increasing flourish. "So, it wasn't an overdose? Perhaps mistaken-identity murder? Wrong place, wrong face, wrong time?"

"Fuck off, Downtown!" said Sawatski. He was surprised that he used the name that he had made a point of never using when addressing the reporter. "Go through channels or go fuck yourself!" He slammed the Crown Vic into gear while at half throttle, narrowly missing the parked car in front of them while kicking up plenty of grit and slush onto Worschuk as they left. Sawatski saw Worschuk in the rearview, hastily brushing off the cold mess from his coat and notebook. He did manage to flip the Crown Vic off before it was out of sight.

CHAPTER
TWENTY-FIVE

Ernie Friday knew that Claire Hebert had gone underground by now. The question was how far. Any of the known hole-up spots were reserved for the higher-ups in the Heaven's Rejects, not the hired help, and certainly not the hookers. The last independent safe house that he knew of was on Battery Street off Burrows Avenue, in a weathered pre-war storey-and-a-half. It was run by a low-level crystal-meth dealer by the name of Martin Biggs. Biggs was on disability, caught in the crossfire of a gas station holdup gone wrong. It was big news for Winnipeg, with the shooter shot dead by three patrol officers, one of whom was hit by a friendly fire ricochet. Biggs was gassing up his truck when it went down, taking a slug in the hip, a reflex trigger action from the would-be robber after police slug number three hit the perpetrator's upper body. A second reflex slug ended up in the back seat of Biggs's rusty Silverado, the entry hole still in view on the passenger side door. Ernie noticed the hole as he parked next to the truck in the back lane.

Ernie banged the reinforced rear door five times hard. From within, he heard the signature shuffling of someone with a walker. The shuffling grew to grunts as Biggs neared the door. "Fuck off, or I'll shoot you with my goddamn shot-gun," said Biggs. This was his signature line, the one he used to scare off neighbourhood hoodlums who thought he might be an easy score for drugs or cash.

"Do that and I'll shoot back, and I don't need a shotgun to hit things like you do," said Ernie, a hint of smile in his thunder. He heard the locks unclasp. Biggs swung open the heavy metal slab. He smiled at Ernie. "That little pussy Beretta of yours couldn't punch a hole through a wet Kleenex," said Biggs, smiling as he waved him in. "You want a drink?"

"As long as it's not alone," said Ernie.

He followed Biggs into the kitchen. It was a respectable state of bachelor clean, dated to the last renovation of a previous owner in the early seventies. Biggs reached up slightly to a built-in shelf, grabbing a half-empty bottle of Seagram's Seven. Ernie took a seat at the kitchen table, lifting a pair of mismatched lowball glasses off of a circular souvenir tray from California. He figured from the vintage that it must have come with the house. The shotgun was not an idle threat; it was leaning against the cupboard door reserved for the built-in ironing board. Biggs poured healthy doubles, clinking his glass against Ernie's as the only indication of a toast.

"Haven't seen you for a while," said Biggs. "I'm hoping it's not something I did. Or didn't do." He chuckled slightly as he raised the glass to his lips.

"Nope, nothing like that," said Ernie, taking a sip. "Just have to check the hole-ups. Even the low-rent ones like yours."

Biggs looked stunned. "Since when is $150 a night low rent? Besides, I got out of that in '09. Making too much off this brain-bake shit." Biggs lifted off the top of a vintage flour can, revealing the packets of crystal meth within. The disability claim, occurring within a police incident, had given Biggs something of a Teflon coating in the neighbourhood. As long as the buyers kept their hours before eleven at night and the noise to a minimum, the unofficial word for patrols was to leave well enough alone. Biggs would also phone in the odd tip, usually on tweakers with burglary beefs that most first-week rookies could spot, though it could take ten of them to finally stuff the suspect into the cage if they were flying. "Look around if you want. They ain't here."

Ernie took a healthy sip. He knew Biggs was telling the truth. Catching the wanted was usually easy enough, especially in a place like this: the slightest residue of female scent, an unexpected creak from a closet, a steady inhale and exhale of movement that no one could ever hold within. Ernie heard nothing. "Anybody else in your inner circle doing this kind of business anymore?"

Biggs took a swig of rye. "Well, it's not like we have a benevolent association or anything. There's a few HR hangers-on that might, but you must be pretty much past that if you're here." Biggs took another sip. He grabbed the *Sentinel* off the kitchen counter, plopping it down on the table and pointing to the front-page story. "Can't remember the last time I harboured a whore," said Biggs. "They tend to get under the radar pretty quick with their own benevolent associates."

Ernie nodded as he put down his empty glass. "This one is definitely a special case. Double rate."

Biggs stopped half-sip. "Double rate?" Biggs looked over at the shotgun, pointing at it like an exuberant child. "Need a partner?"

Ernie smirked at the offer. "I'd prefer one without a fucking walker."

"Fuck you!"

"Fuck you too, you fucking cripple."

The two men chuckled as Biggs shook the last of the rye into their glasses. "Here's the way I figure it," said Biggs. "You've got a coked-up whore-slash-user on the run, can't get a fix and can't call to get a fix. She's got detox to deal with while still trying to get safe. She can't call another whore. They can be just as bad on that shit as she is, which means that whore could call in the tip or off her herself for the cash, especially if she hears it's four grand. That can pay for a party weekend without getting fucked in the ass with a dribbly dick." Biggs took a swill to finish his thought. "Still, it's probably an ex-whore. Somebody she'd trust. And in this town, that's gotta be a pretty short list."

Ernie nodded. "There are a few reformed ones who do that hooker safety outreach bullshit."

"Too risky," said Biggs. "Too high of a community profile, and this bitch is a wanted killer. This is way too much for a hooker with a heart of painted gold to take on."

"What about a business?" said Friday. "I've seen a few. The news loves to talk up that reformed shit."

"Could be," said Biggs. "I think one of them started a pole

dancing party thing. One might be a sex therapist or some-thing."

Ernie looked down at the paper. The *Sentinel* had been increasing the amount of small earlug-style ads on its front page to the point that slow news days were starting to look like Madison Avenue was eating the paper from the outside edges. The tiny ads were cheap, which attracted all manner of businesses. One ad caught Ernie's attention. He pulled it closer to the right bifocal angle. "Wasn't there some ex-hooker who opened a sex shop somewhere?"

Biggs took a sip and rested the glass on his sternum as he thought about it. The recollection hit him mid–glass raise. "Yeah, that dildo shop on Main Street. The Other something-or-other. Right by Arlington."

"Well," said Ernie, as he gulped the glass clean. "That's the closest. I guess I'll start there." Ernie rose to leave. Biggs responded with a wave and the last sip of his glass at the same time.

"And Friday," said Biggs. "You might as well get a clean butt plug while you're at it."

Claire Hebert had finally moved into a sitting position on the couch. Proceeding past that position didn't seem like a good idea with the current state of queasy. She assessed the current location of the wastepaper basket for a potential volley of dry-heaves. She was alone, for the moment. Cindy and Tommy had gone downstairs to assist with the lunch preparation. She looked around the room, still squinting at the little light afforded by the bare sixty-watt bulb overhead. It was a mess of papers and piles of T-shirts and jeans that may or may not have been clean. There were no pictures of Tommy and Cindy. Claire wondered why.

Her first steps were shaky, still affected by the detoxification process. Claire used the desk to steady herself. She knew better than to expect any coke in the top drawer. She set her sights low: antacids, Tylenol, anything to stop the combination of stomach churn and throbbing headache. She found service station–style sample packets of each in the drawer, tearing them open, and tossing the pills in dry, which she immediately regretted. A capped half-empty bottle of water was close to the edge of the desk. Claire reached for it, slightly out of focus. The bottle fell, rolling under the desk. She swore quietly as she reached down to pick it up. The bottle had rolled farther inward than she could reach without having to crawl on all fours. She reached blindly up to the desktop, figuring a stapler, ruler, even a manila file folder would be enough to start the bottle rolling in her direction. She pulled down the ledger of the late Jimmy Stephanos, not realizing what it was until she had removed the bottle from under the desk. She pulled herself up, using both bottle and ledger to steady herself as she sat in the desk chair.

Swigging the water, she flipped open the pages of the ledger. The coded entries failed to register any meaning: a lot of numbers, a lot of columns. No names or places, not even a scrawl of a phone number and first name. She capped the bottle and placed it on the desk without looking. It landed on a lopsided pile of bills and papers, a teetering mess waiting for the slightest rustle to send it to the floor. "Shit," she said, as the pile slid to the floor below. Claire almost fell to the floor to retrieve them, convinced in some strange way that this minor indiscretion of home-office etiquette would be her undoing. On the trip down, the ledger fell with her, opening to its natural spine. She did her best to keep the papers in their semi-organized fashion, stacking them on one side of the open ledger. The bills were the usual variety: Manitoba Hydro, cell phone, internet. The last of the stack was three water bills, as if Tommy had dragged them out as long as possible, waiting until the last day of the estimated bill to call in an actual reading from the meter. The invoices had landed in such a way that the account number was legible at the top of each invoice. *1263734119*. Claire grabbed at the invoices, dropping the last invoice as she hoisted the other two to the desk. "Fuck, fuck, FUCK!" she said, as she reached down for the last time. The loose invoice was covering part of the ledger with a bank of numbers that started with the first three of the water bill. She blinked hard. It wasn't her mind playing detox tricks. She slid the invoice away from the ledger slowly, confirming each matching digit as she moved the paper; it was a lottery she didn't want to win. The panic rose in her face as the numbers matched, one after the other. There were six additional characters on the end of the string that didn't coincide, all with different sequences. She wasn't sure if they were simply there to mask the meter number or if they held something more ominous in their string. She didn't care. *Tommy is in on it*, she thought, *whatever 'it' is*.

As her mind raced, she envisioned that this underworld railroad was something more sinister: a gateway of safety until three bullets find purchase in your head and chest. It didn't take long for her to find the Smith & Wesson in the file box. She stuffed it in the cushions of the couch, memorizing the location of the butt for quick access. She was done for sleep. She was poised for survival.

CHAPTER TWENTY-SEVEN

Paul Lemay wasn't enjoying his upgraded weapon. He fidgeted in the tight cab of the Ranger while Paul Bouchard tried to keep the shifter from popping out of gear. "Quit squirming, you fat fuck," said Bouchard.

"I don't like the way this gun is touching my junk," said Lemay.

"What do you care?" Bouchard chuckled. "When's the last time you could look down and see it?"

"As long as the bitch can find it, that's all I care about." Lemay produced the revolver, stuffing it into his side pocket. "Ahhhh, that's much better."

"I'm sure the gun appreciates being out of your stinky fat man rolls."

"That's not fat, it's pushin' cushion."

"Says you."

"Says me, and my johnson." Lemay still struggled for comfort in his seat, knocking the shifter into neutral. Bouchard had become used to it, quickly jamming the shifter into third. "Jesus," said Bouchard. "Next truck is a fucking automatic."

Lemay was too busy cycling through his phone to respond about transmissions. He had received text messages back from the HR-friendly cab companies; no one had picked up anyone with high heels, no jacket, and a high-end briefcase on the night that Jimmy Stephanos was killed. Either she grabbed a ride with a friend or hailed an indie cab. They could simply muscle the indies, though it probably wasn't in their best interest, especially with all the police attention the Stephanos killing was earning, plus the Cumberland corpse. The Pauls had tried to get close to the HR house, but it was still under guard, with even more tents and white jumpsuit–wearing investigators.

"Any tips?" said Bouchard, still holding the shifter steady.

"Sweet fuck all," said Lemay. "Like the ground swallowed her up or something." He cycled further through the phone, hoping he had missed a pivotal message. "No wonder this gig is double. If I wanted to work for a living, I'd go back to Day Street." Day Street was the epicentre for auto dismantling in Winnipeg, in the oil-parched moonscape of the North Transcona district.

Bouchard checked his phone for a text, just before a downshift. "She's gotta be with some kinda hooker, former or otherwise. You know, some Julia Roberts–kinda skank." The thought triggered a memory. "Take the wheel!" said Bouchard, as he started fishing under the driver's seat.

Lemay instinctively steadied the Ranger. "We got a light in a couple of blocks," said Lemay.

Bouchard fished his hand under the seat, past the fast food bags, coffee cups, and general indifference for the Ranger's interior. He locked on the item of want, pulling forth a piece of the *Sentinel* that had seen better days. It was a copy of the *Weekender*, the replacement tabloid-style substitute for the defunct Sunday edition. Bouchard had the club section folded over, with stars next to the establishments that were hosting karaoke nights. He took back the wheel, steering, reading, and scanning the roadway. "Here's where we start," said Bouchard, handing the paper to Lemay.

The story was adjacent to the Lifestyles page, with a feature titled "The Working Girls; Former Sex Trade Workers Walking the Entrepreneurial Street." The story profiled three former prostitutes with small businesses. One was in Thompson, another in Brandon. The last was an adult toy store on Main Street, near Cathedral. The picture had been stained by spilled coffee, but the caption was still intact. "Jasmine Starr stands in front of The Other Woman on Main Street. 'I just couldn't resist the name,' said Starr. 'It's who I've always been.'" The story went on to tell the tale of Jasmine's days on Albert Street in the early two-thousands.

"That's around the time that this Claire chick was walking Albert," said Lemay. "Better check it out."

Jasmine Starr steadied herself against the washing machine, as Pete, the laundromat owner, thrusted against her backside. Her fleece sleep pants were bunched up around her ankles, about as much primping as she would indulge in for cheap rent. He had reached under her sweater and her loose-fitting bra, searching in vain for a squeal of the slightest delight. In her younger days, Jasmine would have been far more convincing. For this event, she could still shake the ash off her cigarette. She had found a magnetic tool bowl for the ashes, which showed no signs of being dislodged from the washer top by Pete's antics.

"Yeah, you like getting fucked like an animal, don'tcha?" said Pete, his face a festival of contortion and moist sweat.

"Uh-huh," said Jasmine, with the tempo of the thrusts. "Yup. Sure do."

"You like that hammer, don'tcha?" said Pete, building up speed. Jasmine smirked, dangerously close to laughter. She said a little internal thank you to the powers that be for the absence of a mirror for Pete to see her eyes roll. She knew he was getting close. *Finally*, she thought. There were books to cook, labels to stick, and a new shipment of lube to go through. There were just a few more minutes of sweaty laundry guy to endure.

Pete started breathing harder. With it, an increase in the nipple squeeze and breast grab. Jasmine had experienced the manhandling before, but this felt strange. This was beyond excitement. She worried that he might be having an attack of some kind. He then made a strange sound, and the strength of his hands on her breasts increased. This time it hurt. She reached under her sweater to yank the hands off, finding that she could hardly pull the fingers loose. He let out a final gasp, falling like an indifferent sack to the floor. Jasmine attended to her pants first before she turned around. She saw Pete on the floor, sprawled half-naked with an ice pick stuck through his neck into his brain. She looked up just in time to see a balaclava-clad perpetrator and his left hook as it deprived her of consciousness.

CHAPTER TWENTY-EIGHT

Claire Hebert was pacing nervously, the Smith & Wesson now poorly concealed under her left armpit. Tommy and Cindy had yet to return, and the detoxification was only making the story in her head worse. She was past being cool about an attempt to flee. She would draw on the first one through the door. Would she shoot? Would she shoot to wound? Would she shoot to kill? The shakes were so bad, she wondered if she could even get a shot off, let alone aim. She'd also forgotten about the backway into the suite. Cindy walked past her to the computer. "Oh, look, it can walk too," said Cindy. "I guess your back has most of the mileage."

Claire raised the gun and pulled the trigger.

The click got Cindy's attention, as did the additional five clicks in search of a bullet. She turned around slow, though not in fear.

"So," said Cindy, smiling. "Is this the part where you throw that at me, or ask for a do-over?" Claire kept a bead on Cindy. Even a useless gun seemed dangerous enough.

"You wouldn't be smiling so big if I knew where the bullets were for this motherfucker," said Claire. She pulled the trigger once more, discovering that no new bullets had grown in the chamber. The clicks continued. Cindy, annoyed by this attempt at white noise, rose from her chair to remove the gun. Claire felt she still had the upper hand, swinging the gun at Cindy. The barrel sliced her forehead, though not enough of a tap to knock her out. She found herself quickly disarmed by Cindy, who pushed her into the couch behind them. Claire cowered in fear, grabbing a cushion as a shield.

Cindy raised the empty revolver, aiming it at Claire-Bear's forehead. "You best be right with your Jesus, missy," Cindy said as she pulled the trigger.

The shriek from Claire was enough to quicken Tommy's steps double-time up the staircase. He flung open the door in time to find her sobbing on the couch, still clutching the cushion. Cindy was still holding the pistol, now lowered to her side. He was not impressed. He also couldn't draw attention to the fugitive they were harbouring. He collected the gun from Cindy, putting it back in the filing box where Claire had found it.

He sat in the chair at the computer desk, massaging his hands. He wanted to erupt and lash out in all manner possible at both women. He had never laid a hand on Cindy. Claire was another story. This was not a high point in the development of Tommy's character. He had been taught, by those he had done his former business with, that you've got to keep them in line. It never ceased to amaze him how easily she could push his buttons. It was almost as though she wouldn't stop until he struck her. She never cried out. It seemed an eternity before he spoke.

"I talked to the rez," said Tommy, not looking at either woman. "We can get you out probably by Friday, maybe sooner. We need some more personal shit of yours to put in at Brady: jewellery, undies, anything that will hint you're in the landfill."

"You're gonna put me in the landfill anyway," said Claire, using the cushion to muffle her voice. "Especially since I know you're in on it."

Tommy creaked forward for clarification. "In on what?"

Claire threw the cushion aside, revealing the ledger. She threw it at his feet. "You're in this fucking book. You're one of them. So, you might as well load that fucking gun, You get 'em out alright. Right into a hole, you fucking asshole!"

Tommy wasn't sure if anything else would come flying at him. He kept eye contact with Claire as if she still had a gun. He flipped through the ledger, wondering if the pages were as valuable as.Claire-Bear believed. His page flips must have seemed too casual to her.

She grabbed the book and threw it on the desk in front of Cindy. "Take a closer look, bitch," said Claire. "Your fucking water meter number is in there, as if you didn't know."

Cindy looked at Claire, a combination of perplexed and pissed off. She slammed the book into her chest. "Show me where the fuck it is then, Einstein."

Claire raised the book to strike Cindy. "I'll show you where the fuck it is!" Her arc of trajectory to Cindy's face was halted by Tommy before it had a chance to gather any speed. He was more concerned with Cindy; he knew the colour of rage in her eyes. He knew she was on the edge. He grabbed an old chair next to the bed, still holding Claire's arm aloft as her hand clutched the ledger. He moved the chair into position at the desk, so that the three could confirm what she saw. "Alright Bear. Calm down and show us what you got."

Claire complied, almost in slow motion, wondering why she hadn't been struck. Her eyes darted back and forth, from the ledger page in question to those of Cindy and Tommy. She asked Cindy for the water bill. Cindy slid it forward as non-threateningly as she could. Claire moved the invoice down the length of the column, stopping at the number recorded. "There," she said, pointing to the line. "Right fucking there."

Tommy and Cindy peered at the line. The water meter number was easily identified; the first digits in the numeric string. Six digits had been added to the end of the meter number. The first entry looked like it could have been a date — 021379 — though it seemed unlikely, judging from the condition of the ledger. They flipped through the pages, finding the meter number again and again. In all, there were fourteen notations concerning meter number 1263734119. The 021379 digit addendum occurred on seven notations. A new number appeared after each logged reference of the 021379 digit string. Cindy wrote the new numbers on an empty space, at the bottom of the ledger page.

451790

604512

307856

129774

605652

349221

142511

"I have no idea what the fuck this shit means," said Cindy. "I'm just glad we drink bottled water."

Tommy turned her towards him in her chair, gently, but not slowly. He pointed to the area beyond the frosted glass. "Cindy, they drink from the tap. The only water they ever get is from the tap. They wash in it. They brush what's left of their teeth in it. Christ, we even cook —"

Tommy sat back in his chair. He didn't know what the numbers meant. He didn't know why they were in the briefcase of an HR captain. Killing Jimmy Stephanos was all that was needed to ensure a death warrant for Claire. *What do these numbers mean?* Tommy looked over at Claire. "Bear, did Jimmy ever talk about any of this stuff?"

Claire looked at Tommy, somewhat perplexed. "We didn't exactly 'talk' when we got together." She used her fingers to punctuate the obvious non-occurrence in their contract-for-hire relationship. "I don't want to know shit about HRs. Just fuck me, pay me, and leave the extra coke."

Tommy pressed. "C'mon Bear, people talk. Even the ones you fuck for money talk."

"That's why I stay fucked up," said Claire. She had moved back to the couch. "I'm not a threat if I can't remember what they said."

It may not have been the healthiest way to suppress information, but Tommy knew that Claire was right. The less you heard, the less you saw, and the less you remembered was the best way to stay alive while contracting with the HRs. Still, Tommy had to ask. "Bear, did any of the HRs ever talk about fucking with the water?"

Claire was looking up at the ceiling now. "The only water the HRs were ever concerned with was the water that shot out of my snatch." Her concentration was interrupted by Cindy, who had started rustling through the desk drawers. She pulled a vintage chrome flashlight from the recesses of the centre drawer. "Oh great," said Claire. "Now the bitch is going to interrogate me."

Cindy walked past Claire, the flashlight already lit. "I'm going to check the meter. See if there's some basket of fun pills attached to the main. Because that's what always happens in fucking Hollywood." She was almost at the back stairwell to the basement when she added a directive. "Tommy, we still gotta get this cunt outta here, wacky water or not."

Tommy waited until her footsteps diminished down the lopsided staircase.

"Okay, Bear. You got a hunk of something you wear that's got your name on it? Other than your gauch?" Claire smirked at the request. She reached through the neck of her sweater with both hands to release a necklace. It was a necklace that she quickly realized wasn't there.

"OH FUCK! FUCK! FUCK! DOUBLE-FUCK!" She reached around inside her sweater and rooted through the briefcase. She triple-picked her own pockets to be sure. She slammed into the couch, defeated, panicked, and started to cry. Slow at first, escalating to the convulsive wailing of an inconsolable child. "That was the only thing my mom ever gave me!"

She was still in the throes of release when Cindy returned, unimpressed by the display. "What's her fucking problem?"

Tommy was still stunned by what he was seeing. He knew it was most likely tied to the detox, and yet, this felt as though there was something genuine attached.

"There's nothing weird on the meter, I think," Cindy said,

slamming the flashlight into his sternum. "The line coming in is as old as this place. If anyone is fucking with the water, it's from the outside." The flashlight jarred Tommy out of his trance somewhat. "Cindy, did you see a necklace around here? It's uh . . . hey, Bear, what's it look like?"

Claire rubbed at her neck, using her fingertips to somehow assist in the description of the phantom necklace. "It's a gold chain with a locket. It was my mom's. Has a picture of me and her inside." She rubbed at her neck a little more for additional details. "I had it engraved," she said. "Momma-Bear and Claire-Bear." It was just what they needed for the Brady Road Package. Convincing Claire of the importance of parting with it would come later. "When's the last time you saw it?" said Tommy.

"At Jasmine's place," said Claire. "It was after we had the fight."

"The fight?" said Tommy, taken aback. "What fight?"

"I thought she was stealing coke out of the briefcase or something," said Claire. "I fucked up her ear pretty good. She must have grabbed it off me when we were pulling each other's hair."

Tommy pictured the scene in his mind; two working girls beating the shit out of each other. It was hard to believe that Jasmine would still have agreed to help Claire after their brawl, though nothing from this world seemed strange to Tommy anymore. Jasmine was one of a select group of people assisting those who didn't deserve it, ask for it, or care one way or the other. That's what the outsiders saw. Tommy only saw himself in their faces, alongside his own shortcomings. Even in the coke-fried brain of Claire Hebert, there had to be some sliver of good worth saving, something no one had seen yet, not even Tommy. He grabbed his jacket and headed for the stairwell.

Cindy stopped him mid-stride. "You know what happens if they ever find out what you did, don't you?"

Tommy nodded. "I know, Cindy. I know."

"Then, why do it?"

"You know why."

"It won't bring him back, Tommy."

Tommy looked at Cindy close, and with purpose. He glanced over at Claire, thinking of his son's lifeless, crumpled state in the Boscalow that fateful night. He looked at Cindy, squeezing her shoulders just the right amount of tight. "It's not to bring him back," said Tommy, as he kissed her on the forehead. "It's to keep me from going." He reached past her for his homemade cross, the one that had been given to him by the Padre after his suicide attempt. "And I'm not going anywhere."

CHAPTER TWENTY-NINE

Jasmine Starr was starting to stir, though she knew it probably wasn't a good idea. She could still hear the rustling of her assailant in her office. She kept as still as possible, her eyes closed, stifling the reflex need to wipe the moist clots from her nose. Her head was still pounding from the blow. Even in a state of recent unconsciousness, she knew that there was more to this than Claire Hebert murdering an underworld john. She opened her eyes in the finest of slits. Even in a view largely out of focus, the wide-open lifeless eyes of her former landlord were enough to rate a flinch. It wasn't enough to register to the assailant, engaged in noisy rustle with the file cabinet drawers. She waited for what seemed an eternity until she heard the rear door of The Other Woman close. She groaned as she rose with caution, engaged in the self-checks of what did and didn't work on her body. She teetered back to her office, finding equilibrium in the walls and the broken washing machines. Everything that could be strewn was. She found herself angrier at the state of her business records than her wounds.

"Fucking asshole," she muttered as she dampened a paper towel with what was left of a water bottle, one of the few things in the area that hadn't been up-ended. Her nose was surely broken, and the wounds from the Claire-Bear scrap had broken clot. This was stirring up unwanted memories for Jasmine, an old beating that had required surgery on her left eye and had caused the loss of scent. She rocked slowly in the office chair, wondering if this would be the last of the unwanted visitors in search of Claire Hebert. There was still the matter of Pete. Whether he was dead, almost dead, or about to enter the next chapter of his life in assisted living, Jasmine knew she would have to make a call. Any of these scenarios would surely be ending her lease.

Ernie Friday had parked his Parisienne on Machray Avenue, idling as he looked up the back lane to the rear of The Other Woman. The Two Pauls were out of sight, shielded by the north wall of the two-storey laundromat on Cathedral Avenue. Spence and Sawatski chose Cathedral, on the east side of Main Street, hoping to diminish the chance of panic that usually occurs when an unmarked detective car pulls up in front of a target. Tommy Bosco was negotiating a U-turn on Main Street, parking on the east side curb, directly across from The Other Woman. David Worschuk was coming out of The Video Cellar, a couple of blocks south on Main Street, with a new selection of XXX DVDs. That's when Jasmine Starr flicked her lighter in front of her final Peter Jackson. She never smelled the gas.

As natural gas explosions go, the Other Woman blast occurred at the right time for the general populace, with a break in traffic from both directions. The blast wave plus the accompanying debris blew out the side windows on the Guiding Light Econoline. Tommy fell across the engine doghouse, shielding his face from the tempered glass cubes, which had still managed to inflict some minor cuts. He felt the van lurch downwards on the driver's side, thanks to the loose window bars of The Other Woman. The broken steel had punctured the side walls of the tires. A section of the bars had penetrated the driver's side door and the side panel, fusing the door in place. Tommy had already decided on a curbside exit. As he stumbled out of the van, he looked north. He recognized Sawatski, who had questioned him about drug connections when he first returned to Winnipeg. Sawatski had predicted that Tommy would be sleeping in a cardboard box, like the bum that he was, within a year's time. He had even bet a twenty on it. Tommy figured that now wasn't the time to collect. While Sawatski stared at the smouldering aftermath, his partner, Spence, was frantically relaying particulars on her cell phone. Tommy slipped down the narrow passage between two businesses. He checked his pocket: three loonies. It was enough to catch a bus on Mountain Avenue to Jarvis Avenue — enough to get to Freddie the Ford.

Ernie Friday waited to see if anyone was going to emerge from the rubble. After five minutes, nobody did. If there was any remnant of life left in The Other Woman, it would be a paramedic matter, which would lead to a recovery period before useful words could be strung together. Friday was already turning left on Scotia Avenue by this point, heading to Inkster Boulevard. Inkster was far enough away that it wouldn't be blocked off for east-west traffic. He had seen and inflicted enough to know that this wasn't an accident. The Two Pauls felt the same. They had narrowly escaped injury when a sign fixture on the laundromat, a victim of the shock wave and shoddy attachment into the brick façade, fell on the Cathedral side. Neither Bouchard nor Lemay spoke as they chose a slow but steady back lane route. The debris cloud had masked their exit from Spence and Sawatski.

David Worschuk ran as fast as his frame could carry him, dropping the pornography in the snowbank. He fumbled with his phone, informing the City Desk about the explosion and promising video that he would upload to the *Sentinel* site. Like most smartphone videos, it would be full of jiggling and horrible audio, but it would get the drop on the rest of the media teams, who were no doubt en route to the explosion, thanks to their emergency channel scanners. The debris cloud was starting to dissipate, though there was still plenty of mangle from the remnants of The Other Woman to post. He couldn't make out if there was anyone trapped inside. There were no moans of pain or pleas for help. There was only the warble of easily triggered car alarms.

Tommy Bosco dabbed at his face with an old napkin from his pocket, which he had moistened with the cleanest of back lane snow. He knew Jasmine was dead, as well as whomever else was inside The Other Woman. The sirens were getting thicker in the crisp air. He saw police units, fire, ambulance, Winnipeg Gas and Power, and media vans descending on the scene as his trudge arrived at the Mountain Avenue bus stop. He entered the bus that was parked next to the McDonald's, depositing his change as the driver followed him in, a fresh coffee in hand for the rest of his shift. Little notice was given to Tommy and his wounds at the back of the bus. It was just another day in the North End.

Nathaniel was parked in his Chrysler, idling near St. John's Cathedral on Anderson Avenue, barely noticing a funeral in progress in the ancient graveyard. The blast and the sirens had done little to quell the sombre proceedings, with the exception of the younger attendees checking their smartphones and looking towards the direction of the explosion. His Blackberry vibrated on the dash top. Without looking, he hit the power window for the driver's side. A Toyota Prius wearing Buddy's Taxi colours was approaching from O'Meara Street. It slowed to a fast crawl as it neared the Chrysler. The Prius window descended and the driver's arm extended outwards, passing a letter-sized envelope to Nathaniel. There was no need to identify the driver. He clutched the envelope with purpose as the cab continued down St. Cross Street. Nathaniel knew the contents before the envelope was emptied. He held Claire Hebert's locket aloft, letting the sunlight dazzle on the sterling silver case. He flipped open the clasp, revealing a photo of Claire as an infant, held by her mother. Momma-Bear, Claire-Bear. He snapped it shut hard.

CHAPTER THIRTY

Tommy Bosco was playing out the immediate goings-on at the scene of the explosion as he tried to get comfortable on the beaten bus seat. Fire crews would already be in douse mode, cooling the hot spots. The gas main would be in the process of being shut off. It would take at least fifteen minutes before anything resembling a search occurred. They would find Jasmine's body and anyone else who chose the wrong dildo shop that morning. Once that happened, The Other Woman was a crime scene with the sped-up convenience of two Robbery-Homicide badges out front. The tape would already be going up around the scene, courtesy of the first patrol units to arrive. It was only a matter of time until Miles Sawatski noticed the Guiding Light van. The tape, and the damage, would invite a query. Tommy figured that was at least worth a visit, and one that would be without courtesy. Once any cop had decided you were a bad seed, no amount of reformation was going to help; there were no grey areas.

"Con is con," Sawatski had said years ago as he blocked Tommy's exit at the Remand Centre, when he was first released. "And the one thing I know is that you won't disappoint me; maybe not today, maybe not in six months, maybe not for two years. But you will fuck up, Bosco. That's what cons do. And I can't wait for you to fuck up."

The immediate concerns for Tommy were the ones expected by most reasonable people after a traumatic event. That's when it hit him: *what were the cops really doing there?* He knew that Sawatski and Spence were Robbery-Homicide. They were on the hunt for Claire for the Stephanos killing. Jasmine must have shown up somewhere as a known associate from the Albert Street days. Still, it seemed like going through the expected cop motions of a homicide investigation. Had the building not exploded, Sawatski and Spence would have explained who they were looking for. Had Jasmine heard from Claire? Tommy smiled to himself as he thought of the conversation that would never be. Sawatski and Spence would be looking for tells, the slightest hiccup in Jasmine's story. Tommy knew that Jasmine wouldn't crack, which would be a tell in itself. There was a danger in being too stone-faced, too matter-of-fact with the law. What was she hiding? They would thank her for her time, then promptly commence with surveillance and questioning neighbouring businesses, especially those with security cameras. Somewhere in those grainy images was the possibility of Claire Hebert, running frantic, frigid from the cold and lack of outerwear. The laundromat camera could show the truck arriving for the washing machine escape pod. They would probably check with the trucking company. That's when they would see The Guiding Light on the manifest. That's when there would be a knock on the door.

Tommy pulled the stop signal as the bus approached the base of the Arlington Bridge. The dogs in the machine shop compound wagged their tails in recognition as he approached, two bullmastiffs with perpetual slobber hanging from their mouths. Jaime Bachynski's machine shop was never a nine-to-five concern, so a locked compound was a reasonable expectation. The contract work was lucrative enough for the shop to sit idle for weeks at a time. This must have been one of those weeks.

The bullmastiffs followed Tommy to the entrance door of the shop. He let them in for some needed warmth, an invitation they happily accepted. The ancient fluorescent fixtures flickered to life, some faster than others. Tommy started to move the necessary items away from his Ford's exit path. He had little concern for preserving the patina, inviting new and profound scratches to take up residence on the hood and the roof of the cab. The cargo box took longer to empty, filled to the brim with buckets of scrap aluminum shavings. Freddie rose an inch in height to the rear once the items had been removed. Tommy knelt down to assess the fluid stains. After a momentary internal debate, he opened the driver's door and pushed the seat back forward in search of top-ups for the oil and transmission.

As he removed the bottles, he noticed the remnants of duct tape stuck to the seat back, where Claire had attached the brick of revenge hash. It gave him a moment of pause. There were plenty of acceptable reasons for not continuing, reasons that could be presented by far more acceptable people than Tommy Bosco. The residue made him think of Jeremy. The snow would have been too deep to visit his simple grave at the city-owned Brookside Cemetery, another casualty of increasing municipal budget cuts. Brookside was next to the primary runway for the James Armstrong Richardson International Airport. It was just the Winnipeg International Airport when Tommy would take Jeremy to watch the planes. They would sit on Freddie's tailgate, quizzing each other on the types of planes, predicting how smoothly each landing would go. Dinner was two Coke Slurpees and a family-sized bag of Doritos. When he could get to Jeremy, he would always bring the same dinner combination, sitting with him like the old days, watching the planes.

Tommy blinked slow and hard, the usual prelude to his mental reboot. He had told himself many times over, in prayer, and in tear-drenched rage, that he was ultimately responsible for the death of his son. This was a truth he embraced, with the reluctance of any parent who has failed their child. He had never forgiven Claire for the act that led to Jeremy's death; there was no need. Tommy shouldered the responsibility alone. His path had killed Jeremy long before the slugs that tore through his flesh.

He released the hood, adding the required top-ups. He found a better battery hooked to a trickle charger on the workbench, leaving a crisp fifty in its place. As a force of habit, Tommy reached down to inspect the dummy tank, the one that the border patrol had completely missed. The guns, the drugs, and all the money that it had concealed had become worthless metal, powder, and paper in the eyes of Tommy Bosco. They couldn't buy what Tommy wanted. They couldn't buy the life of his son.

Freddie the Ford, like most automotive things in long-term storage, gave the usual start-up protests — a backfire, rough idle, a flickering oil pressure warning light — until finally settling into a reasonable cadence of combustion. Tommy opened the large overhead door with a chain pulley. Tommy pulled the Ford into the yard, flanked by the curious pair of bullmastiffs. He thanked them both as he scooted them back into the compound, wiping their excess drool on his jacket. They were still wagging their tails as he pulled away from the fence.

The smoke was finally starting to clear at Main and Cathedral, though the air was now thick with local media and curious onlookers. The news channels were doing their very similar at-the-scene portions of what was easily worth three minutes of airtime. As far as the media knew, there were two dead, with no mention of foul play. Sawatski and Spence were waiting for the captain of the engine company to give the okay to enter the scene. Somewhere in that commotion, David Worschuk snuck around a barricade, making a beeline for Sawatski and Spence. He didn't notice the fresh ice nodules from the fire containment. Sawatski turned just in time to see Worschuk's legs shoot out from under him. He couldn't stifle the laugh. He leaned down to Worschuk, who was in the throes of real pain. "You know, Dave, for a guy who's always asking where the fire is, you sure don't seem to know what happens when all that water freezes."

"Fuck you, Sawatski! That fucking hurt like a son of a bitch!" Worschuk continued to wince as two paramedics helped him up. Even in his state, he was still able to reach for his voice recorder, which was now sporting the bleeding ink screen of crushed electronics. Making more noise than words, he threw it to the ground. Spence pointed at the infraction. "Better pick that up, unless you want to get brought in for littering, maybe even aggravated littering."

Worschuk struggled to find his normal facial expression and something resembling composure. He gave his reporter's notebook a one-two flip while engaging his pen. "You can write that ticket, and I'll pay it," said Worschuk. "I'll do that right after you tell me why Robbery-Homicide is first on scene at a gas explosion. You got a meter reader with a deep dark . . ." Worschuk hesitated as the pain found new places on his person. "Fuck," he muttered.

Sawatski rolled his eyes before answering in a complete state of mockery. "That's right, Clowntown. There's a maniac on the loose, and he's got a fully charged meter reader and a white panel van with Free Candy painted on the side. He's one sick bastard." Sawatski stopped, realizing that Worschuk was actually taking down what he was saying. He grabbed his notebook, tore out the page containing his explanation, and threw the notebook onto the smouldering roof remnants of The Other Woman. "Whoops! Boy, it sure is slippery here, isn't it?"

Spence smiled along with Sawatski, enjoying the momentary lapse of professional decorum. "Yeah, Sarge. It's downright treacherous. Better watch your step, Dave. If your story doesn't run, they'll have to fill the space with an ad for M&M Meats."

Sawatski chimed in. "They've got those coconut shrimp, right?"

Worschuk was steaming and decided to let some of it vent. "I'm going straight to the PIO on this, and I'll tell them just how professional you guys are. Maybe even the chief. Bust you guys down to school crossing guards!"

Sawatski took the bait. "Even a school crossing-guard gig

trumps being a chain-link mechanic that carries low-grade smack in his asshole."

Worschuk's eyes glared at Sawatski, losing all reason. While his intention may have been to defend his honour, Worschuk's sudden movements, coupled with the ice, sent him crashing downwards, in a slightly more animated dance than the first fall.

Sawatski leaned down to assess his foe. He lifted his boot to Worschuk's head, revealing the steel spike grids he had fashioned into his soles. "It's winter, Clowntown," said Sawatski. "You should be using the right tires."

The paramedics, still none too busy, attended to Worschuk's slip-and-fall number two as Sawatski stepped around him to assess the scene. Spence kept an eye on the firefighters working within the building shell. The street was littered with pieces of glass, window bars, and chunks of wood that had been part of the window frames. Luckily, there were no pieces of people to mess with Sawatski's breakfast. The windows in the building across the street had also been blown out, their draperies flowing outwards to the winter chill. There were three vehicles in the path of the blast: a rusty Cavalier in front of The Other Woman, a late-model windowless Civic on the other side of Main Street, and a battered white Ford Econoline, with flattened tires on the driver's side. All of the vehicles were total losses, the Cavalier looking as though it had been hit by some form of industrial shotgun blast. Two uniforms were getting particulars from the owners of the Cavalier and the Civic. Voices were raised. Sawatski turned to see the laundromat owner's wife at the barricade, concerned about the business.

The mission name on the side of the Econoline failed to register to Sawatski as he tried to jimmy the driver's side door, held closed by the former window bars of The Other Woman. He headed to the passenger side, where he found the door slightly ajar. The door gave a signature old-van creak as Sawatski made a cursory check. Nothing seemed odd about the interior — it was a mess of discarded coffee cups, fast food bags, and free community newspapers. He noticed something black and leathery sticking out from the pile in the passenger footwell. He retrieved the book and opened the cover. "Please return to Pastor Tommy Fucking Bosco, The Guiding Light Mission," he muttered. Sawatski agreed to do so in his thoughts.

Sawatski's phone started to vibrate as he closed the door to the Econoline. *It must be that fucking puppetmaster*. He answered as angrily as one physically could with a cell phone. "What the fuck do you want?"

There was a brief pause, then his partner, Spence, spoke. "I just wanted to see if you wanted a coffee, Sunshine. Then again, maybe you've had enough for today." Spence waved at Sawatski from across the street, standing next to the rookie who had drawn the short straw for java detail. She punctuated the wave with a *What Gives?* shrug.

Sawatski quickly composed himself. "Sorry, partner. Thought you were Tyrannosaurus Ex for a minute. Yeah, the usual, please and thank you."

"Sure you don't want some piss in it, too? You sound like you're a quart low."

"Fuck you, Spence. Fuck you very much."

"No, Sawatski. Fuck YOU very much!" She hung up her cell phone as Sawatski watched. He turned to flip through the Bosco bible, checking for anything that looked unique, half-hoping for a notation of self-incrimination. His phone buzzed again. *Probably Spence*, Sawatski thought, *asking about the doughnut*. Sawatski answered. "Sour cream glazed, as per usual."

Nathaniel paused, but quickly recovered. "I bring you money, Miles. You can buy your own doughnuts." Nathaniel didn't wait for Sawatski's response. "I understand that our dear Miss Hebert is not part of the rubble you're standing in front of right now."

Nathaniel watched Sawatski from two blocks south, just outside the barricade and away from earshot of the crowd. He saw Sawatski's hopeful glances for a face to assign to his aural intruder. Sawatski did not see him.

"It's not her," said Sawatski.

"I know," said Nathaniel. "My operative confirms this."

"This was you?"

"Management always stays out of the hands-on, Miles. But yes, it was my directive."

"You sick son of a bitch. I should —"

Nathaniel cut Sawatski off. "You *should* continue making actual progress, Miles. Without progress, we don't proceed forward. We don't reach our destination. In your case, that's keeping your pension intact, your semi-good name unsullied, maybe a casino security job in a warmer climate. Or perhaps it's public embarrassment, disciplinary action, maybe even time behind bars with some of your favourite people. By the time I'm done with your personal and professional destruction, you may want to consider eating your gun instead of today's special at The Line Up."

Sawatski breathed heavy as Nathaniel talked. He was more intent on listening, trying to decide if he knew this man from the arrests of years past. He wondered if it was a former cop, maybe ex-military. He was still breathing hard when Nathaniel spoke. "Miles, Miss Hebert is obviously in protective custody, but not through any official agencies, as that is my bailiwick. My operative confirms that the ledger was not on the premises of The Other Woman, in its pre-destruction state. She has most likely determined that it has some value, possibly worth trading for. She may reach out to you or a member of your team. When she does, I will need to know all the particulars."

"And what if I can't get you that information?" Sawatski felt the pause to be too long, a possible disconnection. "Hello? Are you there, asshole?"

"Then Headingley Correctional gets you," said Nathaniel. "Happy hunting."

The Two Pauls were hungry. Ernie Friday was also hungry. The chances of them all being hungry for A&W late breakfast fare was slim. The chance that they would all order from the drive-thru window at Main and Inkster was slimmer still. Where it got really skinny was the A&W parking lot. The Two Pauls sipped their coffees as they watched Ernie Friday sip his.

"I wonder where he's going to go next," said Bouchard. He fished around in the takeout bag for a hash-brown patty, keeping his eyes locked on Friday. Lemay nodded, his mouth stuffed to the brim with sausage, powdered eggs, and indifferent biscuits. He was just about ready to speak when he stopped in mid–vocal formation.

Bouchard looked at him strange, then with annoyed concern. "Oh, fuck, don't you go and have a stroke and shit yourself in my truck."

Lemay said nothing, reaching down into the footwell for a newspaper. He flipped down the visors. Bouchard watched with concern as Lemay attached two sheets of the *Sentinel* to the visors with two large spring clips, part of the collection of dashboard debris. There was now something resembling privacy. Lemay adjusted the screens before he spoke. "I'll bet that old fuck Friday can read lips." He tapped at the paper playfully, though not hard enough to tear it. "See this, old man? Bet you can't read through this!"

Bouchard gave Lemay the look that usually accompanies the realization that you're sitting next to Crazy. He looked straight ahead at the newspaper before he spoke, shaking his head slightly. "He's not a fucking ninja, numbnuts. He's just a low-rent shooter who kept the get-caught to a dull roar. You're talking like he's the Matrix Oracle grandmother or something."

But Lemay wouldn't drop his convictions. "It'd be a good skill to have. You could find out where somebody was going before you whacked them, so you wouldn't have to follow so close." The Two Pauls continued to eat their breakfast, Bouchard doing his best to contain his displeasure at how stupid the newspaper drapes must have looked to the rest of the parking lot, and to Friday. He decided to distract himself with work. "It's not just Friday," said Bouchard. "Somebody else is gunning hard for this bitch. I wouldn't even know where to start with blowing up a building."

"You'd blow yourself up first," said Lemay, his mouth full. "Fuck, I'd probably blow my hands off helping you." Lemay chuckled for a moment, losing some egg and biscuit in the process. He cycled through his messages, looking for any-thing that could be a tell. Frustrated, he threw the phone on the dashboard, almost dislodging his newspaper screen. "This is fucking bullshit," said Lemay. "Somebody deluxe came in for this shit. The dead roomie and now this dildo shop bitch. We're fucked before we get started. We should just say fuck it at this point."

Bouchard chewed slowly on his hash brown, half-won-dering if Friday could see through the newspaper blind. "They don't need out-of-town for this," said Bouchard. "That bitch is hiding, but she ain't that hidden. She's going to get seen, and somebody is going to tip it. When they do, we do the job, get some cake, and get some new CDs. I'm getting tired of singing the same old shit, anyway."

Lemay nodded in full-mouth agreement. He swallowed just enough to speak. "We should keep an eye on Friday. He's got a good nose, good leads, might have to take him out too, as a bonus. He's gotta be up for retirement." Lemay pushed the newspaper open to check on Friday. The rusty Parisienne was gone.

David Worschuk parked in the least-travelled section of the *Winnipeg Sentinel* parking lot. He did his best with the dash-board coke bump, using his press card and a plastic clipboard to form the lines. Most of the *Sentinel* editorial team had car-ried on the long history of twenty-six-ounce days. Worschuk had started sampling the cocaine that he had been entrusted to smuggle during his chain-link days at Milner Ridge. He felt that he had reached something resembling moderation, only needing a bump during big stories, when he was trying to get the jump on the other news outlets. He tilted the rear-view mirror, brushing his nose clean of the powder. He exited the *Sentinel* Cavalier slowly, wondering when the next twinge of pain from his earlier falls would present itself.

The newsroom was deserted, with most of the day staff covering the aftermath of the explosion. Worschuk grabbed an empty desk and started flipping through one of his notebooks, recently exhausted of free space. Thankfully, the notebook that Sawatski had tossed up to the smouldering roof at The Other Woman was fresh; Worschuk had finished this one while interviewing Wilson. The cocaine wasn't doing its usual job of arranging the puzzle pieces of chicken scratch. He dragged the mouse next to the computer, waking the screen. *What's the common thread?* Worschuk punched in his login and password for the *Sentinel* archives. He leaned back in his chair, holding his notebook aloft, twisting it left and right in hopes that something would jump off the page. He leaned forward, staring at the search window's flashing cursor.

He started with variations of Claire Hebert's name, finding only minor mentions of prostitution and drug arrests from her junior days on the low track. Basic elements, like prostitution and Heaven's Rejects, were returning too many hits. He pulled a pair of earbud headphones from his pocket and plugged them into his phone. He watched the video taken at the Other Woman explosion. Worschuk felt himself getting slightly nauseous from the jittery movements of the playback. He wondered how many readers of the *Sentinel* were also getting sick from his work.

There wasn't a lot to see. Worschuk had started filming while on the move, with the first initial strides showing more of his feet than the aftermath of the explosion. As the camera steadied, Worschuk had decided on a shaky pan of the entire scene. The front of The Other Woman had been obliterated, shielded by smoke. Flames were visible within the business, with no sign of survivors ready to emerge. Worschuk watched as his pan pointed out towards the street. He had focused in on debris, bits of brick, glass, and the damage they inflicted. He saw the windows blown out across the street, the drapes flowing outwards in the wind. Then he'd filmed the cars: the Cavalier, the Civic, and the white Econoline. The van looked familiar, as though he had just seen the image of it. He stopped the video, and returned to the archival search for prostitution. He squinted at the screen, clicking on something white and wheeled. It was the van from the scene of the explosion, with the same mission name. The accompanying story spoke of the problems of male teen prostitution in the downtown core. Pastor Tommy Bosco of The Guiding Light Mission spoke of the efforts they were making to get them off the street. Worschuk saw the common thread: prostitution. A pastor who dealt in saving prostitutes, parked across the street from the business of a former prostitute, and a city-wide search for a prostitute. "Good things always come in threes," he said, as he pushed himself from the desk and headed for the door.

David Worschuk wasn't the only one who noticed the Econoline. Ernie Friday had made a note of his estranged son's van as he scanned his mirrors before the explosion. There was little in the area to attract Tommy; it was too far north on Main to encounter those in need of the Guiding Light rescue. Most of the other businesses on the block were vacant. He had heard the rumours about escape options for cons on the run, though he never gave it much thought. He was finding too many of them with his gun.

Is Tommy part of the escape route? Ernie had a hard time going there. Of all people, Tommy should have known better. You only needed to get caught once.

Ernie had taken a moment behind the Winnipeg Transit garage to compose himself while attending to another coughing fit peppered with blood on an A&W napkin. He played out the events of the last hour. The explosion had changed everything, regardless of the cause. Police presence would escalate around anything that was remotely related. Ernie figured that most of Robbery-Homicide would be leaning hard on HR associates, who would quickly develop multiple cases of laryngitis. He had a hard time believing that Tommy would lift a finger for Claire Hebert, unless it was five of them, balled into a fist. She may have not pulled the trigger on his grandson, but she helped load the bullets. Ernie wasn't worried about the Two Pauls, or any of the other figures who could be in play. Ernie was worried about Tommy. When he'd had his epiphany, Tommy had shed all allegiance to what his father had stood for, including his name. That was when there seemed to be little point in maintaining their relationship. Giving safe haven to Claire Hebert would be the new normal for Tommy Bosco. It was a normal that was asking for death, or at least tempting it with a pointed stick. Ernie wondered if he could do both: kill Claire and reconcile with his son. He lubricated the thought with a swig from his flask.

CHAPTER THIRTY-TWO

Freddie the Ford wasn't happy. The cold winter snap, coupled with diminished octane from the one real gas tank attached to his frame, had developed into a sputtering cough as the F-150 crested the steep incline of the Arlington Bridge. Tommy knew the drill, coasting in neutral, prodding the gas pedal ever so slightly in an effort to keep the idle speed in the low 700s. He could rev higher once he reached the south slope of the bridge, hoping that the treatment would result in some magical road-going tune-up. As the pair descended the slope, it became apparent that the old Ford needed more warm-up time.

Tommy pulled up to the curb, across from the Canadian Science Centre for Human and Animal Health. The name sounded a lot better than what was housed inside. The Centre's most notable tenant was the National Microbiology Laboratory, where the petri dishes were full of killer viruses with media-friendly names like Ebola and H1N1. If it were any other city in Canada, the not-in-my-backyard placard-waving would have reached a fever pitch. Winnipeg was simply grateful that anyone would spend a dime within its perimeter — plus there were only six months of the year where it was comfortable enough outside to protest.

Tommy kept prodding the throttle, hopeful that Freddie's idle speed would at least settle into the mid-500s. As he monitored the cheap tachometer bolted to the dashboard, he glanced up at the Centre. There was a public driveway to the facility, which looped around the rear of the building to a public parking area and the general reception entrance. There were more cameras than people these days, though Tommy figured that there was a sizable team paying attention to the flickering screens. There was a robust security gate and a fenced compound for deliveries. Tommy remembered the layout from dropping off Jeremy for a field trip with his biology class.

As he studied the glossy veneer of the lab, he noticed a vehicle exiting the driveway. It was a white Ford Transit Connect, a small European van that had been gaining in popularity with local trades. It carried the Winnipeg city crest on the front doors, as well as an amber light bar on its roof. Along the sides were vinyl lettering, identifying the van as a twenty-four-hour emergency unit for the water and waste department. *Probably the best-paying plumbing gig you could get*, thought Tommy as he watched the van head north on

Arlington. He turned back to the tachometer briefly, tapping it twice to ensure it was actually working. When he turned back to the lab, he saw another Ford Transit, identical to the last one he had seen. He watched it wait for clearance in traffic, eventually heading south. If this had been the last van to exit with similar markings, Tommy would have easily passed it off as a deluxe plumbing issue. He smiled as he thought of a level-four plumbing issue, assurance that the water for hand-washing was piping hot at the lab. That's what he would have thought, if seven more identical vans had not exited the premises in the next ninety seconds. *The water — what does this have to do with the water?* Tommy wasn't sure if van ten was the last unit. He figured it was worth a tail. Freddie was finally warm enough to assist.

CHAPTER THIRTY-THREE

Cindy watched the kitchen clock at The Guiding Light. Tommy was taking too long, or at least that's what the cheap clock seemed to be saying. She kept an eye on the stairwell to the room where Claire was hiding while she played out the worst-case scenarios as she scrubbed the industrial stew pots. The first play was the least dramatic, a visit from someone in Vice or Robbery-Homicide, asking about Claire — had anyone seen her — and leaving a business card and the "if-you-see-her" speech. She had handled enough of those to deliver the response in a waking coma. The next scenario grew darker: a mystery man of cold features, cold eyes, cold ideals. He entered, no, glided into the entrance.

He looked at Cindy briefly, and then looked upstairs with an all-knowing vision that exceeded the fantasy of the superhero X-ray. He pulled a vintage Colt .45 with pearl handles from his waistband, ascending quickly and silently until the explosion from the six-shooter. The steps of his descent were heavy, booming through the structure of the entire building, growing louder, harsher. She looked up in time to see the stranger and the Colt levelled at her forehead. The flash from the barrel had the intense white light of a nuclear blast. She felt the dream bullet impact as strongly as a real slug. She dropped the stew pot as she was shocked back to reality.

Cindy reached down to collect the stew pot. As she ascended, she saw a stranger in the front entrance. He wasn't a cop — Cindy could spot them all too easy — though he was inquisitive. He looked around far too much, like he was searching for something, or someone. He walked as though he was in pain, something recent. Eventually, his eyes found hers. Cindy crossed her arms, and set her cordial dial to minimal. "Can I help you with something?" She looked at the stained jacket of slush and grit, deciding to assume the worst. "We're not taking any new clients today."

David Worschuk looked down at the mess he had become over the last few hours. "Oh, this," he said, as he did his best to brush off some of the debris. "It's been a bit of a busy day." He reached into one of his front pockets, producing his business card. He explained the contents of the card as he handed it to her. "David 'Downtown' Worschuk, from the *Sentinel*. I write the Downtown 24/7 column." Worschuk had hoped for some level of recognition from her. She continued to study him and the card, still wondering if the two fit. She handed the card back to Worschuk. "The guy you want to talk to is Pastor Bosco. He handles all of the media stuff."

Time to turn up the charm. Worschuk took back the card, deciding to use it to punctuate his enquiry. "Actually, I was hoping to talk to the front-line people at your mission, like you. Get a feel for what it's like to help those who society has turned their back on. You know, giving back to the community." Worschuk's card danced along with the conversation, the way a rubber ball bounces across song lyrics on a television screen from the seventies.

The woman stood firm. "That sounds all fine and good, Mister Downtown, but this still has to go through Pastor Bosco."

Level one, thought Worschuk. *She knows who I am. Good, bad, or indifferent, she knows I'm kind of a big deal. MISTER Downtown! Fucking awesome!*

The woman turned to the kitchen, pointing out the daily mess that occurred after every meal at the mission. "Plus, you've kinda caught me at a bad time, unless you feel like scrubbing some of these pots while you're taking notes."

Worschuk knew he surprised her when he removed his coat and headed towards the sink. "How's about I wash, and you dry?"

"Whatever," said the woman, grabbing a fresh dishtowel. "You can wash. My fingers are shrivelled like raisins."

Level two, thought Worschuk. *The establishment of rapport.* Worschuk had done the odd charity stint in soup kitchens, usually when someone like Kyle Morgan of the *Sentinel* had decreed it a community-outreach requirement for his staff. The oversized scrub brush and the wall-mounted spray head made easy work of the pots and pans. The woman continued to dry and stack the dishes on the shelves.

"So I was wondering, uh, I'm sorry," said Worschuk, "I didn't get your —"

"It's Cindy," she said. "Cindy Smyth. Smyth with a Y, no E on the end." The woman may have given her name, but she had yet to provide any warmth in her demeanour.

Level three. I got a name. Keep going.

Worschuk did his best to keep his internal level achievements to himself, though he knew he was breaking down walls, which always made him a little giddy. "So, tell me, Cindy, Cindy Smyth with a Y and no E on the end. How long have you worked —"

"Volunteered."

"Sorry. Volunteered at the —"

"A few years."

"Right, a few years. And what do —"

"Everything and anything."

"I see. So, cleaning, cooking, help —"

"And washing the sheets and stacking the Bibles and making the coffee and breaking up the fights and mopping up the shit. Whatever needs getting done, I make sure it gets done."

Level four. She's venting for the first time in a while. Keep going.

Worschuk decided to start getting more intricate with his questioning. "Cindy, tell me about your, as you put it, clients." *That's right, Davey — clients. Make sure she knows you've been listening. Make sure that she thinks you give a rat's ass about these shitbags.* "Where do they come from? What are their stories?"

Cindy thought about it for a moment. Worschuk thought she seemed hesitant, but when she began talking, he saw she had something original to say. "They're the ones who fall through the cracks. They've been falling through the cracks their whole lives, you know? They come from shit, they've only known shit, so they think, they *believe* that all they're worth is a shit life. We try to give them a place, a time in their life that isn't complete shit. They may get out of the shit, or they may go right back into it, maybe even worse than they had it before."

Worschuk realized that Cindy was staring at him. He had stopped washing the dishes, hanging on her every word.

"We're an island," said Cindy. "The Guiding Light is an island in a sea of shit."

Level five. She wants the world to know. She thinks I can help. Perfect.

Worschuk took a moment, making sure that Cindy noticed. If she believed that he was sincere, that his actions were noble, then he might have a chance at a lead on Claire Hebert.

Worschuk did his best to attempt a newfound fervour in his scrubbing. He wanted to look more interested in the task than the question he was about to ask. *Don't look at her when you ask. Make it sound natural, not a big production.*

"I'll bet you get quite a mix in here," said Worschuk.

"It can get pretty interesting," said Cindy. She was moving throughout the kitchen now, stacking the dried items in their places. She seemed grateful for the help of a stranger. "Tweakers, junkies, dudes who put on wigs and, well, you know the rest."

Worschuk did, as did most local newshounds when it came to the male prostitution stories of the previous owner. Now was the time to offer up something of his, the knowledge of what he knew. He was searching for the tell, the slightest of indicators that could confirm the whereabouts of Claire Hebert. Anything.

"Yeah, it's been a busy twenty-four hours for the sex trade."

Cindy felt her back tense up. If it was any other day, the back-handed comment would have not even registered. She was bending over when it happened, placing a pot into a cupboard, turned away from Worschuk. *Shit!* she thought. *This fucker's digging for a lead.* In the nanoseconds that followed, she thought of the best response. Steady, matter of fact, nonchalant. *Don't give him a reason to stick around. Make this place cold.*

"Yeah, I saw something in the *Sentinel* about it. Some working girl and an HR?"

Worschuk wasn't going to get anywhere — and Cindy could see that he knew it. No flinch, no reaction. *Just some recovering addict working in a soup kitchen who can read.* He wiped his hands on a nearby dish rag and retrieved his smart-phone. "Yeah, not a good week to be in the sex trade, or for-merly in it. Did you hear about the explosion on Main Street?"

"The what on Main Street?"

"The sex shop, near Cathedral, The Other Woman or something. I was there right after it happened. Got a video in here somewhere."

Oh God. Tommy!

"Yeah, I think there were a couple of bodies in the place."

Tommy and Jasmine. Oh my fucking God!

Worschuk found the video and pressed Play, handing the phone to Cindy. "Here it is. Sorry, my camerawork is a little shaky."

Cindy fused every fibre together in her tiny frame. *No tells. No tells. Even if you see Tommy cut into twenty-seven pieces, you WILL NOT BUST! DO YOU FUCKING HEAR ME? YOU WILL GIVE THIS FUCKER NOTHING!* Cindy watched what little could be seen from the impromptu coverage: a lot of smoke, car alarms going off, general panic. No sign of Tommy. No pieces of Jasmine, either. She watched as the camera panned to the street. The battered Cavalier, the glassless Civic. The Econoline. Anyone else would have burst. Cindy looked at the shattered van, with the quizzical look of an eight-year-old. Worschuk stared at her hard. Cindy held it together, no tells, no flinches, nothing. Her chuckle subsided to a warm smile as she handed the phone back to Worschuk.

"That piece-of-shit van," said Cindy. "It's always stalling out somewhere."

Nathaniel knew that Sawatski would be tied up with the investigation at the explosion for at least a couple of hours. He knew that Claire was in the wind; though near, probably ten minutes from where he was parked. He had retrieved a long-lens camera from the trunk, capturing as many stills of the crime scene as he could from the rooftop of an evangelical hall just south of the explosion, on the opposite side of Main Street. The lock was conveniently broken off of the access ladder shroud. There was enough of a façade on the wall facing the street to shield his presence, not that anyone was looking.

There was a clear view of the scene. The building had seen mostly cosmetic repairs over the years, which explained how it so easily caved in with the force of the explosion. The laundromat was largely intact, escaping the brunt of the blast with half of the front glass blown out. The wife of the owner had been apprised of the discovery of her husband's body. She was inconsolable, restrained from entering the scene by the largest of the available rookies. Nathaniel scanned the pictures, uploaded to his police-spec laptop. There were no people of concern in the crowd. His next scan brought up the detail on the license plates of the totalled vehicles. The Cavalier and the Civic were clean for wants, though the Cavalier owner was in for an expensive surprise; they had missed their last insurance instalment. The van came back as a commercial registration to a numbered company. Nathaniel dug deeper into the principals. The company was operating as a non-profit, a community mission of sorts.

"Shitbag Central," said Nathaniel as he continued to probe into the owner, a Pastor Thomas Jasper Bosco, no official ties to any mainstream churches. Notable in the query was the criminal background, especially the nature of the charges. Nathaniel respected the art of smuggling. It took a keen mind to pull it off, and Bosco must have had a lengthy career, until his arrest. Nathaniel smirked as he read the details of the arrest. *Son of a bitch was set up.* The searches brought up the untimely demise of Jeremy Bosco, the crime scene splashed across a scanned image from the *Winnipeg Sentinel*. Nathaniel wondered how Thomas Jasper Bosco would have taken the news, how it would have shifted his modus operandi. The Jesus Train was a pretty big shift, though it wasn't squeaky clean. Though not criminal in nature, The Guiding Light had been cited numerous times by the department of social services, as well as for building code violations. Nathaniel dismissed these concerns as part of the territory, as a quick search of similar infractions confirmed that every independent community mission had logged similar complaints. It all seemed very plausible. That's when Nathaniel knew that it needed checking out.

Tommy and Freddie the Ford followed the water department van from a safe distance as it headed east on Logan Avenue, just slightly under the speed limit. If there was a water emergency somewhere, the driver of the van didn't seem to be in a big hurry to get to it. The old Ford had worked most of the storage bugs out of his system by now, settling into an idle speed that didn't need coaxing from Tommy's right foot at the traffic lights. The van squeaked through a late yellow signal at Salter and Logan, leaving Tommy and Freddie at the light, behind a larger U-Haul rental truck. By the time he was able to steer Freddie around it, the water department van was gone. Tommy decided to head back to The Guiding Light.

Tommy was just about to make the turn into the back lane behind the Light when he stomped on the brake pedal. The water department van was parked in the lane, about halfway down the length of the snow-covered ruts. He put Freddie into reverse, keeping the Ford out of sight. Tommy exited the cab as quietly as possible, making sure not to latch the door in a noisy fashion. A heavy vintage downspout on the corner of the building was enough to shield his view, with a gap between the pipe and the building for clandestine watch. The van was running, with soft plumes of white exhaust wafting away from the rear. The driver was nowhere in sight. Tommy couldn't see if there was anyone in the cab. He decided to move closer.

As Tommy entered the lane, he noticed the driver, crouched down, moving snow away from the water main feeding The Guiding Light. Tommy moved quietly to the rear of the van, half-pleased with himself for his quiet approach, half-concerned with what he would do next. He inched his way along the passenger side of the van, keeping his shuffle in time with the snow clearing of the water department employee. As he peered through the passenger window, Tommy saw the usual trappings of any service vehicle: Tim Hortons cups, invoice holders, and a few tools in the footwell. When he looked back at the water department employee, he breathed a sigh of relief; he was turning off the water. Tommy knew it was a distinct possibility after the latest round of bills spilled across his desk. He wished he had kept the cash from Paulie Noonan's wallet at the landfill.

Tommy knew he was going to startle the water department employee from any angle, so he tried to make sure he wasn't in swinging range of the shut-off tool, should it be swung in fear. He headed to the back of the van, to appear as though he had quietly approached from behind. He then found his inner asshole. "Oh, for fuck's sake," said Tommy. "We just paid it two days ago!"

The water department employee did swing around, without using his shut-off tool as a sword. "Jesus Christ, man," said the employee. "You just about scared the shit out of me!"

Tommy continued the role. "You know, you guys got a lot of fucking nerve, turning off the water to a bunch of homeless people." He pointed at the cuts on his face. "Look at this," said Tommy. "This is how they act when they have water. How happy do you think they're going to be without it?"

The water department employee muttered under his breath as he walked over to the driver's door of the van. He reached inside and produced a pink copy of a disconnection order. "Hey, don't come down on me, man," said the employee. "I'm just doing my job." Tommy grabbed the order, acting as though he was reading the fine print. He threw it back at the employee.

"All I know is you'd better get your supervisor on the phone and ask if he wants to get this story on the six o'clock news tonight or not." The employee looked at Tommy's stare for a moment, and then relented. "You know, this shit wouldn't happen if you paid your bill on time. Just so you know." He bit his lip, as he pondered his next move. "Just go pay something. You're like three blocks from city hall."

Tommy turned down the act. "Hey, sorry I yelled at you, man. I know you're just doing your job. How much do I gotta pay?"

"Just something, anything," said the water department employee. "Like even forty bucks will probably make it cool. I'll say I couldn't find the valve, okay? And you'll need this," said the employee, handing the crumpled disconnection order to Tommy.

Tommy smiled his best smile of appreciation. "Thanks man, I'll whip over there right now." The water department employee nodded, and stowed his shut-off tool in the rear of the van. He paused at the driver's door. "And get some louder boots, man."

Tommy waved as he watched the water department van spin through the ruts. He wasn't convinced that this was a simple disconnection visit. He wasn't convinced that there was anything wrong with the water. There was only one thing that he was convinced of: time was running out for Claire Hebert.

CHAPTER
THIRTY-FIVE

Miles Sawatski got into the driver's seat of the Crown Vic as Gayle Spence scanned the car-mounted laptop. "I got nothing on this Bosco guy since that federal rap you told me about," said Spence. She tapped a few more keys. "Nope, just fines and warnings from the city, mostly health and building code stuff."

"Well, this one is looking like a homicide," said Sawatski, knowing full well that it was. "The fire didn't get too hot, and it turns out that the laundromat guy had just enough pants left on to cover his knees, if you get my drift."

Gayle looked up from the laptop. "Okay, so Laundry Man is fucking the other woman at

196

The Other Woman? Brilliant. So, we like Mrs. Laundry Man for this?"

"Maybe," said Sawatski. He wondered if the wild goose–chase approach for the double homicide behind him might be enough to split the pair up, keeping Spence at the scene of the double while he braced Tommy Bosco. He didn't know how much thug he would have to use on Bosco for information on Claire Hebert or any luggage she might have been carrying with a ledger or two inside. He didn't want to drag Spence into his mess. "Why don't you hitch a ride with the techs, see if the M-E can get a quick look at Mr. and Mrs. Crispy?"

"Crispy?" said Spence. "They looked a little blackened Cajun to me."

Sawatski just looked at her the way any partner would when driving home the needed tasks.

"Ugh," said Spence. "I'll find out what I can about the Crispy couple." Spence exited the Crown Vic. Sawatski headed to The Guiding Light.

Tommy was starting to feel the fatigue. He sat in Freddie's cab, listening to the stumbling engine, prodding the throttle every few seconds out of habit. There was too much happening, too much to process. The explosion, Claire-Bear, the cops, the HRs, plus whoever would be freelancing for the hit. This wasn't going to end well. The chances of moving quickly, quietly, to avoid detection, were fading faster than the afternoon sun on a January day.

What does any of this have to do with the water? Tommy went there, to the place of *X-Files* weird. He wasn't sure what he and Freddie had just encountered in the back lane. The water was getting turned off or was in danger of being turned off on a regular basis at The Guiding Light. This was normal. A whole bunch of other water department service trucks leaving the federal virus lab at the same time felt a lot more like a tinfoil-hat conspiracy scheme than a happy coincidence. Even if there was something in the water, there was still the primary issue at hand: Claire Hebert was a walking dead girl.

Tommy weighed his options. One: throw her to the wolves. She had done untold amounts of damage to him if he chose to accept that any of the outcomes that had occurred were in no way related to his own bad choices — but he couldn't walk away. He could feel the sting of the Padre's bible for just thinking it. Two: get her out of town. This wasn't going to be easy. Tommy figured that his chances weren't better than twenty percent. The locket was the key for a clean exit for Claire, and Tommy didn't have it. He hoped it was in the smouldering debris of The Other Woman. What if it wasn't? What if it had been found? It wasn't the cops he was worried about; it was the various soldiers of the HRs. If there was a sliver of information, no matter how slight, it meant that they would be coming. They would not be cordial. They would kill for what they needed to know, even if it was just the next piece in the puzzle. The Guiding Light would burn quick. The residents would die in agony. Cindy. She would try to fight. She wouldn't win.

What does the water have to do with the ledger? Was this more about the pages within and less about the dead HR? Was the throat slit that set the events in motion just an unhappy coincidence? Who was pulling the strings? Tommy didn't believe that the HRs were in the water-doctoring game, assuming that the game was even in play. Jimmy Stephanos was never lauded as anything approaching a mastermind. He was a mid-level manager with the basic responsibilities of a biker gang: drugs, prostitution, and keeping these areas in check through whatever means necessary. If the HRs were involved in anything above these elements, they were subcontractors. Their awareness of the packages, the formulas, and the parts-per-million of the chemical cocktails was most likely limited to the role of bagman. There would be no need to question this area of criminal enterprise, especially if it didn't seem criminal. Whatever the HRs were getting paid, it was enough to look the other way.

Tommy eased Freddie the Ford into drive, depositing him at the rear of the Light, tapping the bumper ever so slightly against the wall to keep the battery from getting stolen. He took his time ascending the stairs, though not the climb of apprehension. He entered his apartment. Claire was sleeping soundly on the couch. She needed it. There would be more bouts of the sweats, the shakes, and generally bad behaviour from Miss Hebert. The stillness of the moment gave Tommy pause to smile. He looked away from Claire-Bear just as Cindy came through the door.

Cindy was shaking. At first, she didn't see Tommy. When she did, the tears erupted. She ran into him hard and held him even harder. Tommy held her close as she convulsed, subduing the sobs, which would have awakened most of the residents.

She pulled back slowly, looking up at Tommy as she cradled his weary face. "I thought you were dead," she whispered.

"So did I," said Tommy. "The piece-of-shit van is though."

Cindy smirked. "Yeah those window bars did a number on it. Did Jasmine . . ."

"It doesn't look good," said Tommy, as softly as he could. "I think she's gone."

Cindy buried her head back into Tommy's chest. He closed his eyes for a moment, enjoying the sanctuary of her arms. He shifted his hands to her shoulders, and she looked at his eyes.

"How did you find out about the explosion?"

"I saw the video."

"What video?"

"The video that the guy from the *Sentinel* took, at The Other Woman, right after the explosion."

"What's his name?"

"I think it was Davey Woros-something-or-other. Big fat redhead."

Tommy rubbed Cindy's arms as he processed the revelation. Things were getting much too busy for his liking. There were only two other people who could be coming through the door of The Guiding Light in short order: a cop or a killer.

Tommy released his hold on Cindy, heading back to the storage area. He whipped back the curtain, reaching for the dangling light string in the semi-dark. The illumination revealed an old wooden step ladder and the roof access hatch in the ceiling. He moved the ladder into position. Cindy knew the drill. She steadied the ladder as Tommy scrambled up, stopping just before the top of the hatch. She handed him a large rubber mallet, a required tool in the winter months to release the ice buildup on the hatch lid. Four solid whacks on the battered tin released the lid. Tommy poked his head up like a concerned prairie dog, scanning the roof for any unwanted visitors. He reached downwards with his loose hand, feeling for the strap of the binoculars that Cindy had retrieved from their case. He ascended to the roof.

The minimal insulation of The Guiding Light meant that heat escaped easily, keeping most of the roof clear from snow during the winter months. The downspouts would quickly become overwhelmed with the ice melt, forming freestyle stalactites of rust-stained ice, gripping each corner of The Guiding Light's exterior. The same insulation properties were in play with the surrounding rooftops, close enough to the Light that no great Hollywood-style leaps were required to change vantage points. It was easy to spot an idling car with the current winter chill. The exhaust smoke would rise in a lazier fashion than that of passing cars. Tommy headed to the front of the building, using the crumbling brick façade as cover.

The first idler was a late model Chrysler 300 with deep tint on the windows. It seemed a little too flashy for the neighbourhood, possibly an HR associate. There was an old Ford Ranger with some form of metal cargo box in the back. He couldn't make out the driver, though he did notice that the passenger was almost twice his size. On the opposite side of the street, a *Winnipeg Sentinel* Cavalier sent up its tailpipe plume, a large driver behind the wheel. *Must be the big fat redhead.* Tommy pivoted, checking the rest of the one-way street. An older rusty General Motors full-sized beast was idling at the curb, its lights turned off. *Nice to see you, Dad. How's Chico?*

Tommy descended the ladder, already wearing his grimace of concern. Cindy caught it. "How busy is it?"

Tommy folded up the ladder, handing the binoculars back to Cindy. "Looks like four asshole wagons, at least five guys. That newspaper guy never left."

"The big fat redhead?"

Tommy nodded. "Dad's here, too. He's driving one of his crusher wagons."

Cindy wasn't fazed by the news that Ernie Friday was on

the short list of nearby kill goons. She snapped the binocular case shut. "What's the plan, Felchfairy?"

Tommy pulled the curtain back just enough to check on Claire-Bear. Her body rose and fell with sleep. He turned to Cindy, the next step already imprinted in the creases of his face.

"Light the match, Supercunt."

Sawatski was about ten minutes away from The Guiding Light, assuming light traffic, when he heard the two-way crackle that dropped that estimate to five.

"All units, be advised. Structure fire, Princess Street at Alexander Avenue, The Guiding Light Mission, Winnipeg Number One responding, ladder required, no alarm, 911 call, traffic coverage required, EMS dispatched, call is active, repeat, active."

"Shit!" Sawatski said as he slammed the Crown Vic into gear and hit the throttle. Rush hour on Main Street was long over, though the opportunities to slip in and out of the lanes easily were few in number. Sawatski interspersed the siren wail with plenty of horn blasts to move the traffic accordingly. He had to jump the pedestrian island curb at Higgins Avenue for a right turn, thanks to a confused older driver who had moved to the right just enough to reduce the size of the lane. Two quick blocks dissolved, leading to the left turn onto Princess Street. The first fire engine was just arriving, tailed by the paramedics and the ladder truck. The Winnipeg Number One station was a mere six blocks from the scene. Sawatski pulled into a fresh spot, vacated a few seconds earlier by a Chrysler 300. He assessed the scene.

Thick smoke was rising from the roof of The Guiding Light. The windows of the second floor gave off the telltale glow of active flames. It appeared that the fire had not reached the first floor, with no smoke or flames present. Sawatski walked over to the engine company captain, a barrel-chested veteran who looked somewhat related to Sawatski. His name tag read Kulyk. The captain shouted above the diesel din.

"I need that snorkel in the air for hot spots on the roof — plenty of old tar up there, so it's going to go quick. Don't know how many we've got on the second floor, but we're probably dealing with smoke inhalation, need to get them out before the roof caves." He scanned the crowd. "Was anyone here inside the building?"

David Worschuk raised his cell phone, filming the scene. "I was, about twenty minutes ago."

The captain motioned him over as he spoke. "Did you notice anything while you were inside? Did you smell anything burning?"

"Negative," said Worschuk.

"Do you know if there are any chemicals inside, explosives?"

"Nothing that I saw."

"Do you work here? Are you a resident?"

Sawatski chuckled aloud. Worschuk looked annoyed. "No, I'm David 'Downtown' Worschuk, from the *Winnipeg Sentinel*."

The name didn't register with the captain. "How many people are inside?"

"I dunno. Maybe fifteen, twenty."

"Anyone in wheelchairs, walkers, canes?"

"I dunno. I'm just —"

"WILL YOU FUCKING IDIOTS SHUT THE FUCK UP? PEOPLE ARE TRYING TO SLEEP IN HERE, FOR CHRIST'S SAKE!"

Sawatski, Worschuk, and the captain turned around to a bearded man in his early fifties, wearing an open bathrobe over an old Domo Gas t-shirt and tighty-whitey underwear that hadn't seen their original colour in some time. He had just come out of The Guiding Light, but he wasn't singed; he didn't even smell of smoke.

"Where's the fire?" said the captain.

"How the fuck should I know?" said the man. "You're the ones with the shiny red trucks." The man was a little hard to understand without his teeth. "You figure it out, Smokey!"

Sawatski stepped up. "Is everyone okay inside?"

The man looked over Sawatski as he tightened up his robe. "Who the fuck are you?"

"Sawatski, police."

"Fuck you! I'm on parole!"

"I'm not here for you, I'm —"

"Yeah, Sawatski, who are *you* here for?" Worschuk filmed him, waiting for an answer.

Sawatski grabbed Worschuk's phone, looking directly at the camera lens. "No comment." Staring at Worschuk,

Sawatski snapped the flip phone in half and handed the pieces back to the stunned reporter. He then approached the door to The Guiding Light. Courtesy of the resident they had just awoken, the door was wide open. Sawatski peered up the stairs at the glow of the flames.

The captain grabbed his arm. "We've got to make sure everything is okay first."

Sawatski looked at him, gently removing the hand from his sleeve. "Don't worry; something tells me it's very okay." The captain and Worschuk watched as Sawatski neared the top landing of the stairs. He looked around the room, chuckled, and then headed back down. The captain grabbed his arm again.

"What is it?"

"It's Christmas," said Sawatski. "Merry fucking Christmas." The two watched Sawatski as he exited the building, still chuckling to himself. Worschuk and the captain ran up the stairs.

There was no fire, but there was Christmas, in the old-school sense. The rear wall of the sleeping quarters had a fire-like glow, courtesy of a half-dozen vintage colour light wheels. The wheels were originally used to light up the equally vintage aluminum Christmas trees from the 1950s and '60s. The wheels were usually a four-colour configuration, though these wheels had been retrofitted with red and orange colour films. The effect on the wall, as seen from the street, was a fully involved blaze, the kind that needed shiny red trucks. At the front of the room, three large smoke machines fed a vent system that was piped to the roof. Half of the residents were still asleep, while the rest were looking out the windows at the commotion below. The captain grabbed his radio, doing his best not to erupt into laughter.

"Dispatch, Winnipeg Number One. False alarm, structure fire, Alexander and Princess. Repeat, false alarm, over."

The voice crackled back. "Roger that Number One. Call cancelled. Over and out."

CHAPTER THIRTY-SEVEN

Tommy and Freddie the Ford rumbled down Alexander Avenue with two additional, yet unseen, riders. Cindy and Claire were in a forced huddle, mashed into Freddie's passenger footwell. The room was at a premium, and the tension was starting to spill over.

"You know, we'd have a lot more room if you hadn't gone for those stupid porn star implants," said Cindy.

"Shut up, bitch," said Claire. "Or I'll start puking on you."

"No puking in the truck," said Tommy. "That shit's hard to get out."

"Where are we going, anyway?" said Claire.

She squirmed as much as she could, searching for comfort. "And some food would be nice."

"Smaller tits would be even nicer," said Cindy.

"Fuck you," said Claire. She punctuated the verbal jab with an elbow to Cindy's chest.

"Fuck me? Fuck you, you dumb cunt!" Cindy started pulling on Claire-Bear's hair, and not the way she liked it.

Tommy drummed the top of Freddie's steering wheel as the old Ford rocked from left to right. The movement was even more noticeable at the next traffic light. "Great way to not attract attention," said Tommy, fiddling with the radio. No one was reporting the "fire" at The Guiding Light. The firefighters and the police must have realized that it was the falsest of alarms. Two-way transmissions were heavily monitored by the local media, and once the false alarm had been verified, there was no need to proceed with the story on the radio, Twitter, or Facebook. Tommy wondered if the big fat redhead, the same one who he'd seen in the *Winnipeg Sentinel* car, had stuck around to get the lowdown. If he had, he might be planning to communicate the nature of the fraudulent call, as it would certainly be amusing to the readership at large. He scanned Freddie's mirrors for the vehicles that he identified from his rooftop perch at the Light. It was hard to tell, with the cab still swaying back and forth from the ongoing footwell skirmish. The exhaust fog didn't help with matters.

Cindy seemed to be getting tired of the scuffle. Tommy noticed she had figured out a hold to restrain Claire-Bear that resembled a half nelson, ever mindful of the possibility of being bitten by her opponent. She gave Tommy a look that simply asked, *what's the plan?*

Tommy gave the rear-view mirror a scan. "You two better

calm down," said Tommy. "We've got a marked car two cars back in the curb lane." His passengers stopped tussling. The police car was a ruse, one that neither Cindy nor Claire-Bear could confirm or deny. The possibility of capture calmed the moment. Things stayed quiet for the rest of the trip to the only safe house that Tommy felt was worth the risk.

He headed towards the library.

Beneath the Riverview Health Centre, a certain Emerson respirator had become a far busier cocoon. The frail figure within listened intently to the emergency channel chatter, hearing none of the news he so desired. There was no need to call Nathaniel; if there had been developments from the front lines on the whereabouts of the ledger, it would have been reported. The time had come to inform those who had even more to lose than the polio-stricken man in the polished breathing tube. He pressed the patient call button three times, paused, then pressed again. Unseen speakers warbled the tell-tale tones of an outside call being placed. It was answered on the fourth ring.

"Jus-just a moment," said the answerer. Voices heard in the background were quickly muffled by the placement of the answerer's handset against their chest. The voices were getting quieter, replaced by the sounds of singular breathing in the background. Something large and door-like made its signature closing sound. There was creaking now, the type that was normally reserved for a well-worn office chair. There was a little more breathing, then a concerned exhalation. "Please identify," said the speaker-bound voice.

"Chancellor, Morley, Peterson."

"Date of birth, please."

"Four, sixteen, thirty-one."

"Code level."

"Black."

The breathing seemed to stop for a few moments, wherever the well-worn office chair was. "Please confirm code level."

"Black, as the Ace of Spades."

The office chair creaked with the response. "Please observe protocol, Mister Chancellor."

"We are past the point of protocol, Mister Finch, far past it."

"Have you confirmed with all operatives?"

"Confirmed."

"Are secondary assets in place?"

"Multiple."

"Confirmed sightings?"

"None."

"Grid?"

"Central."

"Formula?"

"Clean Sweep."

The chair creaked a few more times, coupled with sounds that could only be described as keyboard inputs. "Chancellor, Morley, Peterson. Four, sixteen, thirty-one. Confirming Code Level Black, Central Grid, Clean Sweep."

"Confirmed, Mister Finch. Oh, and one more thing."

"Please observe protocol, Mister Chancellor."

"Mr. Finch, please make yourself available for a discussion regarding our recent transactions. My aide-de-camp will contact you with the particulars."

"Good day, Mr. Chancellor." The line went dead before Morley Peterson Chancellor could respond.

CHAPTER
THIRTY-EIGHT

Sawatski was relieved to see that the number on his call display was known. Spence was finished at the Health Sciences Centre, looking to get picked up. He collected her at the Sherbrook Street entrance, using his visor lights to get the taxicabs to move out of the way.

"They're both pretty cooked," said Spence as she fastened her seat belt. "The laundromat guy was already dead, no smoke inhalation. The inside of his lungs was about the only thing that had any pink left. Puncture wound in the base of the neck probably helped that."

"What about the Other-Woman woman?" said Sawatski.

Spence looked up, noticing that the visor lights were still going. She switched them off as she spoke.

"She was the one who set it off," said Spence. "There was a Bic lighter fused to what was left of her hand."

"Suicide?" said Sawatski. He knew full well that it wasn't. Spence didn't catch it.

"Well, it wouldn't be the first time that someone blew something up because someone blew up about who blew someone," said Spence. "Just seems weird that they find them in completely different parts of the building. Most lovers' spat-icides happen in close quarters." Spence checked her notebook. "The M-E says that Laundry's neck wound was probably a pro. Most amateurs don't angle the ice pick up high enough to scramble the brain. Usually comes out the front of the neck, hits an artery, big bloody mess."

Sawatski changed the subject, and the direction, away from the Robbery-Homicide division and towards Tommy Bosco's mission. There were no city video cameras near The Guiding Light, though Sawatski figured that at least one business might have recorded the alleged escape. He relayed the Christmas-lights ruse and the smoke machine system to a wide-eyed Spence. "Whether she was there or not doesn't even matter at this point. His eminence Pastor Bosco and his girlfriend set the thing up, and they're in the wind, probably with Hebert."

"Do we have another vehicle for Bosco?" Spence started the search on the Crown Vic's laptop.

"Already got it," said Sawatski. "It's a blue Ford half-ton, '89, regular cab, Gordon Thomas X-Ray, eight two eight. It shouldn't be too hard to spot."

Spence nodded. "Ford POS — that Bosco certainly has a type."

The Two Pauls had seen a marked increase in the amount of freelance thugs on the street. Ernie Friday had noticed it, too. He hadn't received any new messages as to the whereabouts of Claire Hebert, with the same being true for the Paul contingent. Ernie's estranged son had done an admirable job of keeping Claire hidden, at least for the time being. The cover of night would help. Freddie the Ford would be easier to spot during daylight hours, assuming that a vehicle switch hadn't already occurred. Ernie was convinced that they would be in a safe house of sorts till the following evening. He found a working payphone flanked by two broken ones in the Robin's Donuts parking lot on Salter Street. There was nothing to report at the Biggs safe house. Ernie wasn't entirely convinced that Biggs was out of the hole-up racket, though he knew that a finder's fee for Biggs would easily be twice what he would make for a couple of nights hiding Claire Hebert. He took a swig of rye from his flask before a refresh of his cigarette. The Two Pauls watched him from inside the donut shop. They had both decided that if they stared at Friday without flinching, they could better combat his perceived ninja assassin powers.

Nathaniel watched the three from the front seat of his idling Chrysler 300. He had just received the Clean Sweep order from Morley Peterson Chancellor. In his five years with the Chancellor organization, there had never been a need to initiate the directive. Nathaniel knew that the Clean Sweep search system was multi-tiered, the ultimate in all-points bulletin. Phone surveillance was a primary pillar of the Clean Sweep system, both landline and wireless. Nathaniel knew that burner and pay-as-you-go phones would be a problem.

It usually took up to forty-eight hours for new pay-as-you-go activations to be logged into the search engines. The burner phones were trickier to flag, though even their clandestine electronic signatures would eventually become identified, especially if the burner was in communication with a known phone. There was still the continuing street-side component of the hunt, plus additional digital assets that had been activated. For now, there was plenty of video.

Nathaniel watched a tile display of grainy video screens on his laptop. The screens were a combination of traffic camera locations, crime prevention pillars, and a selection of private business units that had been easily commandeered, thanks to their wireless nature. The tile of screens cycled through what appeared to be a random sequence. Within the randomness was a search algorithm, tailored to locate the Ford's GTX 828 license plate, as well as any general weirdness, such as 911 calls, internet traffic, and security alarm signals from businesses that should have been closed up tight for the night. Facial recognition markers were also in force, with police mugshots of Tommy Bosco, Claire Hebert, and Cindy Smyth in view on the right-hand portion of the screen. He toggled back and forth between the Clean Sweep screen and the Winnipeg Police Service's Be On the LookOut updates, the same screen that would be appearing on the city's police unit screens. Hebert was wanted in connection with the Stephanos homicide, with Bosco and Smyth sought as persons of interest. City utility trucks had also been notified of the BOLO alert, a practice that had worked well in speeding up the apprehension of wanted fugitives. If a BOLO vehicle or person was spotted, the utility vehicle driver would advise the location of the sighting through the secure police channels.

The next step was to advise the killers-for-hire. Nathaniel

checked another screen on his laptop. There were at least ten quality hitters still in play on the Claire Hebert job, though Nathaniel knew that he had already chosen his short list. When the location confirmation came, he had his pick of the litter as to whom he would send it to. He quickly sent secure messages through a variety of systems to those who had been instructed to stand down. And then there were three: Ernie Friday, the Two Pauls, and Nathaniel's own lieutenant, the one responsible for Claire Hebert's roommate, Jasmine Starr, and the laundromat owner who was in the wrong vagina at the wrong time. Nathaniel was scanning the video feed when the call came in through the car's Bluetooth system.

"Update."

"I've got eyes on Sawatski. Is he still working for us? He sure doesn't act like it."

"It's still to be determined. What's your twenty?"

"One block from location, texting it to you now." The text information flashed up on the information display of Nathaniel's Chrysler. "Do you want me to take him out?"

"Negative," said Nathaniel. "Sawatski is still in play, for now."

"Got it. On your way?"

"On my way." Nathaniel ended the call. He took one last look at the Pauls staring at Ernie Friday before he put the Chrysler in gear.

The old Ford creaked and groaned over the bumps and ruts of the back lane route to the St. John's Library on Salter Street. The branch had recently celebrated its one hundredth anniversary, with plans in place to improve accessibility and facilities within. The St. John's branch was one of three Carnegie libraries that still stood within city limits, constructed through a grant program that steel magnate Andrew Carnegie had first offered in the late nineteenth century. Tommy Bosco checked his watch as they approached the classic brick structure: 8:13 p.m. The branch would be closing in less than twenty minutes.

Tommy parked Freddie on Machray Avenue, next to the library. "All right, ladies, we're home for the night."

Claire Hebert turned towards the heritage building, working the kinks out of her neck from the cramped quarters in Freddie's cab. "What the fuck is this place?"

"It's called a library," said Cindy. "It's like the internet, but without the computer screen."

"I know what the fuck a library is."

"Imagine how much fun it would be if you could read."

"I'd rather be reading your o-BITCH-uary."

"Shut the fuck up, both of you." Tommy was attaching a weathered "The Club" steering-wheel lock to Freddie. "We're going to lay low here for the night. You'll have to spend tomorrow here, too, while I get things ready to leave, so if you can't read, I suggest you fake it."

"Is this guy a friendly?" asked Cindy.

"He's cool," said Tommy. "Bit of an egghead, too. I'm going to get him to look at the ledger, see if there's something in there that might help." Tommy removed the ledger from the dummy tank, taking care not to drop it into the dirty snow. They entered the heavy front doors as the speakers crackled overhead.

"Attention readers: the St. John's branch of the Winnipeg Public Library will be closing in fifteen minutes. Please return all reference materials to their appropriate stations. Please bring all items you would like to check out to the front counter, and please have your library card ready. Please watch your step near the corners of the stacks, as we are in the process of reinforcing their foundations. Thank you for visiting the Winnipeg Public Library."

Tommy saw the message's announcer as they crested the stairs. Steve Galecki was easily the tallest librarian in the city library system, around six-foot-four if you could lay him on a flat surface for measurement. His operating height was more in the realm of five-foot-ten, with a permanent hunch to his frame — the result of years of leaning over to read grainy computer screens for library patrons. His glasses were old and thick with an amber tint that must have been in fashion when they were new, circa 1985. That was the year that Tommy first met him, when Galecki ran a lucrative sideline in the field of fake documents, starting with Tommy's first fake ID. Driver's licenses, vehicle registrations, even the odd passport could be had from Galecki when the age of paper reigned supreme. Tommy had used Galecki's services with decreasing regularity in recent years. The crispness of his early work simply wasn't there. With both of their criminal pasts behind them, Tommy would call Galecki for special shipments of retired library books and magazines for The Guiding Light.

Galecki kept his focus on the library patrons, waiting for the large doors to close firmly shut before he acknowledged Tommy's presence. "Pastor Bosco," said Galecki as he extended his hand for a gentlemanly shake. "You're a little late for story time today."

"That's a crying shame," said Tommy as he shook. "I could go for *The Little Engine That Could* right about now."

"Spoiler alert: he knew he could." He walked past Claire and Cindy, giving them a tip of a hat that wasn't there. He securely bolted the hundred-year-old front doors. "Gwen made some chicken soup for lunch, in case you're hungry. It's on the hot plate in the office." Gwen was Galecki's girlfriend of some thirty years. Tommy had never met her, unless one counted the soups. Galecki had met Gwen while they were both working for the City of Winnipeg archives department, which just happened to be housed in the first Carnegie library for Winnipeg. Tommy smiled at the thought of the ultimate eggheads in love. He motioned Cindy and Claire into the office for some much-needed sustenance. "I guess I should let Gwen know that I'll be a little late."

"I think we'll be okay," said Tommy, giving a head nod in Claire's direction. "Have to get Tits McGee out of town — major heat."

"Should I warm up the laminating machine?" Galecki had already produced the unit from beneath the counter. "In case you need something old school. I've still got some old Manitoba birth certificate blanks I could whip up, pre-techie."

"Not right now. I need you to look at something." Tommy spun and slid the ledger towards Galecki. "We're not sure what it means, but the numbers might be tied to water meters." Tommy opened the ledger to the bookmarked page with the Guiding Light water meter number. Galecki leaned down even farther to investigate, looking anything but comfortable. He flipped back and forth between the pages. He stood up as straight as his frame would allow, pulling a shirt-tail loose to clean his glasses. "Where did you find it?"

"I didn't," said Tommy. "Claire did — in an HR briefcase."

"The one on Pritchard? Razor in the neck, right?"

"Yeah, somebody wants her and this thing pretty bad. The building she was at before she came to me got blown up — killed a friend of hers. We had to sneak out of the mission to get here."

Galecki continued to flip pages, rubbing his chin. "You're sure the heat's not just payback for the HR?"

Tommy rubbed his forehead to find the right words. "There's too much going on for payback. If this book is the key, then it might be worth safe passage."

"Safe passage? For how many?"

"That remains to be seen." Tommy saw the worry creep across Galecki's face. "Listen, Steve, we can leave right now. No sense in —"

"I think I know what this is," Galecki said.

"What is it?"

"It's something that's been going on for a very long time." Galecki pulled the standard issue librarian's counter chair closer for support. "Something that a lot of people thought had died when the people involved in it were dead and gone. I've got papers on it back at the house."

"Can't we just Google it?" Tommy added an arm sweep to the request, pointing to the empty public-computer terminals.

Galecki chuckled at the suggestion. "That's the problem with the World Wide Web, my friend. It knows all, and it sees all. My personal library isn't online. The only tech I've got is the microfiche. That reminds me." Galecki moved to the phone on the counter, dialling an outside line. Galecki took a moment for pleasantries with Gwen, and then informed her he would be home shortly with a friend who required the microfiche reader warmed up, and maybe some soup, too.

Tommy continued to voice his concerns after Galecki hung up the phone. "Steve, you don't have to get messed up in this. We just need a place to crash till we make a run for it."

Galecki flipped through the ledger in a casual manner. "If this is what I think it is, you won't make it outside the Perimeter Highway." Galecki looked up at the clock. "I'll start the wagon. We need to check my archive."

Galecki disappeared out of the side door that bordered the back lane, propping it open with an ice chipper. Tommy heard the telltale sounds of something old and creaky. It must have been old; Tommy counted eight pumps of the accelerator pedal. Tommy peeked out the side door in time to see the car start. Galecki was known for his love of vintage Plymouth cars. He owned a restored 1958 Belvedere convertible as well as a robin's egg–blue 1958 Plymouth Suburban station wagon that had belonged to his father. His winter beaters were just as legendary and always followed a station-wagon theme. The latest was a dark green 1972 Plymouth Fury Sport Suburban, held together with what was left of the woodgrain panelling. The winter wagons always wore the same vanity plate: BEATER. Galecki would find his winter heaps in farmers' fields and barns, and stitch them together with his cache of spare Mopar parts, which was sizable. He would usually be able to drive the wagons for at least a couple of winter seasons until a rookie traffic cop would pull him over for a roadside inspection, which usually ended with the wagon's plates being removed and a call for a tow truck. This was the third season for the Fury, and Galecki knew he was driving on borrowed time.

Galecki came back inside, leaving the Fury running and unlocked. Tommy was concerned. "Shouldn't you at least throw a Club on it?"

"Power steering's shot," said Galecki. "None of the kids around here have the upper body strength."

Tommy explained the plan to Claire and Cindy, making sure that they knew to keep off of the computers — they'd have to resist the urge to check for updates on their escape. Cindy was already consulting the library's newspapers, looking for anything that could help. Claire had found a new couch in the office to convalesce. Tommy helped Galecki scrape the windows of the wagon as it warmed up. He tossed the ledger onto the front seat.

A few blocks down from The Guiding Light, David Worschuk nursed his pride with a coke bump and then fired up his backup phone. Luckily, the actions of Miles Sawatski had not fractured the all-important SIM card, which held the majority of his contacts. Worschuk didn't have an on-board police scanner, but there was a unit that ran 24/7 at the *Sentinel*. He connected with the night editor, who recorded a police BOLO that was getting repeat airplay: a blue 1989 Ford F-150, plate number GTX 828. Worschuk then sent a text to a contacts group titled FOD: Friends of Downtown.

Lookin for blue '89 F150, GTX 828, Murder First. Big Reward! Text with tips. Thanks from the D.

The "Big Reward" never amounted to much for the tipster. In Worschuk's eyes, the big reward was the mention in the Worschuk story for the assist. He thumbed through his contact list, hoping to find someone, anyone, who could put him closer to the scoop he so desperately needed. He slowed his sweep as he hit the Ls. He hit the contact and waited for it to connect. It took three rings plus a fumble that could only have meant the contact was driving. "What up?" said the voice.

"Little Bill?"

"D-town? Shit. Lemme guess, mofo: the Double-Dee-Dave needs to top up the tank with some premium, right?"

In most cases, this would have been the purpose for the call. Little Bill was one of the better-known drug dealers in the North End, working out of a pool hall on Main Street near Bannerman Avenue. Big Bill was his father, currently in Stony Mountain for a string of violent assaults, most of them tied to collecting on bad drug debts. He would be out in 2023, with good behaviour. Little Bill was keeping the ship afloat, distributing a good portion of the HRs' shipments. The *Sentinel* was a steady customer, from the press room up to the executive offices. The standing discount was ten percent. Worschuk checked his stash just to be sure.

"Tank is full, Billy. What I need is intel — trying to crack the Stephanos whack before the *Sun* and the *Freep*. Hear anything?"

"Naw man, that bitch gotta be underground by now. That was some cold shit. That's what happens when you pay for it. I never paid for it. My daddy never paid for it. You pay for it and you might just pay for it, you know what I'm saying?" Little Bill talked as street as he could, which always sounded comical to Worschuk since Little Bill's last name was Bernstein and he'd grown up in Transcona.

"So, everyone's looking for her, right?"

"Like those little chocolate eggs at Easter, man. Every hitter in the two-oh-four be locked and loaded. Bitch need a helicopter to rise above this shit."

Worschuk felt the scoop slipping further from his reach. For a moment, he thought about asking to connect with one of the hitters, knowing full well that Little Bill would have laughed it off. "Thanks, Billy. If you hear about a takedown, shoot me a text."

"Yeah, that be a messy scene fo sho. And Double-Dee, they be looking for some words too."

"Words? What kind of words?"

"Like words, man, a book or something that Stephanos had — got words, numbers and shit. They wants it back."

"What's it for?"

"How the fuck should I know, man? Hey! This better not be on no wire or something, man. My daddy ain't the only one who can fuck you up, motherfucker."

Worschuk calmed Little Bill down, assuring him that no recording was taking place, which wasn't true. His phone had a silent recording app. It was faster than taking notes and easier to consult when he was writing his column. Worschuk confirmed that everything was cool with Little Bill before he disconnected. Things were starting to make sense, especially with the amount of resources that had been afforded to catch a killer of a known criminal. This wasn't just a revenge job; it was a recovery mission. He frantically dialled another number. It answered after two rings. "*Winnipeg Sentinel*, City Desk."

"It's Worschuk. I've got a late story breaking. Give me thirty minutes."

Miles Sawatski knew that Winnipeg Police Service technology was on the job to find Tommy Bosco's F-150. License plate scanners had been installed on a third of the city's marked police cruisers with at least three cars per district rolling per shift with the scanner set up. The scanners were mounted on the opposite ends of the cruisers' roof-mounted light bars. The technology was originally designed for slow passes of parking lots, though as with most technical advances, the systems were now able to capture plate images at patrol speeds. If a cruiser got a hit, they had been instructed to send in an unmarked to set up surveillance with a direct call-out to Sawatski as the lead investigator.

Sawatski had dropped off Spence for the night at her house on Atlantic. He promised to call if there were any developments, though he hoped that he could somehow keep her out of his mess. The best scenario was a report of a body, or bodies, preferably not cops or innocents. As long as one of them was Claire Hebert, he could relax. *What if Bosco has the ledger?* He thought about the scenarios. Would he hand it over? Would he try to bargain with it? Or would Sawatski have to pull his throwaway piece and silence him for sure? The Smyth girl: he might have to kill her, too.

Sawatski knew that sleep wouldn't come. He drove north on Main Street to the Salisbury House at Matheson Avenue. A few dollars later, the steam from a long-simmering chili was warming his face. Similar zephyrs of warmth rose from his coffee. He hoped that the day would come when this would be nothing more than a ritual for a retired night-owl cop. The Sal's location he had chosen had recently gone back to twenty-four-hour service, though most of the locals had figured it was still a ten p.m. shutdown. The place was deserted. Out of habit, Sawatski sat with his back to the wall, able to see both entrance points as well as a commanding view of the sidewalk traffic. His jacket was unbuttoned, his Glock within easy holster reach.

The front and rear doors were equipped with entry chimes. The kitchen space and the restroom real estate created a hallway, or a blind spot to anyone wearing a badge, so Sawatski heard the chime before he saw the person that had activated it at the rear door. Sawatski kept his hand close to his Glock. In three seconds, he knew that there was no need to worry. The Sal's patron was Constable Billy "Bangster" Sangster, wearing his signature grey longshoreman toque and a well-worn leather coat that he had dubbed his Serpico jacket. He seemed a little unclear as to how the path of a Salisbury House restaurant worked at first, taking a moment to scan the regular offerings of red velvet cake and petrified chocolate donuts. He decided on a slice of lemon meringue and a large black takeout coffee. He still hadn't noticed Sawatski when he received his change. He smiled upon the recognition, sliding into the booth. "You know, you need some heavy fuel to win the Sawatski Stretch."

"So I hear," said Sawatski. "But that pie will hit your ass like a brick."

"Don't discount a little ass-play," said Sangster. "The world needs a few more dirty girls that know where to stick their vibrators." Sangster seemed intent on finishing the meringue in as few bites as possible. "Talk about a long fucking day," he said between shovels. "You and Spence get any traction? And what about that fire that wasn't a fire?"

Sawatski leaned forward, rubbing his eyes without taking off his glasses. "Yeah, that was fucking hilarious. They got out, but we've got the BOLO out on the truck, Bosco, his live-in, plus Miss Hebert. I don't think they've got the hardware to cause a problem. We've just got to make sure that the take-down is epic. When ten cars surround you, you tend to go from lion to lamb pretty quickly."

"Didn't the live-in tenderize that Kildonan Park asshole better than Tenderloin Meats does a prime rib?" said Sangster.

Sawatski leaned back into the vinyl bench. "She's harmless, Bangster. It's not motorcycle weather, and I highly doubt that she's going to show up to the surrender with a full-auto under her arm. We're just playing whack-a-mole on this one."

"What about the barbeque at the porn shop? Did anything show up at the autopsy?"

Sawatski shook his head. "It looks like a pro offed the laundry guy. He was dead before that Jasmine something-or-other flicked her Bic for the kaboom."

Sangster had reached the final remnants of the pie crust. "Yeah, this whole thing is getting weird. Can't believe we haven't got a tip or a body by now. I mean, we've got bodies, just not the one we're looking for. The white shirts are trying to deflect it, but you know the shit's going to dirty us before it dirties them." The "white shirts" were reserved for the administration-level staff of the police service. They usually weren't seen for the day-to-day media reports unless a comment was required to keep the populace calm or to deflate a growing scandal. Three bodies within twenty-four hours related to the case, major property damage, and no arrests would mean that the white shirts would be getting plenty of starch.

Sangster gobbled up what was left of the meringue, pushing the plate towards Sawatski. "I gotta jet."

Sawatski nodded at the exit. "Hot date?"

"Hot enough," said Sangster as he buttoned up his coat. "Catch you on the flip side." Sangster was about five steps from the table when Sawatski called to him.

"Hey, Bangster, forget something?"

Sangster turned around to see Sawatski holding his takeout cup. "Shit," said Sangster. "I'd forget my head if my toque wasn't holding it on."

"Sweet nectar of life, right?" Sawatski held the cup aloft for an easier grab.

"You got that right, brother. I'll see you tomorrow."

Sawatski nodded as he watched Sangster exit the way that he had entered, to the rear parking lot. He waited for the door chime to ring before he moved quickly to the front counter. Near the cash register he saw a monitor that was displaying the four camera feeds for the restaurant's security system, most likely a deterrent to would-be thieves. He watched as Sangster walked past the camera to an idling silver Chrysler 300. Sangster got in on the passenger side, handing the coffee to the driver. *Bangster wouldn't drink Sal's coffee if you put a gun to his head*, thought Sawatski.

Sangster was freelancing just like him, but for whom? He grabbed a nearby Sal's order pad and pencil to record the plate number: 729 DWN. The city-owned police cars had used plates starting with an A prefix since the mid-nineties, recently switching to F, G, and H-prefix plates. There was only one full-sized Chrysler product in the fleet, a marked Dodge Charger Enforcer that was purchased for evaluation against the newest Ford Police Interceptors. The Charger's brakes couldn't hold up to the pursuit requirement, and the car had been demoted to a marked community affairs unit. Whomever it was, it wasn't a cop. It also meant that someone was looking at the movements of Sawatski's Crown Vic, thanks to the now-standard GPS tracking system on the police fleet. Sangster was part of the union committee that had recommended the GPS system to speed up response times for officers needing assistance. Every member of the service had access to the live GPS movements of the fleet, 24/7, through car-mounted laptops or a secure smartphone app. Sawatski continued to watch the screen, hoping that the driver would get out for some reason, any reason, for a basic ID. As Sawatski watched, one of the night staffers ambled up to the counter. "You want to order more chili?" said the counter clerk.

"No thanks," said Sawatski as he watched the screen. "I think I just lost my appetite."

Nathaniel sipped on his Sal's coffee while Sangster gave him the lowdown on his conversation with Sawatski. "He's not saying a lot that helps, and I don't think he's got it in him to whack the hooker and her Dynamic Duo. The guy's a total fucking liability at this point."

"We don't need a dead cop right now," said Nathaniel, checking the camera feed on his laptop between sips. "If it can somehow happen during the takedown, and it's clean, then you have my full authorization. But let me be clear: we can't have any witnesses. We need the ledger, and we need to ensure the silence of the Hebert extraction team, which may have just unwittingly added the good sergeant to its ranks."

"Bullshit," said Sangster. "Sawatski won't help anybody but himself. What's in it for him?"

Nathaniel took a stiff swig of the Sal's coffee to punctuate his thought. "Every man has a moral compass, Sangster, even you. Every man has the ability to chart a course away from his true moral north, and a precious few have found the justification needed to do just that. The world needs men like that, Sangster, men like us who can see the bigger map."

Sangster was impressed by the statement. "Wow, when you say it like that, I feel like one of the good guys."

"We are the good guys, Sangster. Did Sawatski say anything else?"

"Yeah, he actually gave me a compliment."

Nathaniel smirked. "Please tell me it wasn't for that ridiculous toque of yours."

"Nope, it was for the laundry guy. He said I did him like a pro."

Galecki's station wagon had an exhaust leak somewhere. Tommy felt the headache begin about two minutes into the drive. It was anyone's guess where the leak was coming from: a rusted muffler, a cracked gasket, or one of the holes in the floor that had been hastily fixed with sheet metal and pop rivets. He rolled down his window a crack to help diminish the toxic gases. The dashboard lights flickered constantly. A play-by-play of the out-of-town Jets game vibrated the front speaker.

As Tommy opened the window, Galecki stepped the defroster fan up one speed to compensate for the frigid air. "I think it's the Y-pipe," said Galecki, fully aware of the safety concern within. "And the weatherstripping needs to be replaced on the back window."

So, that's where that rattling is coming from, thought Tommy as he looked at the rear pane covered with yellowing frost shields. He remembered hearing that driving with the rear window down on a station wagon could cause exhaust to roll in, probably affecting the cognitive development of the kids who sat in the rear-facing third-row seat. Tommy figured he had dodged that bullet: he would always call shotgun with Ernie Friday.

Galecki lived on Alfred Avenue, a block east of McPhillips Street. The neighbourhood had gentrified over the past decade, with many of the post-war boom houses wearing new siding and windows. Casa Galecki was the exception; the house was built in 1909 and still wore many of the original exterior decorative wood trimmings. Much of the paint had flaked away from the original craftsmanship, along with the shingles, eavestrough, and many of the front porch floorboards. Tommy was surprised at the level of dilapidation and how it failed to take away the significance of the original architecture. They drove around to the back lane, where a large gate on an equally large fence had been opened, rolled to one side on a metal wheel-and-track system. Galecki hit a button on a garage door–style opener, and the gate started to roll back to its closed position as they came to a stop.

"Just like the rich folks do," said Galecki, punctuating his dig at class and society with a signature snort.

The pair ambled past the garage up to a rear porch that wasn't doing much better than the front. "It's a little spongy in spots," said Galecki, so Tommy placed his steps exactly where Galecki's landed. He tapped the door with "Shave and a Haircut, Two Bits," which didn't seem like much of a secret knock to Tommy. From within, a series of six latches unbolted. The door opened to reveal a petite blonde in her mid-fifties.

So Gwen IS real, thought Tommy as they shuffled into the

rear mudroom. She wore simple clothes, including an oversized cardigan that must have been from Galecki's closet. She adjusted her reading glasses as she looked up at the guest.

"Gwen, this is the infamous Tommy Bosco," said Galecki.

"Good evening, Mr. Bosco," said Gwen, with a voice that sounded like it could have been culled from a society page of a bygone era. "Welcome to the library. Would you care for Earl Grey or chamomile?"

Tommy remembered that one, or possibly both, of those things were tea. "Uh, sure, thanks, Gwen. I guess the grey one, please."

Gwen smiled graciously as she took both of their coats and hung them on a vintage mirrored stand that had started life in a much grander house. The interior of the home was best described as organized chaos. There were stacks of books everywhere, situated in some of the neatest stacks imaginable. It appeared that the stacks were concerned with lining up the dimensions of the books first, mingling a variety of subjects together. Even with the multiple stacks, the house was spotless, filled with an eclectic array of bric-a-brac. Add a few price tags, and Galecki's home could be easily transformed into an antique shop.

While Gwen readied the tea, Tommy followed Galecki into the living room. A tubular chrome table of 1950s vintage was taking up most of the centre space. On top of it was a Bell & Howell microfiche reader, humming the way that vintage technology tends to do. Next to the machine was a selection of microfilm reels and microfiche slides.

"It's like the internet," said Galecki. "But without all those annoying cat videos." The Galecki house cats didn't seem to mind the dig; they were too busy occupying the comfortable chairs.

Galecki started off with a well-worn box of slides, scanning through them at a frantic speed that only his librarian superpowers could understand. The same was true when he switched over to the spinning microfilm, forwarding and reversing in a fashion that Tommy found reminiscent of the procedure used to dislodge an old car from the snow. "Eureka!" said Galecki, as he landed on a black-and-white image of a white-haired man in thick black spectacles. "Say hello to Dr. Donald Ewen Cameron."

Tommy looked at the picture for a moment, not entirely sure what the grainy image signalled to Galecki, or anyone else. He figured it was his job to break the silence. "Uh, okay. And who is Dr. Donald Ewen Cameron?"

Galecki looked at him, puzzled. "You don't know about Dr. Cameron?"

Tommy shrugged. "What is he? A chiropractor or something?"

Galecki went to answer, and then paused to think about what Tommy had just said. "Well, not exactly, but I guess in a way he was, except that he wasn't adjusting your spine, he was doing the Snap-Crackle-Pop to your brain."

Tommy didn't understand a word of it. "Steve, explain it to me like I'm five."

"Very well," said Galecki. "You'd better pull up a chair." Galecki started to flip through more of the microfilm panes, stopping on a postcard of a brick institutional building, dated 1950. "Back in the fifties, they called this the Brandon Hospital for Mental Diseases, and after that the Brandon Mental Health Centre. In the beginning, it was just a good old-fashioned nuthouse, the Brandon Asylum for the Insane."

Tommy looked at the building, noticing its tightly manicured grounds and its regal stone staircase. There was something off about the place: it was as though the asylum's worst patients had been locked up in the cellar while the promotional picture was being taken. The image literally gave him the creeps.

"Cameron was the new whiz kid on the block for psychiatry in those days, when the whole idea of psychiatry was still wearing short pants." said Galecki. "He landed in Brandon around 1929, and they put him in charge of assessing every loon that came through the door. It wasn't like today; there were no 'c'mon get happy' pills to dole out. There was frontal lobotomies and electroshock therapy, and they did an awful lot of that." Galecki flipped forward a few more slides to an image of nurses in crisp uniforms, standing next to what looked like a cage attached to the top of a hospital bed. "Apparently, they loved to experiment on the schizophrenics. They'd strap them down in those cage beds and aim 200-watt heat lamps at them for hours, just to see how they'd react. Scary shit. Cameron left Brandon in '36, and he went on to do a whole pile of big-time head-shrink stuff, even went on to psych-evaluate some Nazis at the Nuremberg trials after World War Two. The biggest big-time of all was at the Allan Memorial Institute in Montreal. You ever hear of the Sleep Room?"

"The what room?" said Tommy.

"The Sleep Room," said Galecki. "It was all part of this CIA mind-control study called MKULTRA, and Cameron was the resident Dr. Frankenstein. They'd knock you out with drugs for a couple of months, and then they'd spic-and-span your brain to the point that you had to relearn how to talk, piss, and shit. They were messing with LSD, trying to build a real live Manchurian candidate. People went into the Allan to be treated for depression and walked out not even knowing their own kids."

Tommy finally nodded that he understood. He remembered seeing the remake of *The Manchurian Candidate* with Denzel Washington, at the time unaware that there was a black-and-white version before it with Frank Sinatra in the same role. Mind control, assassins, and government black-ops — *what did any of this have to do with a cheap-ass ledger?*

"What happened to Cameron?" said Tommy.

"Died in '67," said Galecki. "And even that's a little trippy. He left the Allan in '64, and right after he left, the Institute did everything they could to distance themselves from anything associated with Cameron's methods. So, in '67, he goes for a hike with his kid and keels over, dead as a doornail. Heart attack, maybe a poison CIA dart in the neck for all we know. They didn't even get around to investigating the CIA mind-control stuff until '75, which worked out really well for them, since they started incinerating the really bad stuff back in '73. A little thing called Watergate probably had something to do with that."

He was losing Tommy again, and Tommy was glad when Galecki decided on fast-forwarding to his summation. "The thing is this: weird government-funded stuff has been going on here for a long time. Cameron might have been at the Allan in the fifties and sixties, but the guy had a lot of influence and a lot of friends. Maybe, just maybe, they were still doing stuff in Brandon. Maybe they were injecting prisoners with LSD at Stony Mountain Penitentiary. Maybe the whole polio epidemic in the fifties was an experiment in germ warfare. It's all a big fat maybe, but THIS —" Galecki felt the need to stand and hold the ledger aloft to drive home his point, "*this* could be the smoking gun that everyone has been looking for."

"Everyone?" said Tommy.

"A lot of people have been messed up by governments over the last hundred-ish years," said Galecki. "Mustard gas in World War One, radium water at the corner drugstore, lead paint, red dye, cyclamates in your diet soda, and whatever else they're sticking in the food, the smartphones, and most of all, the water. That's how you can get to everybody, through the water. You've gotta drink it sometimes, you've gotta cook in it, you've gotta clean in it. Hell, we're all about sixty percent water. There's no better bullet than water."

Tommy thought about what he had seen at the federal lab, the city water department trucks, and the entries in the ledger, especially what appeared to be the water meter number of The Guiding Light. What did the meter number actually prove? There was nothing red and shiny attached to the water main, no flashing blue light with a skull-and-crossbones symbol to tip him off. Maybe the water meter number was just another way to put down an address instead of actually writing it down. It still didn't explain the pent-up interest in a working girl who murdered a low-life who probably had it coming. There was more to this ledger — a lot more than he ever could have imagined.

Miles Sawatski let the new pieces of recently acquired information settle into place as he poured his takeout coffee at the 7-Eleven near Kildonan Park. With the exception of a few Crown Victoria catnaps, Sawatski was approaching thirty hours without a proper dream. Sangster was definitely dirty, but who exactly was he working for? Whoever it was didn't drink Timmy's. *Is the Sal's coffee man also the president of the Toilet Tank Bank at The Line Up?* thought Sawatski. Sangster had obviously tracked Sawatski to the Salisbury House, and, thanks to the hard-wired GPS system, he would continue to track him in any police unit. If he drove back to the Public Safety Building,

Sangster would follow and easily assume that Sawatski had switched out the current Crown Vic for his personal car, which probably had a hidden GPS tracker on it by now. He couldn't grab another detective unit, since his badge number would appear on any police vehicle that he signed out, also appearing on the live GPS feed. He didn't know if there was a tap on his phone. He had to get to Spence to tell her the tale that no cop wants to tell their partner. Sawatski didn't care about the consequences anymore. For the first time in a long time, Sawatski felt like he was a cop again.

"Mileage, is that you?" Sawatski popped out of his trance and looked up at Jim Fletcher, better known as the Repo Man. He was pouring his coffee into an oversized mug on the opposite side of the self-serve coffee station. Fletcher was the go-to guy for vehicle repossessions in Winnipeg, having run a successful bailiff service since the early nineties. He was pushing a fit fifty, with a well-manicured salt-and-pepper moustache and goatee combination. He must have been on the job from a recent seizure as he was still wearing his high-visibility orange parka. "They still got you driving the Crown Vic? I thought they were all retired by now."

"Hey, Fletch," said Sawatski. "Yeah, I wish. I guess they've got to pay for the new station first." Sawatski looked outside at Fletcher's idling rig, a very shiny International flat deck wrecker with an equally shiny BMW 7 Series strapped to it. "Is that a new one?"

"They both are," said Fletcher. "Get this: the truck's a repo, too! Only cost me seventeen grand at the auction."

"That ride makes a lotta sense for the Repo Man." said Sawatski. "Hey, isn't your yard around here somewhere?"

"Yeah, we took over that old Dodge dealer's compound on Partridge," said Fletcher. "Locks up tight, nice high fence, keeps the neighbours happy. Hey, if you know anybody looking for cheap wheels, we've got the towing auction next week."

"Anything good?" said Sawatski. "I kinda need something." Sawatski paused and looked around the store first before he leaned in closer. "Actually, Fletch, I kinda need something right now."

Fletcher nodded in kind, mimicking the store-wide scan. "Message received and understood. Besides, you never know when I'll need backup. It's almost like a reality show some days. Aren't you up for retirement soon? I could use a quality guy."

"Yeah, quality," said Sawatski. He thought about just how little quality he had recently exhibited. "Let me get your coffee, Fletch. It's the least I can do."

Sawatski followed Fletcher the short drive to the towing compound. The lot had approximately two hundred cars lined up for the next auction. It was easy to spot the newest cars for the sale, as they weren't completely buried in snow. He had explained the GPS problem on the Crown Vic without getting into all the details as to why he had to ditch it. "Deep undercover stuff, I get it," said Fletcher as he flipped through the auction list for cars that still had active tags. "Looks like you've got your choice of classy or trashy," said Fletcher.

"Classy?" said Sawatski.

"That would be the 1996 Jaguar Vanden Plas," said Fletcher.

"And what about the trashy?"

"Oh, I can't tell you; I've got to show you." Fletcher disappeared into the shop while Sawatski waited. He hadn't even noticed the dogs in the compound, who seemed more interested in getting ear scratches from Sawatski than barking at a new stranger. Inside the shop, something roared to life with a low grumble. The overhead door started to rise. The exhaust fog was thick as the trashy wagon ventured forward. Sawatski blinked. He could vaguely remember the period of automotive customization known as vanning, though as memory served, it had lasted about as long as disco. The painted theme on the sides looked like a cross between *Star Trek* and fantasy porn, with plenty of airbrushing that never quite hit the mark of artistic merit. The exhaust left through dual side-mounted pipes, while the tires and wheels looked equally vintage, accented by Iron Cross windows in the rear and a tubular chrome grille up front. Sawatski figured it was probably a Chevy, though it was hard to tell with all the custom touches. Through the windshield, he could see Fletcher grinning like a Cheshire cat, with a string of dingle balls dancing above his head. He put the van into park, kicking down the high idle before exiting. "So whaddya think?"

Sawatski stared at the cartoon-like breasts of one of the Barbarella-esque space swashbucklers. "So, where's that Jaguar?"

"Yeah, about that. It's nice, but the big kitty doesn't like the cold." Fletcher pointed to the Vanden Plas inside the shop, its hood wide open. "I think it needs an alternator, or a starter, or maybe a boat anchor and a good stiff push down the North Main boat launch."

Sawatski quickly realized that the boogie van was his only choice. He arranged for Fletcher to follow him with the van to the District Three police station on Hartford Avenue, about three minutes away from the compound. Sawatski knew that Sangster would be watching the Crown Vic move on the GPS map. The stop at the station wouldn't have seemed suspect, as the cold weather often wreaked havoc with the in-car laptops. There were backup units at all the districts for quick changeovers. Sawatski parked the Crown Vic at the rear of the station, bringing in the laptop to the desk sergeant. He quickly swapped it for another unit and then headed over to the detectives' section. The desks were deserted except for a uniform who had ducked in to have a conversation with his girlfriend, a chat that sounded anything but PG. The uniform was surprised to see Sawatski. He quickly ended the call, nodding to Sawatski as he left.

Sawatski put the laptop on one of the desks, firing up Constable Herridge's desktop computer. He lucked out with the password, though it was probably even money that Herridge's password would be the same string of digits that most cops used for their desktops; his badge number, which was on various pieces of department correspondence. Sawatski had one thing left to check through official channels. He punched in the license plate he had seen in the Salisbury House parking lot: 729 DWN. The plate came back to a 2008 Chrysler 300-C, registered to the Department of Weights and Measures for the Province of Manitoba. Sawatski figured that it had to be a bogus tag.

Sawatski was preparing to go offline. There would be no Crown Vic to track, no laptop signature in motion, and no cell phone to ping from the transmission towers. The boogie van was clean, as far as he knew. He found a universal charger that fit his phone in an unlocked desk drawer, making sure to put all the phone alerts into bedside mode. He stuffed the phone under the desk, plugging it into a power bar that was hidden by a tangled mess of electrical cords. If anyone was currently watching him, it would appear as though Sawatski was checking on leads for Claire Hebert. Sawatski waited till the hallway to the rear was clear of any uniforms. The camera that had the view of the exit was at least twenty years old. Sawatski could have easily pulled the coaxial cable off the camera, though a dead camera was sure to get someone's attention. As helpful as cameras had been to modern policing, there had been instances where a recording could hurt a case, rather than help it. Sawatski removed a small jar of Carmex lip balm from his jacket pocket. He figured his chances were fifty-fifty that someone would be watching the hallway camera feed at that moment. He took a generous swipe of the balm and quickly spread it over the camera lens. He slipped out the back, his image obscured by the greasy smear. He headed over to the side street where Fletcher was waiting with the boogie van. "That must have been some dump you took in there," said Fletcher.

"It was a stinker," said Sawatski. "Just wait till it hits the fan."

CHAPTER FORTY-THREE

Everything was quiet at the St. John's library branch. Cindy busied herself with the newsprint of the day while Claire tried to relieve the boredom. She wandered through the stacks, wondering if any of the volumes present had a chapter on what she should do next, if there would be a next anything to indulge in. If everything did go according to plan, Claire knew that the party was over. She was fast approaching the age where her unique talents were unemployable. She hoped that she might be able to hoodwink some rich old man into a comfortable lifestyle, with trips, clothes, and a few credit cards with her new name on them. She knew that it meant she would still be

245

a whore of sorts. At least she wouldn't have to worry about carrying a razor in her boot anymore.

Claire wanted a cigarette, but she didn't feel like asking Cindy for it. She checked a librarian's desk near the front entrance. The top drawer was locked, though the lock looked old and tired. A look under the desk blotter revealed a dull letter opener. With a little leverage, the drawer slid open and a pack of Peter Jacksons presented itself, with a lighter stuffed where three cigarettes had previously been. She gave little thought to the No Smoking signs as she lit the cigarette. A half-full cup of cold coffee became the ashtray. The desk had pictures of its occupant, a heavy-set woman with mousy grey hair, with at least two cats accompanying her in each picture. The cup must have been part of a birthday bouquet. Claire pondered the quotation on the cup. "It's nifty to be fifty," she said as she exhaled.

"Yeah, like you'll ever find out." Cindy was leaning up against one of the stacks near the desk. "Toss me a dart."

Claire was getting too tired to be annoyed anymore. She threw the pack wide and feeble, but Cindy was quick on the draw. One of their stomachs grumbled. "Let's see if the cat lady has any kibble," said Claire-Bear. The bottom drawer revealed a meagre picnic: a six-pack of generic diet cola and a package of equally generic crème-filled cookies. The pair ate, drank, and smoked.

Cindy finally broke the silence between them. "So, you sliced up that Stephanos pretty good."

"Well, it's not like I had any experience," said Claire-Bear. "Not like you."

Cindy smirked. "Yeah, the Kildonan Park Incident. I thought they'd lock me up and throw away the key for killing that piece of wife-murdering shit. Next thing you know, I'm getting interviewed by that Cloutier dude on CJOB, getting free shit all over town. The Triumph dealer even fixed my bike for free!" Cindy took a reflective drag, exhaling just as long. "Yeah, they all said I was a hero, but I sure as hell didn't feel like one. But I'd damn well do it again. It's the only solution for some of these assholes."

"Amen to that," said Claire. She paused, realizing what she had just said. "So are you, like, 'born again' like Bosco?"

"Tommy's not born again," said Cindy. "He's just trying to be as little of an asshole as possible."

"I remember when I had a little asshole," said Claire. "That was a long time ago."

"Surgery is probably your only option there," said Cindy. "As for personality, you're still a little bit of an asshole. Actually, more like a —"

"A cunt?"

"Your words, not mine. But yeah, you're a little on the cunty side. You might want to work on that."

Claire stood up, looking at some of the books on the stacks, and wandered into the religion section. She pulled down a weathered King James edition. "Is there really an answer in all this prehistoric shit?"

"Yes and no," said Cindy. "It's basically the world's oldest self-help book, and like any self-help book, it has some of the answers. The rest you gotta fill in for yourself."

Claire flipped through the thin pages, hoping that the answer would somehow spring forth from the page and allay her fears. She closed the book shut and looked at Cindy. "Well, I think I'll just work on being less cunty for a while." The two women almost managed an in-unison smile then, which came to an abrupt halt as the side door opened. "It's just me," said Tommy. "Don't start throwing *National Geographics* at me."

The two women came around the corner carefully. Tommy was already doling out the bounty from the A&W bags; Mama Burgers, Teen Burgers, and a few orders of onion rings. As they devoured the contents, Tommy relayed the conspiracy theories that Galecki had told him, which had continued during the ride back to the library. "Steve says that they even sprayed chemical stuff into the air around the city in the 1950s. Cadmium-something, I think."

"Is that stuff bad for you?" said Claire.

"Well, it doesn't exactly sound good," said Tommy, in between bites of his Teen Burger. He picked up the ledger, which had now earned a few blotches of onion-ring grease. "Maybe what they're doing now is even worse."

"But how can they get away with it?" said Cindy. "You can't steal a grape at the grocery store without someone taking a video of it and putting it on fucking YouTube."

Claire rustled in the bags for condiments, which seemed to have been forgotten by the night shift staff. "As interesting as all this shit is, it doesn't change the fact that the cops want me in jail, and the HRs want me dead."

Tommy pondered the dilemma as the discussion went on between Cindy and Claire-Bear. If they were going to make a move, the best time to avoid the police would be around 5:45 a.m. With a shift change at six a.m., the patrol units coming off duty would be making a beeline for their respective stations, hoping that no emergency calls would be going out. Freddie the Ford was just as wanted as they were, so they would have to move fast. The first thing to go would be the license plates to confuse the intersection cameras. They could take the trucking routes that left the city, which were far less travelled by regular traffic. Tommy knew that all it would take to end the run would be one cop or one of the thugs gunning for Claire, which included Papa Friday. The chances continued to be slim to none. "What we need is a fucking miracle!"

As if on cue, the phone at the St. John's library started to ring. The three fugitives looked at the desk phone together as it warbled. After the eighth ring, Tommy figured that it must have been someone who knew the additional extension numbers within the library and knew which phones weren't equipped with the voicemail greeting of the main line. Tommy reached carefully for the handset that predated call display. He looked at Cindy and Claire for some form of confirmation that his next move would be to answer. They nodded. Tommy swiftly picked up the handset. "Thank you for calling Gondola Pizza, would you like to hear about our specials?"

There was a chuckle on the end of the line. "You don't have greasy Gondola down there, you've got A&W. I should know, I bought it for you."

Tommy breathed; it was Galecki. "Way to scare the shit out of us, Steve. What's up?"

"I think you better fire up the computer and look at the *Sentinel* website. That Downtown 24/7 dude just threw a wrench into the works. Gwen noticed it on her laptop while I was dropping you off. Use the one at the counter; I'll call you back in five." The call disconnected. Tommy motioned to Cindy. "Check the *Sentinel* website. Apparently, we're on it."

Cindy fired up the sleeping work station. As promised, the Downtown 24/7 story was posted as breaking news. The three fugitives took turns scanning the meat of the story. The headline read: "HR killer on the run, may have underworld ledger."

"Oh, shit fuck," said Tommy.

"That fucking idiot," said Cindy.

"What does it mean?" said Claire.

"It means we've got to get out of here, now," said Tommy. "It's one thing for the cops to have a hard-on for you for the Stephanos slice, but now they've got a chance to fuck up the HRs in the process. Basically, now you're wanted with a side of fries."

"But we don't even know if this book has anything to do with the HRs!" said Claire.

"Doesn't matter," said Cindy. "If the cops think it's something, it's something until they figure out it's nothing. Tommy's right — we gotta move."

The phone started to ring. Tommy answered hard on the first ring. "Steve, I gotta switch cars with you, Freddie is too hot, the cops are gonna be all over it. And Steve —"

Tommy stopped talking. The line was silent, though it was anything but dead. It wasn't Galecki on the phone; it was someone else, someone who had the smarts to know that certain things were worth watching, things like phone traffic on lines that shouldn't have any traffic, alarms that hadn't been activated, and internet activity on supposedly sleeping computers. Tommy had fallen into a basic technology trap. He ripped the handset off the desk, smashing it to bits in front of Cindy and Claire. "We're not going anywhere; they know we're here."

Nathaniel disconnected his call to the St. John's branch of the Winnipeg Public Library. He flipped a coin deciding who to send in: heads, Ernie Friday, tails, the Two Pauls. He knew that Sangster would be busy tracking Sawatski's movements, even though he could see that Sawatski's Crown Vic was still at the District Three station. Whether he chose heads or tails, his pick would be within ten minutes of the library. He removed his hand from the coin on the top of his hand. He sent the message to the winner of the toss.

Nathaniel confirmed that the clip on his Glock was full, and then attached his Osprey 45K silencer to the barrel. He then plugged in the address on the Chrysler's navigation screen for the other end of the St. John's Library call, a Stephen J. Galecki. He tapped Go on the screen and put the Chrysler into drive.

Tommy, Cindy, and Claire-Bear were looking for anything that resembled a weapon. The library had three expired fire extinguishers stored in the basement, an old wooden step-ladder, and an oversized push broom. There was also a pair of rechargeable drills plugged into their charging stations. "Grab those drills and see if there are any screws," said Tommy as he hoisted the ladder up on his left shoulder. "If someone's coming, they're going to be here real soon."

Tommy had an idea: use anything and everything he could find to slow down access to the library. He tripped on one of the brackets that had been attached to the side of one of the book stacks on the way into the main level. He scanned the selection of furniture. It was mostly plastic chairs, institutional tables, and a few study carrels. The carrels were firmly attached to each other and had probably started life with the original construction of the library, their flat-headed screws covered with decades of protective lacquer. He tripped on another of the reinforcement brackets for the book stacks as he checked the office for anything that could help. Two vintage tanker desks took up the small space, loaded down with enough files in their locked drawers that they wouldn't budge from their positions. As Tommy exited the office, he tripped on yet another support bracket, falling next to one of the stacks. He looked at the bracket that was next to his head, which had been screwed to the sides of the stack with Robertson screws. "Hey, Cindy, you got those drills?"

"Yeah, I got 'em."

"What kind of screwdriver do they have in them?"

"Looks like the square one."

Tommy got up from the ground, greeted by Cindy with the two drills. "Are they charged up?" said Tommy.

Cindy first answered with the drills, pressing their power switches for a confirmation whirl of their respective drill chucks. "Ready to spin," said Cindy. "What are we screwing?"

"Hopefully each other later," said Tommy. "For now, it's all these brackets." There were six oak book stacks in the main library area, each stack about eighteen feet in length. Tommy and Cindy busied themselves removing the screws that held the vertical sides of the stacks. Claire wasn't sure what to make of the recent activity, though she had finally reached the point of wanting to be useful. "What can I do to help?"

"Start grabbing books from the second-lowest shelf," said

Tommy. "Grab the ladder and start stacking them on the top shelves as fast as you can."

Claire took to the task with a speed and agility that neither Tommy nor Cindy had thought existed within her. The book stacks that had been removed of their anchor screws were starting to sway slightly as Claire-Bear continued to pile the various volumes on the highest shelves.

The plan was to use the unstable stacks to pin their attacker, or attackers. Tommy would position the ladder at the rear stack, next to the wall. When the attacker or attackers arrived, Tommy would send the stacks crashing forward, putting his legs against the wall and giving the stacks the best shove he could muster. The problem was how to draw the attacker, or attackers, into the stacks and keep them in such a position that escape would be highly unlikely. If the attacker(s) heard any commotion at the back of the stacks, they would make a beeline for the noise. The challenge was to lure them mid-stack and keep them there. Tommy was trying to figure out how when he tripped on one of the books that Claire had removed from the second-lowest shelf. He bent down to pick it up and smiled.

"Hey, Cindy, you feel a little slippery?"

"Well, it would be nice if you took me to dinner first."

"I mean slippery in tight places."

"Like I said, dinner is a good place to start." Cindy had figured that Tommy meant something else by now and was heading over to his position when they all heard the sound. It wasn't the boiler, the clank of the steam radiators, or the buzz of the fluorescent tubes overhead. It was the sound of someone trying the latch on the front door of the St. John's Library.

Claire almost lost her footing on the ladder when she heard it. She kept it steady as she looked at Tommy for direction. He motioned her down the steps and then pointed to the ladder, adding a new pantomime to indicate its new location at the back of the stacks. Claire moved the ladder as quietly as possible, then hid in the office, as per Tommy's wordless direction. Tommy explained his next wordless plan the best he could to Cindy, who had now become the decoy. Cindy nodded that she understood, without looking thrilled about it. She was crouched down in the middle aisle of the stacks when she thought of something. As Tommy watched, he wanted to cry out to make her stop. It only took ten steps from start to finish, but it was a huge gamble. Cindy grabbed the ledger off the front counter. As she returned to her position, the front door flew off its hinges with a deafening crash.

Like most explosions, this one came with the expected haze, as well as various bits of rubble and splinters. The smoke that moved inward from the event burned Cindy's lungs. She remembered a similar burning sensation, when her car had slid into the back of a city bus two winters ago. The plume from the exploding airbag tasted exactly the same.

Outside the library, the Two Pauls were disconnecting the twelve-volt car battery from what was left of their improvised airbag-firing wiring harness. The trio inside did hear their attempts to unlatch the door by hand, but they had missed the additional soundtrack stylings of Paul Bouchard, who had knelt down to slice off the rubber weatherstripping on the bottom of the front door with a box cutter. With the gap exposed, Bouchard slid two airbag membranes under the door, a sound which may have been mistaken inside for the shuffling about on the other side of the door. The pair stood to the side of the front door, shielded by its identical heavy oak twin. The blast from the air bags pushed the door upwards with violent force, snapping it in half at its mid-section. Bouchard and Lemay stepped inside, each fanning the air with one hand and holding their recently acquired firearms in the other.

"Okay, story time's over," said Bouchard. "Give us the bitch and the book, and maybe we'll leave you breathing." It was a hollow promise from the Two Pauls; Bouchard and Lemay would have to kill everyone inside to ensure their continued anonymity.

As the assassins started up the staircase, Cindy stepped out from behind the cover of the book stack. She held the ledger aloft. "Hey, assholes! Looking for this?" She immediately darted back into the stack as the first volley of shots was fired. Tommy had figured that shots would come, making sure to stack plenty of thick, heavy books in the line of fire. The literature did its job for the most part. Puffs of exploding paper followed Cindy as she ran. She wriggled through the space on the second shelf that had previously been populated by books, as the Two Pauls entered the stack. They had expected to see her running at the midway point of the skinny aisle and already had their guns aimed to fire at a target that simply wasn't there. They walked forward slowly, looking all around for another position that had given her safe haven.

"Hey, assholes! Over here!"

The Two Pauls turned quickly, looking through a space on the fourth shelf where the books had been removed. Cindy was smiling and waving at them, then disappeared as quickly as she had appeared. The Two Pauls stuck their guns through the shelf access, firing at the general position of their antagonist. Bindings and pages continued to explode around Cindy as she readied her last line of defence. As the Two Pauls moved towards the centre of the stack, they were hit by a volley of books at eye level, as though they had been lobbed at them with spectral hands. They looked through the stacks at Cindy, who was standing in the book stack aisle that was bordered by the wall of the library. She had pushed the books onto the Two Pauls with an oversized push broom, with a handle that was long enough to cover the width of an additional book stack. Cindy smiled at them, knowing what was coming.

"Book 'em, Bosco!"

Tommy Bosco had readied himself when Cindy had entered the last aisle through her second-row wriggle. With the cheesy tag line uttered, Tommy moved his legs off the ladder and onto the wall, pushing with full force onto the book stack. The stacks fell forward onto the Two Pauls as Tommy held the stack he had just pushed for the ride to its final resting place. Like the exploding door, there was plenty of dust that presented itself from the collapsing stacks, which seemed to be as noxious as the exploding airbags.

Tommy peered through the opening in the stacks to see if there was anything to report on the condition of the would-be assassins. The domino effect had appeared to dispatch Paul Bouchard instantly, his eyes in a wide-open death stare, with a portion of the shelves lodged in an area best used for his former windpipe. Paul Lemay was equally crushed, though he had yet to make his final exit. His injuries appeared to be in his chest, most likely the spears of broken ribs that had penetrated his organs and major arteries. As he bled out internally, Tommy noticed that Lemay still had his gun in his right hand. Lemay looked at Tommy with bugged-out eyes, wheezing as he tried to will the revolver into firing position. The revolver fell out of his hand instead as he wheezed once, twice, three times. Then he was quiet.

Cindy and Claire tried to look through what was left under the fallen stacks, satisfied that no one would be wriggling out to cause them any more trouble. Claire looked up at

Tommy as he started to move himself off the debris. "Aren't you supposed to say something, like, you know, Goddish?"

"Sure thing," said Tommy. He stopped and casually clasped his hands together. "Dear Lord, thank God these guys are dead. Amen."

"Amen," said Cindy.

Claire didn't know what to make of it all, though she figured it was better to be safe than sorry. "Uh, yeah. Amen, man."

If the trio was expecting a Hallelujah from on high, it didn't come. What did come was the sound of a vibration. Tommy listened, and then realized that it was coming from the pocket of one of the assassins. He reached down between the shelves and tore open the Velcro pocket flap on Paul Bouchard's jacket, pulling out a well-used Samsung Rugby flip phone. The phone was new enough that it registered the incoming calls on an exterior LCD. The caller was simply Unknown. *Why not*, Tommy thought. He flipped open the phone to chat. "St. John's Library, home of the Fugitive Brigade, how may I direct your call?"

There was silence at the other end for about five seconds, much like the silence that Tommy had previously heard on the library's landline. Then the voice spoke. "Good evening, Pastor Bosco. Would you happen to be in the company of the two men I sent to collect you, your lover, and Miss Claire Hebert?"

Tommy bent down and looked at the two fresh corpses before he answered. "Well, they're a little indisposed for the rest of eternity right now. Good effort though, a really good effort. But we've got to get back to the matter at hand, Johnny Unknown. I'm guessing that you've probably got a few more fuckers out there gunning for us, one of them a close family relation, but we've still got this book that everyone seems really concerned about. I wonder . . ."

"What exactly do you wonder, Mr. Bosco?"

"I wonder how much this little book may be worth to you and the rest of your people."

"And why, Mr. Bosco, would there be other people involved in this affair?"

Tommy had to think about that for a moment. "Well, I suppose the easiest way to put this is that this much asshole factor couldn't possibly come from one guy; there has to be at least a committee or something, wouldn't you agree?"

Nathaniel stretched his legs in his Chrysler as he idled on Alfred Avenue. The flames were just starting to be visible in the windows of Steve Galecki's former home as Nathaniel removed the silencer from his Glock. "You are correct, Pastor Bosco, so I would highly advise that your next course of action reflects that. I want that ledger, you want Miss Hebert out of harm's way, and you want little to no consequence to befall you and Miss Smyth, correct?"

"Yeah, that would be about the size of it. So you'll play ball?"

"Oh, don't worry, Mr. Bosco. The department always plays fair."

"Awesome sauce," said Bosco. "Tell your posse to stand down. We're going to go get some coffee. Give us a call by three a.m., or we go to the media. They're better than the cops."

Nathaniel disconnected the call. He looked over at the smoke starting to rise. He keyed through the contacts on his screen until he found Chancellor. The call was answered on the second ring.

"Nathaniel, it's either very good news or very bad news at this hour. Which one is it?"

"We're almost done here, Mr. Chancellor," said Nathaniel. "What I need to do is arrange a tour." Nathaniel waited a few seconds for a response, listening to the predictable cadence of the Emerson respirator. There was a long sigh before Chancellor spoke.

"Nathaniel, for the life of me I can't understand why we must put ourselves in peril for such an exercise. This isn't bad television; this is very serious business. Simply get the book and kill them all. I'm not in the mood for company."

"I realize that, Mr. Chancellor, and killed they will be. This is simply a ruse. I have spoken to the good Pastor. He is under the impression that we are willing to negotiate for the safe return of the ledger. It is a good impression for him to be under. Yes, it will involve some theatrics on our part, but the end result will be the same. They cannot reveal what they'll never be able to tell. With containment, on-site, we can ensure success."

The Emerson respirator continued to breathe for its occupant. It seemed like an eternity until Chancellor spoke. "Alright, Nathaniel, bring them to me. Meet me in the main hall. I'll advise Mr. Finch of the plan, and insist that he attend. He needs to see the lengths that we go to for the greater good."

"Understood, sir. Will advise when I am at the location." Nathaniel ended the call without any further pleasantries. He put the Chrysler into drive and pulled away from the burning home of the late Steve Galecki, Gwen Addams, and at least four cats all named Cat. Galecki never saw the point in naming something that wouldn't come when you called it.

Miles Sawatski had used almost five dollars in change to get his partner's attention. He pitched a combination of loonies and quarters at the rear windows of Gayle Spence's house for at least five minutes until she noticed. He saw her gun in the window first. She was obviously sleeping, probably on the couch, which is where most hard-working cops end up for the night, when he started to pelt the glass with cash. She poked her head out the back door. "Mileage, what fucking time is it?"

"Time for pants," said Sawatski, pointing to the granny panties below her flannel top. "And this just in: I'm going off the reservation."

"Hey, that's my line!" said Spence, still rubbing the sleep from her eyes. "Fuck. Give me five minutes."

Sawatski was pleased that Spence was more or less in on his plan, a plan that was still very loose. She demanded coffee in its largest form, and Sawatski obliged, driving to the 7-Eleven on McPhillips at Mountain. He even sprang for the massive refillable take-out cup that resembled a carafe and the midnight edition of the *Winnipeg Sentinel*, which was free with any size coffee purchase. He told her about the Toilet Tank Bank at The Line Up and how the whole Claire Hebert case had been tainted by the anonymous requests from the get-go. He told her about Sangster and the need to run silent while he figured out what to do next.

Spence sipped her coffee and listened, occasionally picking at the button-tufted crushed velvet pieces of the boogie van interior. She attempted to make some sense of the whole situation. "So basically, there's Stephanos's murder, which is probably self-defence for Hebert. That's the easy part. Then there's this briefcase thing and whatever Pandora's Box is waiting inside. Sangster just might be a professional hitter-for-hire, which makes whatever you did pretty small potatoes, we hope. Let's face it: the best-case scenario right now is that you get fired. Just fired."

"I know," said Sawatski. "I'm cool with all of that, but there are way too many bodies piling up here. We've gotta shut this whole thing down, and right quick."

Spence agreed. "What we need is all the help we can get, and it may not be from people you like, like, uh . . ." Spence felt the need to scan the parking lot at that moment. David "Downtown" Worschuk just happened to be parked three spaces to the right of Spence, in the process of inhaling another clipboard coke bump in the *Sentinel* Cavalier, unaware that the boogie van next to him had just been deputized. "Now, there's an asshole we can use." She pulled her badge from her pocket. Sawatski went to unlatch his door. Spence stopped him. "Take a break, Mileage," said Spence. "This one's on me."

Worschuk was in the process of reading his latest efforts on the Claire Hebert case on his phone when he was startled by the sound of metal tapping the side door window. He still had the rolled-up bill of cocaine-dusted Canadian Tire money in his nose when he looked up at the person holding the detective shield. "You got a doctor's note for that NeoCitran powder, Clowntown?" said Spence. "I'm guessing the answer is no, so let's step out of the car."

Worschuk complied with Spence's orders, though he already had a story to tell as he rose from the driver's seat. "Hey, it's not what it looks like," said Worschuk. "I'm working this story on the increase in recreational cocaine use, so I wanted to make sure I had a good understanding of the effects of the —"

"Save it, Worschuk," said Spence. "You're not getting busted, you're getting your big scoop." She led him over to the van and opened the sliding door. Sawatski had already moved to the common area of the boogie van, seated on a low lounge chair of red crushed velvet. He had found an RV-style table for the steel base that protruded from the middle of the shag-carpeted floor. "Have a seat, Clowntown," said Sawatski. "It looks like we're going to be working together."

The sight of Sawatski immediately killed Worschuk's coke buzz. He slid onto the half bed at the back of the van, and Spence discovered that her passenger seat swivelled. Sawatski and Worschuk were still looking at each other as though each was a different strain of dog shit stuck to their respective shoes. Spence checked the miniature fridge on the floor behind the driver's seat, finding a six-pack of Coors that didn't appear to be of the vintage of the boogie van. "Let's all have a drink and talk this thing through," said Spence, placing the six-pack on the miniature table. "We've got stuff, you've got stuff, and it's going to be a big story."

Worschuk crossed his arms like an upset tween. "Not until your partner calls me Downtown."

"Oh, for fuck sakes," said Sawatski. He took a hit of a tepid Coors to temper his resolve. "Okay, *Downtown*, we know you found out about the ledger. We know about it too, not that anyone has any idea what it's for. We know there's a hit in place for Hebert. We know that Bosco and his girlfriend are in on it somehow, at least aiding and abetting. They're running, they're scared, and it's only a matter of time until we catch them or a hired goon sprays their brains all over a wall. So, enlighten me, Downtown Twenty-Four-Fucking-Seven, what the hell is it that you know that we don't?"

Worschuk smiled at Sawatski, leaned over, and picked up a can of Coors. He opened it carefully, half-expecting that one of the detectives in front of him had shaken up the beer before placing it on the table. He took a long chug from the can, wiped his arm with his sleeve, and gave a mighty sigh of approval. "That's a lot, Sawatski. I guess the only thing you don't know about is the magician."

Spence leaned in. "What magician?"

"A magician," said Worschuk. "A real, live Doug Fucking Henning, except this one doesn't make rabbits disappear, he makes people go poof."

"People?" said Sawatski. "What kind of people?"

"Bad people," said Worschuk. "People you're looking for or the other guys are looking for. More than a dozen of them last year alone, right under your nose. You know them better

264

as the ones at Brady Road." Worschuk leaned in for effect. "Did you know they never found a body or even a piece of a body in there?"

Sawatski listened closely to Worschuk's tale. There was an element of truth to what he was saying. Brady Road had been treated as the scene of a homicide investigation before, though the last few years had been particularly busy. Sawatski had even bought a new pair of rubber boots that weren't as slippery as his old ones after falling twice in the slick garbage. They did find personal effects, clothes, even a few pieces of dental work, but not a single chunk of meat. Then it hit him: "Bosco's the magician!"

"Yeah, that Guiding Light guy!" said Worschuk. "That Christmas light fake fire thing was fucking genius!"

"Yeah, well, he's in the wind," said Spence. "How the fuck are we going to find him?"

As the three discussed their dilemma in the back of the van, the arrival of a certain light-blue Ford F-150 was a well-kept secret.

CHAPTER FORTY-SIX

Tommy Bosco took a moment to admire the breasts of the boogie van's space warriors as he opened Freddie's driver's side door in the 7-Eleven parking lot. Cindy and Claire exited through the passenger side. Freddie was now wearing a new set of plates, thanks to the Two Pauls and the remaining battery power in the library drills. The former assassins had parked their Ford Ranger in the small parking lot behind the library, shielding it from view, and the key to the Ranger was somewhere beneath the debris of the library-book stacks, in the pocket of either Lemay or Bouchard.

Freddie now wore CEA 477; it was a commercial truck plate assigned to one of Bouchard's wrecking yard employers. Tommy didn't need any tools to remove the magnetic company signs that were stowed behind the Ranger's bench seat, which was why Freddie the Ford now appeared to be in the gainful employ of an outfit called Home Team Auto Parts. No one had appeared to have heard the various commotions at the library, or had cared to investigate. The screws that Cindy and Tommy had removed from the stack brackets came in handy, as did the debris of the fallen stacks. The shelves on many of the stacks had broken free, looking very much like the vintage of the wood used on the former front door of the St. John's Library. Four shelf lengths covered the door opening easily. From the street at night, it still looked as though the door was in place. The lengths were fastened to the remains of the door frame with the bracket screws, with just enough battery power left in the second drill to drive the last screw into place. Tommy checked the institutional clock that still hung over the library's front door: 2:20 a.m. It was definitely time for a coffee.

The ride from the library to the 7-Eleven had taken a little more than five minutes. Cindy and Claire had moved into more natural seating positions within Freddie's cab. They had yet to see any marked police cruisers or hired hitters on their tail. Tommy figured the voice was a man of his word, though he knew this was a temporary reprieve at best. He still held out hope that he could get Claire out of the city, without the Brady Road addendum. As for him and Cindy, Tommy was wondering if they would also need to hop on the back of a blacked-out snowmobile, driven by a crazy Swedish-American wearing Russian army surplus night goggles. The night was still young.

The 7-Eleven door warbled its over-the-top chime warning as the three entered the store, quickly followed by the stock "Hello!" from behind the counter. Tommy took a glance at the newspaper stacks at the front of the store. There weren't any mugshots of the trio on the front page of the local papers, though he figured that the *Winnipeg Sun* would come up with their usual oversized representation of the wanted fugitives with their morning edition. A potential headline popped into Tommy's head: KILLER'S LITTLE HELPERS.

The two staffers of the 7-Eleven were busy making notations in their inventory logs, paying little attention to the new patrons as they spoke in a language that Tommy couldn't understand. Tommy quickly poured three coffees, opting for double-double fuel without asking Cindy and Claire their preference. A digital clock over the front door signalled the time as 2:35 a.m., twenty-five minutes away from the expected call from whoever was pulling the strings. He checked the battery of the phone that had once belonged to one of his intended assassins — three bars left.

Inside the boogie van, things were starting to calm down. "The only way we're going to find out what's really going on is to find Hebert and her low-rent Bonnie and Clyde before the rank and file does," said Spence. "If Sangster is in on it, he might be planning on an accident to hush the whole thing up."

"And I get the exclusive, right?" Worschuk appeared to be running on genuine adrenaline now, though it could have been the remnants of the coke.

"Yes, Dave, you get your scoop," said Sawatski. "But how are we going to find these guys?"

Worschuk looked straight ahead out the windshield. "I think I just did!"

Sawatski and Spence positioned themselves for the same view as Worschuk's. Tommy Bosco, Cindy Smyth, and Miss

Claire Hebert were in the process of paying for their purchases. The staff at the 7-Eleven had yet to take a break from the last-call bar patrons, a time of night when no one seemed to care how old the rolling hot dogs under the heat lamp were.

"Holy shit!" said Spence. "The whole gang's in there!"

Worschuk immediately went to take a picture, though Sawatski quickly nixed the idea with his hand on Worschuk's throat. "Don't be fucking stupid," said Sawatski. "If you spook them and they run, I'll put you in Brady myself."

"How do you want to do this?" said Spence. She had already drawn her service Glock.

"Put it away," said Sawatski. "Bosco knows who I am. I'm just going to have a little talk with him first. They don't know who's gunning for them yet, so any gun is a bad gun, even if it's a good guy." Sawatski took out his service Glock, putting it on the crushed velvet engine doghouse of the boogie van. Spence could see that he still had his backup piece on his ankle holster, a Kahr P380, which she knew he would hang on to, just in case. Sawatski opened the driver's door of the boogie van, making sure to adjust his pant leg over the small automatic. He headed for the front door of the 7-Eleven. He would have been the first through the door, but an older gentleman with jet black hair had beat him to it, leaving his rusty Pontiac Parisienne idling in the parking lot next to the light-blue F-150. *Not a great idea in the North End*, thought Sawatski. *That's how a car becomes public transportation.*

Ernie Friday had been doing the dull hitman work for the past two hours, criss-crossing the grids of streets and back lanes that were south of Mountain Avenue. He knew Freddie the Ford better than anyone, and a couple of magnetic business

signs on the doors would do little to hoodwink him. Ernie
had passed by Tommy and his former truck on Salter Street,
shortly after the escape from the St. John's Library. Friday
had toggled off the rear brake and running lights of the
Parisienne, allowing him to turn around and follow Tommy
at a safe distance. He made a detour south on Radford Street,
then a quick blast west on College Avenue to McPhillips.
The curb lane was clear, which allowed Ernie to observe
Tommy, Cindy, and Claire-Bear inside the 7-Eleven as he set
up his camera-jamming array. There were no cops around,
just some sort of get-together going on in an old boogie van
with a big fat red-haired guy and some short-haired native
girl. Ernie was tired, so tired that he hadn't felt the buzz of his
pager, alerting him to stand down from the task at hand He
wanted to get this done and over with.

Sawatski pulled the door handle, which wasn't the only thing
getting pulled at that moment. The black-haired man pulled
an older Beretta from his right pocket, raising it up to Claire
Hebert's chest. Instinct took over; Sawatski kicked the old
man hard in the back of his right knee, causing him to fall
to the right and point the Beretta upwards at a forty-five-
degree angle, which ensured that no one at the counter
would be hit by the stray bullet that immediately left the
chamber. The older man's mass took out the end cap potato
chip display with ease, adding a fresh gushing cut to his forehead. His Beretta had slid across the floor to another woman,
who picked it up without a moment's hesitation, firing two
warning shots into the ceiling. *That must be Tommy's girlfriend.*
Hebert had dropped to the floor, using Tommy Bosco's legs

as a shield. Bosco was still trying to pay for the coffees, though it was rather difficult as the 7-Eleven employees had run out the back door when the gun went off. Sawatski couldn't understand their language, but he understood the universal reaction to flee, especially when it was a minimum-wage job.

Sawatski had reached his P380 by now and had it levelled at the woman's chest. "Winnipeg Police!" he yelled. He was going to tell her to kick the gun over to him, but he was still restraining the older man, who would probably have appreciated the return of his hardware. "Throw the weapon towards the back of the store, get down on your knees, and interlace your fingers behind your head. Do it now!"

"You BETTER be a fucking cop!" said the woman, sending the Beretta sailing towards the Wonder Bread.

Spence was crouched outside the store, waiting for a signal from Sawatski. She came in when the Beretta went flying, retrieving it before assuming a watchful eye at the rear of the store. "Everybody, calm the fuck down," said Spence.

"What's the matter, Friday," said Tommy, his finger hovering over which bags of peanuts he wanted at the display. "Getting a little slow in your old age?"

Ernie Friday was sitting against the crushed stack of chips, holding a wad of pocket-found paper towel to the cut on his forehead. "At least I've made it to old age," said Ernie. "The way you're rolling, you'll be dead before sun-up."

Tommy threw two five-dollar bills on the counter for the coffees and the nuts. "C'mon, Friday, what are you getting for this anyway? A couple of gees?"

"Double rate," said Ernie, wincing at the pain. "Oh, and I'll need that book she came with, too."

"What? Her little black book?"

Ernie glared at Tommy, the kind of glare that any father would give to an insolent son. "You always were a smartass, just like your mother."

"Well, Mom was smart enough to get killed by that drunk driver," said Tommy. He smiled as he bent down to look at Ernie without fear. "Sure beats living with a piece of shit like you."

Sawatski watched as Ernie leaned in close. "I'm gonna wipe that smirk right off your face, *Pastor . . .*"

Tommy leaned in closer. "I'd like to see you fucking try, *Father . . .*"

Sawatski had had enough. "Okay, save this family reunion shit for Dr. Phil. Let's start with you, Bosco. You're up on harbouring, aiding and abetting, probably a fake arson, if there is such a thing, and I'm willing to bet you've got a tail light out on that Ford POS out there." He turned to Cindy. "Miss Cindy Smyth. You've got all that, plus the firearms charge you helped yourself to just now." Sawatski turned to look at Claire. "And as much as I'd like to pin a medal on anybody who whacks a Heaven's Reject, I've got at least manslaughter pending for you, little missy." Sawatski looked down at Ernie Friday. "And last, but certainly not least, Grampa Fonzie here gets attempted murder. And —"

Sawatski looked up to see Worschuk filming the rundown of the charges on his backup cell phone. He hung his head and shook it. "Downtown, turn that thing off before I stick it up your fat ass!"

Worschuk kept filming. "But you said I'd get the scoop on this!"

Sawatski grabbed the phone from Worschuk and tossed it into the deep fryer behind the counter. "You get the scoop, dummy, not the goddamn play-by-play." Sawatski rubbed his eyes. "Is there anything else that anyone here wants to tell me?"

"You may want to send a car over to the St. John's Library," said Tommy. "I think a couple of guys might have had an unfortunate reading accident."

Ernie laughed at the statement; he knew it was the Two Pauls. His laugh turned into a cough, a nasty one. Tommy looked down at him in time to see the blood hit a clean section of the paper towel. He wasn't sure if he felt anything about it. Ernie was as good as done for the attempted murder on Claire Hebert in the 7-Eleven. The jammed cameras wouldn't be much of a defence against two cops. Still, there was a twinge of something deep behind the closed doors of their relationship. Tommy wondered if whatever it was had any chance of being found at all. Someone had to try. Tommy extended his hand to his father. "C'mon, Friday, let's get your ass out of all that melted snow."

Ernie looked up at his estranged son, then his watch. "As long as I'm home by seven," said Ernie. "Someone has to feed Chico."

"Who's Chico?" said Worschuk, having switched to his notebook.

"That's his cat," said Tommy as he hoisted Ernie up. "She'll purr you to death." Tommy checked the time on the wall: 2:58 a.m. "Hey, cop," he said, looking at Sawatski. "I'm expecting a call in a couple of minutes."

"A call?" said Sawatski. "And who the fuck is calling you at three in the morning?"

Tommy smiled. "I guess the best way to put this is it's the guy, the guy who gave my old man the job, plus those two dead guys at the library, which was totally self-defence, plus whoever else is in on this bullshit."

"And what the hell does he want?"

"A deal," said Tommy. "An old-fashioned Winnipeg deal."

CHAPTER FORTY-SEVEN

When the clock struck three a.m., Tommy's recently acquired cell phone started to ring. After the third ring, Sawatski nodded at Tommy to answer. Tommy hit the speakerphone button. "Good evening, Mister X, right on time, as promised."

"Punctuality is one of life's many virtues," said the voice. "I trust that you will extend me the same courtesy for our meeting this morning."

Tommy went to talk and then stopped just before he formed the next words. Sawatski had a strange look on his face, a look that seemed to speak of recognition of the caller.

"Mr. Bosco, are you still there?"

Tommy picked up where he'd left off. "Sorry, Mister X, you broke up a little there. Give me the details."

"Very well, Mr. Bosco. It is now 3:01 a.m., Central Standard Time. At four a.m., I expect you and your party to arrive at the Riverview Health Centre service entrance, at the rear of the complex. I trust that you are aware of the location."

"At the end of Morley," said Tommy. "That's towards the river, right?"

"That is correct, Mr. Bosco. I expect to see you with Ms. Hebert and Ms. Smyth, as well as the ledger."

Tommy figured that he had to ask the "what if" question. "What if I decide to take the girls and the book and get the fuck out of Dodge?"

There was a slight pause before the voice spoke. "Mr. Bosco, considering your proximity to Mr. Galecki, I suggest you check on his well-being for the answer to that question. I look forward to seeing you soon." The line went dead.

Tommy paused for a moment, realizing what the voice had just told him. Galecki's minimal assists had signed his death warrant. He looked at Sawatski. "Okay, cop. What's the deal? How do you know this guy?"

Sawatski knew he had to come clean to this impromptu task force. He turned to Worschuk. "Listen up, Downtown, everything I say now is off the record. Don't tweet it, don't Facebook it, don't say a fucking word about it. I've got a feeling it pales in comparison to what's about to go do down."

"Lucky for you, my phone is extra crispy," said Worschuk, as he wrote down his notes. "It's a good thing my pen still works."

Spence stepped in with the baggie of coke that she had retrieved from Worschuk's front seat. "I'm sure this blow still works, too, Downtown. Maybe I should tweet that out, too."

Worschuk grumpily put his pen and notebook in his pocket. "I better win an award for this shit."

Tommy pressed Sawatski again, and Miles explained how he knew The Voice, though that was all the information he had on the man. Claire, having detoxed enough to feel her emotions again, started to tear up when Sawatski explained how the man had confirmed that he was behind the explosion that had killed Jasmine Starr at The Other Woman. He told Tommy about Sangster and the car wearing government plates. Sawatski knew that Sangster wouldn't be watching the District Three station forever; he had probably gone in for a cursory check to discover that Sawatski was nowhere in the building. "I'll bet twenty bucks on Sangster as this asshole's hired hitter."

"What does Sangster drive?" said Tommy.

"An old brown Crown Vic — a detective car he bought at auction," said Sawatski. "It's some kind of low-rent hot rod, Mustang motor or something in it."

"Can we track it?"

"If he's got a laptop in it," said Spence. "It won't come up as his badge number, but it should be easy to spot on the real-time. He's probably got a laptop with him if he's tracking Mileage."

Tommy looked at Ernie Friday. "Whaddya say, Friday — a hitter taking out a hitter?"

Ernie dabbed at his forehead, pleased to see that the cut had finally clotted. "And the attempted?"

Sawatski chimed in on cue. "What attempted?" He reached his hand back to Spence, who handed him Friday's

Beretta. Sawatski handed the gun to Ernie. "Do you think you can do it without a bullet?"

Friday smiled, pocketing the automatic. He looked outside at his idling, full-framed box Pontiac. "Yeah, I think I've got a workaround."

Worschuk asked, "So what the fuck am I supposed to do? Sit around and wait for you guys to figure this out?"

Tommy turned to Worschuk. "Well, the first thing you need is a new cell phone." Tommy grabbed a stack of pre-paid phones off the rack at the front of the store. He left two fifties on the counter to cover their rent. "Okay, let's fire these up and figure out how the speakerphone works."

Cindy walked up to Tommy. "Tommy, what did Steve tell you?"

Tommy wanted to tell her what had happened, what the voice had led him to believe. Steve was most certainly dead, as well as Gwen, and the cats he called Cat. He decided that his friend would be understanding of the delay in his mourning, considering their current situation. "He said a lotta weird stuff when I went to the house," said Tommy. "Something to do with all this CIA mind-control shit. Then there was all those water trucks."

"What water trucks?" said Sawatski.

Tommy laid out what he knew: the water department emergency trucks leaving the federal virology lab, the truck behind The Guiding Light, and the notations in the ledger. He topped it all off with the Coles Notes version of Galecki's conspiracy theories. "There's a lotta weird shit going on, and I think we're about to find out what it's all about."

"You know you're walking into a deathtrap, or worse," said Sawatski. "This is shit that nobody is supposed to know."

Tommy smiled at Sawatski. "I think that's why they call

it a government conspiracy. Besides, I've got an ace up my sleeve."

"Bullshit," said Sawatski. "You've got a pair of threes and you know it."

"Maybe," said Tommy. "That all depends."

"Depends on what?"

"Depends on whether you feel like being a super cop this morning."

Sawatski looked at Bosco. "Yeah, I think I'm up to it." He looked over at Spence. "How about you, partner? Ready to toss your career?"

"On one condition," said Spence.

"Name it."

"Promise me that we're going to blow up some serious shit."

"Don't worry," said Tommy. "I've got just the firecracker." He grabbed the rest of the prepaid cell phones as they headed to their vehicles.

Billy Sangster was fuming. He knew that he had spent too long waiting for Sawatski to emerge from the District Three station. Nathaniel had informed him of the current plan, how the tour of the facility at the Riverview Health Centre would lay everything and everyone to rest. He was pushing his Crown Vic hard on Osborne Street South, a serious rumble emanating from the custom exhaust system under full throttle. He checked the clock on the car radio; it was coming up on 3:30 a.m. It was closer to 3:40. The old Crown Vic's radio seemed to lose a few minutes every week.

The Clean Sweep protocols had been suspended for the time being. If Tommy and his confederates decided to make a break for it, they would be easy to reactivate. Sangster was dealing with another worry: where was Sawatski? His laptop hadn't shown any movement of Sawatski's personal car from the Public Safety Building garage. Then there was the coffee stop at Sal's, which was starting to feel a little hinky. He didn't think that Sawatski had the balls to come after him directly. If push came to shove, Sangster figured that he could break his neck in less than sixty seconds, ninety if Sawatski fought hard. It didn't seem like a fair fight.

Sangster hit the turn signal for the left onto Morley. As he made the turn, he realized that he had to make a detour. An old Chevy boogie van was blocking the right-hand side of the street, flashing its emergency lights, and a big fat redhead wearing a floppy toque and oversized scarf that covered his face was holding up a set of jumper cables in earnest. The left-hand side of the street was clogged with parked cars. Sangster knew that a left turn would put him into a back lane that didn't meet up with a street until he passed an oversized block. Most of the city's residential back lanes had become impassable, thanks to reductions in the snow clearing budget. Taking a right turn would lead him down the back lane to Bartlet Avenue. Running parallel with Morley, it would get him to the Centre just as quickly, if not quicker.

David Worschuk held the jumper cables aloft a little longer, until Sangster's Crown Vic had moved far enough down the back lane. As the car turned left, he lowered his scarf from his face to use one of the new prepaid phones that Tommy Bosco had "borrowed" from the 7-Eleven. "He took the detour," said Worschuk. "He's heading your way."

He gave the thumbs-up signal to Cindy and Claire, who were watching the scene from behind the velvet-covered bucket seats.

"Roger that," said Spence, who was at the end of Bartlet Avenue in Freddie's cab, looking on as Tommy Bosco and Ernie Friday readied the Parisienne, which Friday had already reported as stolen from his Bowman Avenue address. The cheap prepaid phone was smart enough to have a web browser, which allowed Spence access to the police service GPS tracker. Sangster's laptop was an official police unit, and she could see the Crown Vic moving west on Bartlet, with an IT department code in place where the badge number would normally have been. She hoped that Sangster wouldn't see the badge number she was using, the one from the laptop that Sawatski had borrowed from the desk of Constable Herridge at District Three. "Are you guys ready? He's coming down the street. Gotta kill the phone!"

Tommy Bosco's voice crackled through the speaker. "Just let me put on the Clubs."

Ernie Friday was at the back of the Parisienne, holding the rear axle aloft with an old floor jack from Freddie's truck bed. The rear tires were in a steady state of forward rotation. According to the speedometer, the elevated Parisienne was travelling at a speed of about sixty kilometres per hour, with the cruise control engaged. He watched as Tommy attached two steering wheel locks to each side of the three-spoke steering wheel, each positioned to hit the windshield of the Parisienne if it tried to turn left or right. Tommy tilted the wheel as far upwards as it could go, pushing the ends of the respective Clubs against the glass for tension. He gave the thumbs up to Friday, jumping over the snowbank to a safer position. Friday gave the jack a harsh counter-clockwise twist. The Parisienne fell, grabbing the ice hard with its old-school studded winter tires. Like most city streets, Bartlet Avenue was anxiously awaiting the arrival of the city graders to remove the heavy ice ruts that ran the length of the street. For the Parisienne, the ruts had transformed it into a 4000-pound slot car.

Friday watched as the Pontiac picked up speed. All its lights were dark. He knew that the timing would be a simple stroke of luck. If Sangster spotted the Pontiac in time, he might have the opportunity to take a side street detour to avoid it. If the ruts weren't too deep, Sangster could simply move out of the way. These possibilities assumed that Sangster would be paying the utmost attention to the road ahead.

Something appeared to be wrong with the street lights on this section. The problem was Miles Sawatski. With a pair of vise-grips and a set of insulated wire cutters, Sawatski had spent the last ten minutes opening the inspection panels on the light standards and cutting the power to four of the Bartlet Avenue street lights, which had recently been changed over to the new LED style. He didn't even feel an electrical tingle in his fingers when he made the snips. He saw Sangster fly past at Fisher Street, where he had parked the *Winnipeg Sentinel* Cavalier for his part in the clandestine operation.

Sangster was the last to know what was coming. He was giving half of his attention to the glow of the laptop, hoping for a hit on Sawatski. The chances of traffic at this hour on a residential side street were minimal at best. For a moment, he was distracted by what appeared to be a police signature at the end of Bartlet Avenue, which disappeared just as quickly. It was the distraction that Sawatski had been hoping for. Sangster didn't see the square-box Pontiac until it was ten feet away from the Crown Vic. He jammed the brakes hard, but they were of little consequence. The force of the crash obliterated the front sheet metal of both cars, while the rear end of each car rose about three feet in the air on impact before crashing down. There was no Hollywood-style explosion; the only smoke that rose from the wrecks was the steam from the fractured cooling systems. The sound wasn't enough to rouse the neighbours; they probably thought it was the snowplows that had finally arrived to carve down the ruts.

Sawatski went to check on Sangster. Like most cops, Sangster would seldom buckle up; it was a carryover behaviour from the days of uniform patrol, when gun belts and bulletproof vests were deemed bulky enough that the police service members got a free pass on mandatory seatbelt use. Sangster was crushed by the force of the intruding firewall, the buckled floorboards, and the steering column. The air bags had blown on impact, though their effectiveness was tied more to the use of the seatbelts. The airbag was effective at one thing: prolonging the misery of Sangster's final exit. He was still breathing in gurgled spurts when Sawatski peeked through the shattered passenger side window. "Hey, Bangster, you're not looking so good. Need a Timmy's?"

"You're a dead f-f-f-fuck," said Sangster. He tried to move what was left of his shattered arms to reach his Glock. His arms didn't respond to his requests, nor did his legs. "I c-c-c-can't feel my f-f-f-fucking legs. You put me in a f-f-f-fucking wh-wh-wh-wheelchair." Sangster was coughing up blood now. The broken ribcage shards were doing their damage.

Sawatski had zero sympathy to offer. "Listen, Bangster, I'm going to pay our former boss a visit. Any pointers you'd like to give me before you check out? We haven't had the pleasure of a face-to-face yet."

"You're g-g-g-gonna burn in th-th-this, Miles," said Sangster, his breathing even more laboured.

Sawatski noticed the flicker first, from underneath the mangled hood of the Parisienne. The impact had severed its fuel line, allowing the gasoline to trickle onto the hot exhaust manifold. The flame that ignited caught the dust-packed sound insulation under the Pontiac's hood. Sawatski looked down; he saw the gasoline that was pouring out from the Crown Victoria's fractured fuel system. He looked in at Sangster and smiled, then turned his head to acknowledge the flames.

"Yeah, about that . . ."

Sawatski turned back to Sangster. His eyes were wide open and still. Sawatski checked the laptop that illuminated Sangster's death stare. The police-issue bracket had held up better than Sangster. Sawatski pressed the power button for a count of five, using a microfibre cloth as a fingerprint shield. The interior of the Crown Vic went dark. The wrecks burned slowly as Sawatski pulled away in the *Sentinel* Cavalier.

Tommy checked the time on Bouchard's phone; it was 3:57 a.m. Three minutes left until the expected meeting with the nameless man, a man who was about sixty seconds away from his temporary side-street base of operations. He knew it was a sucker play; Johnny Unknown didn't sound like the kind of person who was going to let anyone walk away from this. *Wheeled away on a crime-scene gurney is more likely*, Tommy thought. If it was just Tommy in the body bag, that would be one thing; the problem with the current four a.m. arrangement was that Mr. Unknown was expecting Tommy, Cindy, and Claire-Bear to be in the front seat of Freddie's cab, along with the ledger.

Tommy had no gun. Spence and Sawatski had each offered up their backup pieces, but Tommy had refused. He knew that Mr. Unknown would be clearing them and Freddie's cab for any form of weapons before a deal was struck for the ledger. Tommy hoped that there was one thing that Mr. Unknown didn't know about: Freddie's custom fuel tanks.

As instructed, Tommy steered Freddie down Churchill Drive, towards the service access road for the Riverview Health Centre. Cindy and Claire-Bear sat quietly in the cab. There had been little discussion as to how the events would unfold once inside the complex. "Listen, ladies," Tommy said, "the truth is we simply don't know what we're walking into here. They might just cap us the second we're inside. Or maybe, and it's a big-ass-Lotto 6/49 maybe, we give them this stupid book and then we all go for pancakes."

"Fat chance of that happening," said Cindy as Tommy turned Freddie into the hospital property.

Tommy had few options to consider for their route. The rear service portion of the newest hospital building was cordoned off by a locked metal gate. The service road continued past the gate, towards what looked like a steel storage building. Tommy followed the tire tracks to the building, stopping in front of an industrial galvanized steel overhead door. There was no need to honk. The door started to rise automatically, as though a sensor had been tripped when Freddie the Ford rolled up. Tommy pulled into the building, which appeared to be a storage shed for the landscaping equipment. He pulled up to the rear wall, surprised at how minimal the depth of the building seemed to be on the inside. Tommy went to turn off the ignition key to the Ford, but the storage shed had other plans. The wall in front of them started to descend into the floor. Even the gardening hand tools attached to the wall went along for the ride. Beyond the wall was a concrete ramp that descended below the surface in a gentle slope.

The route down was a winding one, though it didn't seem as though it was heading too deep below ground. Tommy approached a large red arrow painted on the wall of the next curve. Additional lettering accompanied the arrow in white script: STOP AHEAD IN 10 METRES. Freddie the Ford let out a squeal from his power-steering pump as Tommy rounded the corner. Another roll-up door appeared, this one painted with additional lettering: PREPARE FOR SCAN. As Tommy applied the brakes, Freddie and his occupants were bathed in a strange purple light, with an even stranger buzzing noise accompanying it. The light wasn't overly intense; it felt like natural light. After fifteen seconds, the light and the buzzing ceased, and the door began to rise.

The underground facility was a busy hub of activity. The walls were constructed of thick limestone blocks. Four of the emergency water department vans were parked at some form of loading bay, with long umbilical cords of intertwined cables attached to truck-mounted equipment, accessed through the sliding side doors. Tommy had not seen anything beyond the front seat of the van that had been parked at the rear of The Guiding Light. The vans were being attended to by water department employees, if their uniforms could be believed. In the mix were other employees, smartly dressed in crisp white lab coats. Their shoes gleamed like patent leather, their shirts, slacks, and haircuts looked freshly pressed. Two of them were even wearing bow ties. Tommy couldn't read any names on the lab coats, but he did make out an embroidered patch of a buffalo on their sleeves.

"Tommy! Brake!" The warning came from Cindy.

Tommy had almost run into one of the lab coats, who looked slightly annoyed as he walked past Freddie's driver's side door. Tommy read the badge as he went by.

"Manitoba department of weights and measures," said Tommy. "Funny — I don't see any scales anywhere."

As Tommy inched forward, he noticed a silver Chrysler 300 parked next to one of the vans. Next to the Chrysler was a 2009 light-green Ford Escape Hybrid. It came from an era when one of the best ways to identify a hybrid vehicle was to splash it with a green that should have been left on the leaves of the trees that inspired it. Most of the early-generation hybrid and electric vehicles in the province were used by government departments. This Escape had the Manitoba provincial markings on the doors, as well as the current interpretation of the mighty buffalo. There was no government department listed underneath.

Tommy wasn't quite sure of where to park the old Ford, until he saw the man with the ponytail. He didn't have a gun in his hand, though Tommy could easily make out the bulge and the straps of his shoulder holster under his sport coat. He motioned Tommy to park next to the Escape. Tommy whispered to Cindy and Claire, as clearly and as purposefully as he could. "All right, ladies, just follow my lead, and don't forget the ledger."

Cindy opened the passenger door; she waited at Freddie's tailgate for Claire and Tommy. She assessed the threat; Mr. Ponytail was fit, armed, and righteously sure of his abilities. He stood with his hands clasped in front of his belt buckle, a few hints of old tattoos peeking out from his shirt cuffs. He wore dark blue jeans, a crisp white shirt with no tie, and two days of stubble. He was definitely tired. Cindy wondered how much sleep he had lost trying to find Claire Hebert.

"Good morning, Pastor Bosco," the man said. "I am Nathaniel Goodwin. On behalf of the Department of Weights and Measures, I would like to welcome you and your party to our King George facility."

"King George?" said Claire. "Even I know there's no King George anymore. It's Queen something-or-other."

Nathaniel chuckled. "You are correct, Miss Hebert. The King George facility refers to the original structure, the King George Hospital." He pointed to the blocks of prehistoric limestone. "As you can see, the original foundation has held up extremely well. Now, if you could all please follow me . . ."

"Aren't you going to search us?" said Tommy.

"We already have, Pastor Bosco," said Nathaniel. "It was when you and your party stopped at the entrance door to the loading area."

"That purple light," said Cindy. "What was it?"

Nathaniel smiled at Cindy. "Think of it as a quicker version of an MRI machine, Ms. Smyth, without all that annoying claustrophobia." He turned to Tommy. "Pastor Bosco, I see you have the ledger. May I?"

"Have at 'er," said Tommy, tossing the ledger at Nathaniel. He caught it with one hand, without the slightest hint of a fumble or flinch. Nathaniel flipped through the ledger to ensure that none of the pages had been removed. It was completely intact. "Everything appears to be in order. Now, if you could all please follow me."

"Do you need our phones?" said Tommy.

Nathaniel produced his phone, holding the screen up to Tommy. There was a red X where the coverage bars should have been. "We don't have to worry about any interruptions, Pastor Bosco. None whatsoever." Nathaniel walked up to a set of hospital-style doors, placing his thumb on some form of scanner next to the door frame. The doors popped open, and Cindy and Claire followed Nathaniel into the brightly lit corridor. Tommy stood at the threshold. Nathaniel turned and asked, "Is there a problem, Pastor Bosco?"

"Just wanted to lock my truck," said Tommy. "It's got a pretty nice tape deck." Tommy lifted an aftermarket key fob from his pocket, surrounded by the rest of his keys. He pressed the lock switch twice, resulting in Freddie's lights flashing and the signature warble of a cheap car alarm.

"That must be some tape deck," said Nathaniel.

"Pioneer Supertuner," said Bosco. "Never ate a tape."

"If you could all please follow me," said Nathaniel.

CHAPTER
FIFTY

The group continued down the bright white corridor. Like the parking garage access, it wasn't without its twists and turns. As they rounded one of the corners, a new set of security doors appeared. They were much more involved than the first set of doors, constructed of some type of shiny alloy and without handles. Nathaniel stepped up to a retinal scanner to open them. The doors popped open like the last set, though there was a noticeable burst of air from within, as though this area had its own air-exchange system. Claire brushed her hair out of her eyes as they entered.

The new room was the opposite of hospital antiseptic. The walls wore dark oak panelling

291

from top to bottom. Crystal ceiling fixtures and wall sconces cast considerable light. The furnishings were ornate. Tommy wasn't sure if they were authentic antiques or reproductions, though they did fit the room well, regardless of their provenance. What didn't fit was the polished Emerson respirator at the rear of the room. A nurse wearing a cape and an old-style nurse's hat was attending to the occupant of the shiny metal tube. Jazz played, with plenty of piano infused. The nurse acknowledged the arrival of the party and then left through a door that looked like it was part of the oak panelling.

"Good morning, Mr. Chancellor," said Nathaniel. "I would like to introduce Ms. Cindy Smyth, Ms. Claire Hebert, and Pastor Thomas Bosco."

Chancellor did not speak at first. A small panel opened in the ceiling above his head. A box lowered from the ceiling towards him. To the left of the group, a panel started to open on the oak wall, revealing a large plasma television. The image popped to life almost instantly. Cindy grabbed Tommy's hand as the close-up image of the ancient man's face appeared. A video camera appeared from another sliding panel. Tommy looked over at the shiny metal tube. The man inside was looking at a video image of them from his vantage point. Tommy figured that it wasn't anywhere near as creepy as the one they were now observing.

"Good morning to you all," said Chancellor. "My name is Morley Chancellor. I am the chief executive officer of the King George Branch of the Department of Weights and Measures."

"And what the fuck is the Department of Weights and Measures?" said Claire.

Chancellor was visibly annoyed by the F-sharp. "It is Miss Hebert, correct?"

"Yeah, that's right. So apart from the Oscar Peterson over the speakers, what the fuck is this place?"

Chancellor was intrigued. "You know jazz?"

"A little," said Hebert. "I had a regular who wouldn't shut up about this shit — I had to crank it up while I did him."

Chancellor felt the need to enlighten her. "This is Wheatland, from 1964. That year was my eleventh anniversary in this shiny cocoon that you see here. Do you know about the Manitoba polio outbreak of 1953, Miss Hebert?"

"Yeah, I think I heard about it in school, before I dropped out."

"Do you know what polio does, Miss Hebert?"

"It looks like it fucks you up something royal."

Chancellor chuckled at the comment. "You are correct in that, my dear. Poliomyelitis is a cruel disease, more like a thief that comes in the night. I was working for the department in Brandon in 1953 when I contracted it."

The Brandon reference piqued Tommy's interest. "Where was that in Brandon?"

Chancellor smiled again. "You are an inquisitive sort, Pastor Bosco. As your friend the late Mr. Galecki had told you, our efforts were concentrated at the Brandon Hospital for Mental Diseases. I was working as a research chemist for Dr. Cameron's team. You may be aware of Dr. Cameron's work with those suffering from the effects of schizophrenia during the 1930s at the hospital. The work continued through the 1930s and the 1940s, all under the watchful eye of the good doctor, regardless of his travels or country of residence. I joined the department in 1951 and immediately became immersed in Operation Artichoke: a CIA-funded program that concentrated on the latest in chemical advancements for mind control, a precursor to the MKULTRA program. You must understand that time was truly of the essence. There had been reports of American and Canadian soldiers subjected to brainwashing techniques by Red Chinese agents during the police action in Korea. The idea was . . . fantastic. To think that any mind could be captured, filtered of all its information, then wiped clean of the experience and reprogrammed at will. It was as if the hand of God had been presented to us."

"Who did they experiment on?" said Tommy.

"There was a wide selection of candidates available," said Chancellor. "Many of them were brought in from the Canadian Forces Base in Shilo — volunteers for the cause against the Red Menace, if you will. We could only go so far with experimentation on the soldiers, which limited much of our testing to sensory deprivation. Then there was the shiny new toy: lysergic acid diethylamide. You probably know it better as LSD.

"The hospital had a steady supply of test subjects: the chronic schizophrenics. Dr. Cameron believed that schizophrenia was curable. Brainwashing sounds so evil in its cold-war context, but it had the potential to be truly noble. This was truly the intent of the good doctor. But what of the un-corrupted mind? Could the grey matter of the sane be just as malleable? This is where the soldiers came in. Truly, the bravest of soldiers. Unfortunately, history has chosen to demonize the work of Dr. Cameron and his confederates. It is for these reasons that the work continues in secret."

"So, it's still going on in Brandon?" said Tommy.

"The glory days of the Brandon facility are now just a matter of classified historical record," said Chancellor. "The hospital is now the site of the Assiniboine Community College. It seems almost prophetic; a place where clean minds are infused with knowledge, in a place where minds were wiped clean of theirs. As for the study of the human mind, much of it is going on right here at the King George."

The opposite side of the room began to open, the oak panelling sliding to reveal an observation window. Tommy, Cindy, and Claire inched closer to investigate. The window gave view to a space approximately one storey below, which was populated by at least twenty hospital beds. Tommy recognized the beds from the photos that Galecki had shown him of the old asylum; the beds were equipped with cages. They did look a little less draconian than the ones from the 1930s, though their intentions were still enough to incite horror. The ward was a busy place, even at four in the morning. A group of lab coats were busy checking a plethora of monitors, intravenous drips, biomedical sensors, and respirator pumps. The patients appeared to be calm. There was the odd movement under the bars of the cages, though none of it seemed to be of a painful nature or motivated by a need to escape its clutches. Tommy did notice one thing that all the patients had in common; they were all elderly.

"The Riverview Health Centre has been a most generous, if completely unwitting, partner in our research here at King George," said Chancellor. "As far as anyone at Vital Statistics is concerned, all of the patients here have passed away in the last three years. They left no family to mourn their passing, no friends to send them flowers, no one to pay for cable TV in their hospital rooms. Their fate was to simply die alone. Thanks to the department, they have been given a second chance."

"A second chance?" said Tommy, trying to contain his outrage. "A second chance at what, exactly?"

"To contribute to the greater good, Pastor Bosco," said Chancellor. "I could have chosen to close my eyes to science when polio took away my body, and yet, I knew the department would need my talents for as long as I could draw breath, even if that breath came courtesy of a silver mechanical torpedo. Life is full of checks and balances, Pastor Bosco, yin and yang, good and evil. It is full of weights and measures."

The door that the Chancellor's nurse had exited opened, revealing a man in a dark-blue suit with an aluminum briefcase. He seemed frantic. He made a beeline for Nathaniel.

"What's going on?" said the man. "I thought they would be —"

Nathaniel shook his head at the man, who quickly ended his query. He looked at the newcomers, then at Chancellor's respirator.

"Pastor Bosco," said Chancellor. "I would like to introduce Mr. Tobias Finch from the Department of Weights and Measures. Good morning, Mr. Finch."

"Good morning," said Finch.

"Is there a problem, Mr. Finch?" said Chancellor.

"No, no problem at all Mr. Chancellor. It's just that . . ."

"Just what, Mr. Finch?"

"It's just that I don't know why I'm supposed to be here."

"I'll be glad to explain that to you now. Nathaniel?"

Nathaniel grabbed Finch from behind, sinking a small hypodermic needle into his neck. Finch fell to the floor, partially in pain and partially from the concoction that was now coursing its way through his bloodstream. He loosened his necktie to try to alleviate the breathing strain. "What . . . the fuck . . . was that?"

"Patience, Mr. Finch," said Chancellor. "I felt it best that a demonstration of our latest protocol be in order for Pastor Bosco and his party, especially after learning of your extracurricular activities with our monthly stipend from our generous benefactors. Nathaniel, could you please assist Mr. Finch with the appropriate equipment?"

Nathaniel removed his Glock from his holster and handed it to Finch. Finch reached for the gun instinctively, seeming somewhat groggy from the recent injection. He confirmed that a round was ready in the chamber.

"Mr. Finch," said Chancellor. "It has come to my attention that you have recently purchased a vacation cottage in the Nopiming Provincial Park. Is this correct?"

Finch was trying to fight the answer, then relented. "Yes, yes Mr. Chancellor. That — that is . . . that is correct."

"And where did you acquire the funds for such a transaction, Mr. Finch?"

"I, uh, uhm, I . . . took . . . the . . . I took the money."

"From which account, Mr. Finch?"

"Dis . . . discretional. Discretional Funds."

"Mr. Finch, what was the amount of the unauthorized withdrawal?"

"Th-th-thr-three . . ."

"Three what, Mr. Finch?"

"Three . . . hundred . . . ninety . . . thousand."

"Thank you for your honesty, Mr. Finch. Now, there is one task left for you to complete. The department has identified a threat."

Tommy, Claire, and Cindy watched as Mr. Finch stopped his stuttering. He looked at the trio in front of him, the Glock grip now firm and purposeful. "I understand," said Finch. "Please name the threat."

Chancellor smiled on the oversized plasma screen. "You are, Mr. Finch. Please remove the threat."

Finch placed the Glock against his right temple and fired, dropping to the floor dead. Cindy and Claire were holding on

297

tight to Tommy's arms. Nathaniel collected the Glock from Finch's right hand and returned it to his holster.

"Still too much hesitation," said Chancellor. "Nathaniel, make a note of it."

"What the fuck was that for?" said Cindy.

"A demonstration," said Chancellor. "A simple demonstration of just how far we have been able to progress from the days of sensory deprivation and morphine-induced comas. Mind control used to take months for a subject to comply. With the right dosage, a request to the subject can occur with great speed and with no concern to the subject's well-being. This particular activation of an asset provided us with both a truthful admission and a call to, for the most part, immediate action. An assassin can be anyone, anywhere, at any time. Today, the suggestion must be spoken directly to the subject, but we must remember that communication has become much more than the spoken word. Unfortunately, the one thing that the worlds of Instagram, Twitter, and Facebook cannot guarantee is action. Mass, unquestioning, unwavering action. The only thing that can do that to a populace is a virus."

"A virus," said Tommy. "That's what the water trucks were doing at the virology lab!"

"Correct, Mr. Bosco. The federal virology lab has something of a freelance section, a few like-minded individuals who understand the need for the department to exist for the greater good. The water department trucks, while identical to the City of Winnipeg units, are staffed by our members."

"And the Heaven's Rejects? How do they fit into all this?"

"Simple well-paid hall monitors," said Chancellor. "The criminal element ensured that the collection of water samples would go unnoticed, since all of the monitored locations were chosen for their — how should I say this — 'colourful' residents. A filthy man in a filthy establishment draws little to no attention. If a drug transaction occurs in a Manitoba Housing domicile, it's only fair to assume that the dealer might need to use the facilities. A few specimen jars, some training with a portable parts-per-million sensor of our own design, and a few dozen ledgers from an office supply store were all that was needed to monitor the delivery of the virus."

"You keep talking about a virus," said Cindy. "So, which places have it?"

"Oh, I'm sorry," said Chancellor. "Let me clarify: the virus is already active in the entire water supply."

"Whaddya mean, the entire water supply?" said Claire. "You mean the entire city?"

"Precisely," said Chancellor. "The good people of the City of Winnipeg have been ingesting this virus for decades. You probably know it by names such as cadmium, zirconium, or manganese. These substances, as well as others, are allowed to flow at what appear to be the most minimal levels through the water supply, bringing no harm to those who ingest it. The injection that Mr. Goodwin supplied to the late Mr. Finch is an example of what can be done with the right mix of nanoparticles."

"Nano-what-icles?" said Claire.

"Nanoparticles," said Chancellor. "Imagine the smallest particle that you can perceive. Now imagine that particle a thousand times smaller. Imagine that this particle can hitch a ride on other particles. Imagine that the concentrations of the nanoparticle are so small that they could never be traced, since no one would even be looking for their existence in a forensic test. Imagine . . . an invisible bullet, waiting to be fired by a random trigger."

"Okay, asshole," said Tommy. "What the fuck is attached to The Guiding Light that looks like a water meter?"

"Oh, it is a water meter," said Chancellor. "It monitors usage, rate of flow, all those things that result in a monthly bill, but your water meter is special, just like sixty-seven others within the Winnipeg city limits. Your meter is also an activator for the nanoparticles."

"What kind of nanoparticles?"

"Whatever kind we desire, Pastor Bosco. The recipe could be for general complacency, a state of calm throughout the populace, or perhaps a call to arms, a revolution in a volatile land. Or, it could be used to keep the fracas normally associated with an unofficial halfway house from occurring at all, wouldn't you agree Pastor Bosco?"

Tommy thought about what Chancellor was saying. Things had been very quiet at The Guiding Light for the last few years, especially after some much-needed work on the water-supply pipes. He had often wondered if the calm was the by-product of his search for the greater good. He had no idea that it was chemically induced.

Chancellor continued. "Some of the activation mixes have been formulated to open certain pathways in the wiring of the brain, such as the control of free will. Take the recent example of Mr. Finch. The injection he received from Mr. Goodwin was merely a highly concentrated portable activator. We can easily create the perfect assassin, an operative who completes their mission without question, then removes themselves as a potential threat."

"You mean suicide," said Tommy.

"Potato, po-*ta*-toe," said Chancellor. "While an expendable assassin is an important asset to possess, it pales in comparison to an idea, a belief that must be defended at all costs. An idea that is universal to a large group. An idea that can be activated as we see fit."

"Who the fuck is the We in this bullshit?" said Claire.

"The list is a long and distinguished one," said Chancellor. "There's the law-and-order categories, the greater-goodniks, as I like to call them. Then there's the revolutionaries. History may speak of their magnetism as the catalyst for the change that occurred. The truth is that many of them had a little help from the department." Chancellor smiled, almost chuckling as he formed his summation. "Pastor Bosco, think of the world as a ship, an ever-evolving, ever-expanding vessel of tremendous size and complexity. Now imagine this vessel as rudderless. That is what the department is, Pastor Bosco. It is a wheelhouse for the world."

Tommy crossed his arms in front of him. He looked down at his weathered Timex Ironman, which was cycling through its stopwatch function. "So, what's the next big threat?"

Chancellor smiled. "Unfortunately for you, Ms. Smyth and Ms. Hebert, it is the removal of the threat. The work we are doing here is far too important to jeopardize. I do hope that you understand."

"Oh, we understand completely," said Tommy. He looked over at Nathaniel, who was attaching his silencer to his Glock out of habit. "Can I make a final request?"

"What do you desire, Pastor Bosco?"

"Would you allow me and my friends a moment to pray?"

Chancellor's video image looked at Tommy in high definition. "I don't see why not, Pastor Bosco."

"Would it be all right if we kneel?"

"It would be perfectly satisfactory."

Tommy went to kneel. He realized that Cindy and Claire were having a hard time wrapping their heads around the idea. He had to pull their arms down hard to get them to join him on the antique rug. He closed his eyes.

"Dear Lord, thank you for bringing us to the end of this most incredible journey. Thank you for keeping our trespassers from bringing us harm, like those two douche bags at the library, that dirty cop that we blew up on the side street, even my dear old dad. Thank you for these men, especially the one named Nathaniel, for not checking for anything other than a gun on me or Cindy or Claire-Bear. Thank you for the incredible reception on our supposedly dead cellular phones; isn't that right, Sergeant Sawatski?"

"It's like I'm standing right next to you," said Sawatski, his static-laced voice coming from somewhere on Tommy's person. "Are you about ready to wrap this thing up?"

Nathaniel moved over to Tommy quickly, removing the phone of the late Paul Bouchard from his front pocket. He looked at the screen. The signal showed full bars. He threw the phone against the wall, cracking open its case.

"Warmer," said Sawatski.

Nathaniel checked Cindy's jacket, finding the other phone. He dropped it on the ground and smashed it with his boot heel.

"Getting warmer," said Sawatski.

The voice was coming from Claire's hoodie, which she had borrowed from Jasmine Starr before she left The Guiding Light. Nathaniel retrieved the phone and stomped it into bits.

Tommy looked at the image of Morley Chancellor on the video screen. There was a genuine look of surprise on his face. Tommy smiled back at him with his best shit-eating grin.

"In the name of the father," said Tommy.

"And the son," said Claire.

"And the Holy Spirit," said Cindy.

"Now and forever," said Sawatski, wondering if anyone could hear him through the mangled phones. He figured that at least one was still working. He had dropped phones into toilets that could still dial out.

"Amen," said Tommy. He grabbed the girls and fell face forward to the floor.

Nathaniel had his gun drawn, looking in every direction. Where was the threat? He had three people lying on the floor, with no weapons. There was no hammering at the secure doors of the main hall. He ran over to the video display at the door; no one was trying to get in. He pulled out his cell phone and hit a speed dial number. The call answered on the second ring.

"Loading dock, Smith speaking."

"Smith, its Goodwin. Do we have a breach?"

"Breach? What breach? It's four in the morning. You could hear a mouse fart down here."

Nathaniel thought for a moment as to where to check next. Then he remembered something that Tommy had done on the way in. "Smith, go check that old truck parked on the end."

"What? That piece-of-shit Ford?"

"Yes, do it now." Nathaniel heard the footsteps of the guard as he walked over to Freddie the Ford. He heard him jiggle the door handle.

"It's locked up tight," said Smith.

"Does it have a tape deck?"

"Does it have a-what deck?"

"A tape deck. You know, for tapes!"

"Uh . . . yeah, looks like one I used to have in my Chevelle.

Pioneer Supertuner, I think. Hey, I think I smell something burning."

Nathaniel looked down at Tommy, keeping his gun pointed at his head. Tommy lifted his head up to look. "What the fuck is going on?" said Nathaniel.

"Yeah, sorry about that. I thought I had timed it right."

"Timed what right?"

"The Father–Son–Holy Ghost shit. It should have happened by now."

"What should have happened by —"

That's when it happened. It had seemed silly to Nathaniel at the time. Who would make sure that their old, rusty, piece-of-shit truck was locked to protect an old, gummed-up, piece-of-shit tape deck?

Tommy had thought up the idea years before, shortly after Freddie the Ford's unscheduled tank dump of contraband on Highway 75. He wondered what he could do to destroy any evidence of illicit cargo, if the situation required it. He thought of wiring up a chunk of plastic explosive, with remote detonators and such, though the idea of hitting ruts and cracks with a fragile bomb on board seemed like a recipe for disaster. He came up with a much simpler system, using a twelve-volt power inverter, an engine block heater, and a length of cannon fuse that was normally used with fireworks. When Tommy locked up the old Ford, the key fob had triggered the "on" circuit for the cigarette lighter, which the power inverter was plugged into. The block heater element was plugged into the power inverter and mounted underneath the hood. Tommy knew that it would take a little longer to bring the block heater up to temperature with the twelve-volt battery, as opposed to plugging it into a live 120-volt AC circuit.

The length of fuse was a specialty piece, designed to burn underwater, which made it a good candidate for all-weather mounting underneath Freddie. Tommy went one step further, wrapping the fuse in a protective plastic loom. The loom made the fuse look like just another piece of underbody wiring. Tommy mounted a simple tin box over the business end of the block heater, using zip ties to secure the fuse to the heated element portion. Tommy had done a few tests when he had first installed the system, just to make sure that the fuse would eventually light without connecting it to an explosive end source. It took about fifteen minutes to ignite. Then there was the matter of how long it would take for the fuse to reach its destination. The all-weather nature of the fuse meant that it would burn much slower than a typical fireworks fuse. On this particular morning, it took exactly seventeen minutes and thirty seconds for the fuse to hit Freddie's primary gas tank. Tommy had made a point of topping it off before heading to the four a.m. meeting. He'd sprung for premium.

When Freddie's tank blew, the hot shrapnel caused a chain reaction, igniting the Escape, then the Chrysler, and the three Ford Transits that were parked nearby. The lab coats, water truck drivers, and Smith the security guard died instantly. The force of the blast sent a concussion wave through the rest of the King George's foundation, buckling the alloy doors to the main hall and shattering the observation window that gave the view of the patients' ward.

Crouched down, Tommy, Cindy, and Claire-Bear escaped the brunt of the concussion. Nathaniel did not. He was thrown into the plasma screen that had most recently displayed the shocked face of Morley Chancellor. He lay unconscious at the base of the smashed screen, surrounded by pieces of splintered oak panelling.

Tommy made quick checks of himself, Cindy, and Claire. Cindy grabbed Nathaniel's Glock, sweeping the room for any additional threats. The nurse who had attended to Chancellor before the meeting burst through the service door, firing a long-barrel Smith & Wesson .357 Magnum, with little thought to precision. Cindy fired two shots at the nurse's centre mass, dropping her to the floor.

Tommy was moving towards the iron lung.

Cindy edged over to Claire; she was hit in her left forearm, bleeding heavily. Cindy pulled the cape off the dead nurse, clawing at a piece of the lining for a tourniquet. She tended to Claire as Tommy approached Chancellor. There was no escape for the old man, though he certainly looked as though he had enough venom in him to cut Tommy down with his stare.

"You realize that you have accomplished nothing here today," said Chancellor. "The work of the King George has been shared with many like-minded individuals throughout the world. Control is the only key to fighting chaos."

"Maybe so," said Tommy. "There's only one problem with that theory."

"And what is that, Pastor Bosco?"

"Who gets to decide?" said Tommy. "Who determines what chaos actually is? Sure, it can be a bad thing, with explosions, starvation and death. But there's an awful lot of good chaos out there, too." Tommy looked over at Cindy tending to Claire's wounds. "You might even say that chaos can bring out the best in us."

"You're a romantic fool, Pastor Bosco," said Chancellor. "Don't forget; I have friends in very high places."

Tommy looked away from Chancellor, for a closer inspection of the Emerson respirator. He followed the electrical cord from the pump motor to the floor plug. He unplugged the cord and held the end up to a wide-eyed Chancellor. "Like I said, *Morley*, sometimes, chaos can bring out the best in us." Tommy dropped the cord onto the floor. The air pump of the Emerson respirator came to a stop. Chancellor struggled, pressing his patient call button for a nurse who would never come.

Tommy turned to check on Cindy and Claire. "How bad is she?"

"She'll live," said Cindy. "It looks like it was a clean-through shot."

"It fucking hurts like hell," said Claire. "That old guy got any morphine on him?"

"Not that I could see," said Tommy. "Now let's see about —"

"Tommy!" said Cindy. "Where's the ponytail asshole?"

Tommy turned to where he had last seen Nathaniel. He was gone. So was the ledger.

CHAPTER FIFTY-ONE

Sawatski thought there would be more to it. As he waited for the underground explosion that Tommy Bosco had promised, he took a quick scan of his eclectic team. Spence had been making notes on the speakerphone conversation that they had overheard, as had been Worschuk, ensured of the scoop that would give him another thick layer of Publisher Teflon. Ernie Friday was standing outside the open sliding door of the boogie van, halfway through his last Peter Jackson. He was checking on the cellular booster that took up the rest of the space in his well-used briefcase, the booster that had enabled the underground communication. The LED display was jumping back and forth between two and three bars. Friday had explained, as he set up the antenna, that the whiz kid who had put together his jammer had thrown it in for free. "I've never used it before," said Ernie as he familiarized himself with Sawatski's Kahr. He had told Sawatski that his Beretta was jamming. *It would jam up his freedom royally*, thought Sawatski, *if the forensics team ever got a hold of it.*

The shock wave knocked Ernie's cigarette out of his hand; it landed inside the van on Worschuk, who swatted the embers into submission. The snow on top of the blast area rose up about two feet off the ground, leaving a general outline on the surface of where the blast damage extended to. Sawatski scanned the area with his Glock drawn. There weren't any obvious exit points on the surface. He didn't know if Tommy, Cindy, or Claire had survived the blast. Sawatski also didn't know who would be emerging first: friendlies, or a threat.

Like most hospitals, the Riverview Health Centre had a network of underground tunnels. Nathaniel had escaped from the main hall through a hidden side door on the opposite side of the room when the nurse had started shooting. He was in rough shape. The glass from the window had left some deep cuts, leaving a steady trail of blood droplets as he navigated the ancient tunnels that had once connected the King George to the rest of the complex.

He made his way to one of the secret entrance points, having some difficulty with the scanner system that allowed the wall to move. He was now in a janitorial station, off of the main tunnel that accessed the day hospital and the Princess Elizabeth Building, which had originally been a long-term care facility. The building now housed the administration offices for the Centre. Nathaniel figured that it should be fairly quiet at this hour. Any security staff that had been alerted to the blast would have been coming to investigate from the main hospital. He was in the clear. He clutched the ledger tight to his chest, walking as fast as he could with the glass shards in his legs. He needed to get the ledger out and hidden, hopeful that the information within would be of benefit to the multiple global partners that had invested in the King George. He smiled through the pain for a moment, thinking about the potential payoff that the ledger could bring him. He fumbled in his pocket for his keys. He found his set for his backup car, a nondescript Chevy Malibu that was also registered to the department. The car was moved around the Riverview site on a regular basis, cleared of snow, and topped off with gas when required. His last text stated that it was parked on Oakwood Avenue. He hit the remote start. The key fob warbled back its confirmation. There would be time to decompress later, to process the anger at himself for allowing Bosco and his crew to see the inner workings of the department. Nathaniel had three immediate Gets: Get Out, Get Safe, and Get Stitched Up.

Sawatski and Spence took the boogie van around the back of the complex to check the day hospital while Worschuk and Ernie used the *Sentinel* Cavalier to check out the front. Sawatski saw that smoke was billowing out of the storage shed where Tommy had entered the underground facility. Various members of the hospital staff were starting to emerge from the other buildings.

"Winnipeg Police!" said Spence. "Get back inside!" They couldn't be sure if anyone emerging from the scene was a

Riverview employee, a King George operative, or both. Spence wasn't taking any chances.

Sawatski left the van, moving towards the front of the Princess Elizabeth. Worschuk and Friday were approaching from the opposite direction, stopping the car near the entrance. Then came the sound of something trying to open a frosty Winnipeg institutional door handle. The sound alerted Sawatski, who started running towards the main entrance of the Princess Elizabeth. Ernie exited the Cavalier, moving with Sawatski towards the steps. The door burst open. Nathaniel exited to the cold morning air.

Sawatski aimed his Glock at Nathaniel from the right-hand side of the staircase, using the standard law enforcement stance. Ernie Friday stood on the left side of the staircase, mimicking Sawatski the best he could. He pointed the borrowed Kahr at Nathaniel's centre mass. Sawatski could tell that the man he previously knew as The Voice was in rough shape. That made him even more dangerous.

"Winnipeg Police!" said Sawatski. "Drop the book, get down on your knees, and interlace your fingers behind your head. Do it now!"

Nathaniel started to chuckle to himself. He dropped the book to the ground. Then he reached inside his sport coat.

"Don't do it!" said Sawatski.

Friday fired first, hitting Nathaniel in the right shoulder. Sawatski fired three shots: a miss, a left shoulder graze, and a direct hit in Nathaniel's sternum. Nathaniel fell to his knees, then forward, sliding down the icy steps face first. He was able to muster one last exhalation of frosty vapor before he expired.

CHAPTER FIFTY-TWO

Sawatski was confirming Nathaniel's death when the door at the top of the stairs opened again. Tommy, Cindy, and Claire emerged from the Princess Elizabeth entrance. They had followed one of the interior tunnels that bordered the main hall, which connected up with the path that Nathaniel had taken. Cindy took the lead, with Nathaniel's Glock. Spence saw the group emerge. She ran over and gingerly took the Glock from Cindy, who started to shake after she had released it, falling into Tommy's arms. There were plenty of sirens approaching as the group descended the front steps. Sawatski was checking Nathaniel for ID, and for whether he actually had a gun. The holster was empty.

312

"I think this was his," said Spence, handing the Glock to Sawatski. He gave the gun a quick wipe with a microfibre rag from his pocket, palmed it with Nathaniel's dead hand, then stuffed the gun back into Nathaniel's holster.

"There," said Sawatski. "Now he was armed."

"I highly doubt that's going to play out with forensics," said Spence, who was busy wiping down the borrowed Kahr that she had just retrieved from Ernie Friday. She put the gun in her pocket, adding plenty of fingerprint personalization for good measure. She walked up to Friday and started rubbing her right hand on his sleeve. "Just need a little gun jizz," said Spence. "As long as there's a whiff of it, the shooter board won't have a conniption."

Sawatski surveyed the scene. The first set of fire trucks was arriving, along with a few marked patrol cars. As senior officer on scene, Sawatski would be the point person for any police enquiries, including those of the white shirts. He turned to Worschuk.

"Well, Downtown, how do you think this is going to play out?"

Worschuk smiled, closed his notebook, and put his pen back in his pocket. "Whichever way you want it to, Mileage, whichever way you want it. We've got a name for a story like this in the newspaper business."

"What's that?" said Sawatski.

"Job security," said Worschuk. "This shit is going to take years to tell."

"Hey," said Ernie. "Do any of you assholes have a dart?"

Worschuk produced his pack. Ernie took a long drag, exhaling like some kind of storybook dragon.

Sawatski walked over to Tommy, Cindy, and Claire. "So, about this whole Stephanos thing."

"What about it?" said Tommy.

"I'm starting to think that it's a slam dunk for self-defence." Sawatski turned towards Spence. "I mean, that's what it looks like, right partner?"

Spence nodded. "Oh yeah, it was totally self-defence, partner. Totally self-defence."

"Can you make it stick?" said Cindy.

"Sure, we can make it stick," said Sawatski. "We're the good guys!"

"You better be sure," said Claire, holding her injured wing.

Spence flagged down one of the arriving ambulances to attend to her. She recognized one of the uniforms that was on scene. "Hey, Jason!"

The uniform nodded. "Whatcha need, Spence?"

Spence pointed towards Claire Hebert. "Need you to follow this one in to Health Sciences, twenty-four-hour guard. The Stephanos thing."

"You got it," said Jason. He motioned over his partner to join the protection detail.

Tommy walked over to Ernie, who was leaning up against the railing next to Nathaniel's corpse. "So, it's probably time for you to get out of here," said Tommy.

"Probably," said Ernie.

"Think you'll retire?"

Ernie smiled. He flicked his cigarette butt to the ground, crushing it out with his boot. "I think so. I'm getting too old for this shit."

"Guess I'll see you around."

"Guess so."

Ernie started walking away, down the access road in front of the Princess Elizabeth. Tommy looked back at the scene: Cindy, Claire, the big fat redhead guy, and the cops that weren't as bad as he thought. He called out to Ernie, "Hey, Dad!"

Ernie stopped. He turned back to look at Tommy. "Yeah?"

"We should get a coffee some time."

"Yeah," said Ernie. "We should, son." Ernie smiled back at Tommy. He kept smiling as he disappeared into the darkness.

Cindy left Claire, who was being attended to by two paramedics. She put her arms around Tommy. "That was one hell of a weekend, Felchfairy."

"You got that right, Supercunt." Tommy looked over at the spot where the snow had flown up from the explosion. "Looks like I'm gonna need a new truck."

"Maybe," said Cindy. "Then again, you do need a new van." Cindy looked over at the boogie van, with its doors open, its engine idling, and the keys in the ignition.

Tommy smiled at her. "On one condition."

"Name it."

"Trim the dingle balls, so I can see out the windshield."

CHAPTER
FIFTY-
THREE

February 3, 2016
The Winnipeg Sentinel

FEDERAL VIROLOGY LAB LINKED TO
EXPERIMENTS ON RIVERVIEW GROUNDS.
WINNIPEG STILL UNDER BOIL WATER
ADVISORY

By David Worschuk

The RCMP Major Crimes Unit announced today
that additional evidence of 'unique chemical
compounds' has been discovered at the home
of a Winnipeg biochemist who was employed
at the National Microbiology Laboratory in
Winnipeg's North End. A hazardous materials

team from the laboratory, as well as members of the Winnipeg Police Service Emergency Response Team, attended to the home of Jason Matthew Pokrant at 88 Mattinee Bay in North Kildonan. The compounds were removed without incident.

Mr. Pokrant locked himself in one of the Level 4 containment labs at the federal facility on January 29, ingesting a lethal dosage of active viral cultures, including the Ebola virus. It is believed that Pokrant died soon after he ingested the lethal viral cocktail. His body has yet to be removed from a secure section of the Arlington Street laboratory.

"There is no threat to the public at this time, including the neighbourhood that surrounds the National Microbiology Laboratory," said Heather Barnes, Communications Coordinator for the facility. "The laboratory is world-renowned for its safety systems, with zero events of loss of containment occurring since the facility opened in 1999."

Pokrant's apparent suicide note, which appeared in the January 30 edition of the *Winnipeg Sentinel*, detailed his work with the underground laboratory, which was housed in foundation remnants of the King George Hospital, which was demolished in 1999 to make way for the Riverview Health Centre. Pokrant spoke highly of Morley Chancellor, the reported head of research at the facility, in the note. Chancellor, who had worked at the Brandon Hospital for Mental Diseases in the early 1950s, was found clinging to life in the underground facility during the early morning hours of January 25. He was transferred to the Health Sciences Centre, where he remains on life support.

The City of Winnipeg water department has continued to analyse the chemical composition of the water supply since January 26, when information first came to light regarding the use of experimental compounds in the Winnipeg water supply. "We simply don't know what we're looking for," said David Witwicki, water quality manager for the City of Winnipeg. "We are continuing to advise residents to boil water first before using it for drinking and cooking."

Retailers in and around the city have sold out of much of the available bottled water stocks. The prime minister's office announced today that Canadian Forces personnel from across the country are in the process of shipping bottled water to the city, using military transports.

The RCMP announced today that it has discovered additional evidence in regards to the extent of human testing for experimental compounds in Manitoba. Oscar Willington, an eighty-seven-year-old resident of Brandon, led RCMP investigators to a hidden storage room in the former Brandon Mental Health Centre. The facility was closed in 1999 and is the current site of the Assiniboine Community College. In 1949, Willington was working as an orderly at the centre. "I can still remember the screaming from the off-limits wards," said Willington, who reportedly saw Dr. Donald Ewen Cameron at the facility. Dr. Cameron officially worked at the centre from 1929 to 1936, though unconfirmed reports have recently come to light that he continued to experiment on patients in Brandon as late as 1953.

Dr. Cameron, who died in 1967, was a key figure in one of the darkest chapters of Canadian medical history, experimenting with LSD and brainwashing techniques on unwitting patients at the Allan Memorial Institute in Montreal from 1953 to 1964. The experiments were funded by the U.S. Central Intelligence Agency, under the code name MKULTRA. Val Orlikow, the wife of long-time Winnipeg North MP David Orlikow, was one of Cameron's patients. Orlikow, who died in 1990, first spoke publicly about her experience for an ABC News exposé on CIA mind control in 1979. "I thought that this was the coldest and most impersonal treatment that anyone could give to anybody in the world," said Orlikow, who was being treated by Cameron for post-partum depression in the late 1950s. "I can't imagine the mentality of people who would do this." Orlikow sued the CIA, winning an out-of-court settlement in 1988. As part of the settlement, the CIA admitted no wrongdoing for the experiments that Orlikow was subjected to.

The discovery of the underground facility, which occurred during the early morning hours of January 25, continues to reveal connections to the Weights and Measures Branch of the Manitoba government. Tobias Finch, the deputy minister for the department, was found dead of a self-inflicted gunshot wound at the scene. Nathaniel Goodwin, listed as an employee of the department, was shot and killed by Winnipeg Police Service Detective Sergeant Miles Sawatski and his partner, Detective Constable Gayle Spence. The detectives were recently cleared of any wrongdoing by the Officer-Involved Shooting Board.

February 5, 2016
The Winnipeg Sentinel

DEATH OF VETERAN DETECTIVE IN FIERY CRASH YIELDS FEW CLUES

By Staff Reporter

The Winnipeg Police Service is appealing to the public for any information on the events surrounding the fatal collision that claimed the life of Winnipeg Police Service Detective Constable William Sangster during the early morning hours of January 25.

Sangster was driving his personal car, a dark-brown 2004 Ford Crown Victoria, on Bartlet Avenue, when he was involved in a head-on collision with a 1986 Pontiac Parisienne that had been reported stolen. Sangster died at the scene. Neighbours in the vicinity of the crash reported loud noises at about 3:45 a.m. on the morning in question, which were assumed to be from snow removal equipment. The driver of the Pontiac fled the scene.

The city's 311 enquiry line logged over thirty complaints from residents of Bartlet Avenue in the days leading up to the crash, due to heavy accumulations of ice, which had created deep ice ruts that may have contributed to the head-on collision. Anyone with information on the crash is asked to contact the Winnipeg Police Service Investigation Unit.

February 21, 2016
The Winnipeg Sentinel

RIVERVIEW ADMINISTRATOR FORMALLY CHARGED, SUPPLIED PATIENTS FOR "KING GEORGE" FACILITY

By David Worschuk

The latest twist in the story of human experimentation on Manitobans culminated in the arrest of Joseph P. McIntyre, chief administrator at the Riverview Health Centre. McIntyre, 57, appeared before a judge at the Manitoba Law Courts Building this morning, charged with multiple counts of patient endangerment. McIntyre pleaded not guilty to all charges.

The discovery of the underground facility, which was apparently known as the King George, revealed the existence of 24 patients who were being administered a variety of drug compounds. The patients ranged in age from 77 to 92, and were all listed as deceased at the Manitoba Department of Vital Statistics. Steven Cooper, the Crown attorney for these proceedings, explained to the court that the patients were chosen systematically, having no family or friends who would be enquiring as to their welfare if they suddenly died.

"The tactics used by McIntyre are what we would expect from an Orwellian novel," said Cooper. "There are few words that can describe the level of suffering that these patients have endured." The patients, whose names are under a publication ban, have been sent to various area hospitals for treatment. Two patients have reportedly died from the effects of the King George treatments.

November 17, 2016
The Winnipeg Sentinel

SENTINEL REPORTER RECEIVES PRESTIGIOUS AWARD

By Staff Reporter

David Worschuk, Crime Reporter for the *Winnipeg Sentinel*, has received the prestigious Journalist of the Year Award from the National Newspaper Awards jury. Worschuk, a seven-year veteran of the *Sentinel*, was honoured in Toronto for his coverage of the Riverview Health Centre scandal, which revealed a decades-old legacy of human experimentation in Manitoba. Worschuk is currently writing a novel about the case, which is scheduled to be released by the newspaper's Sentinel Press next year.

January 26, 2016
Kijiji Manitoba, Used Cars and Vehicles

WANTED: Looking for 1988–1996 Ford F-150 regular cab pickup truck, two-wheel drive. Any engine / transmission combination. Body must be good enough to pass safety. Must have dual tanks. Call Tommy at 204-929-3673.

At ECW Press, we want you to enjoy this book in whatever format you like, whenever you like. Leave your print book at home and take the eBook to go! Purchase the print edition and receive the eBook free. Just send an email to ebook@ecwpress.com and include:

- the book title
- the name of the store where you purchased it
- your receipt number
- your preference of file type: PDF or ePub?

A real person will respond to your email with your eBook attached. And thanks for supporting an independently owned Canadian publisher with your purchase!